AUTUMN LETTERS

A Novel

By

Michael Frederick

Dedicated to my beautiful mother Toni

Special thanks to Mariam Kirby

for all her good work.

Novels by author:

White Shoulders

Ledges

The Paper Man

Missouri Madness

Shy Ann

Summer of '02

March, 2004/1st printing/10,000 copies

First Burn

One phone call can decide who we become. Sixteen-year-old Mark Freeman knew before the end of the first ring—it was a warning from God, but he couldn't prove it. The phone's peal transformed itself into the dull, ominous sound going on and on inside the boy's head in late September of 1965, in Wichita, Kansas.

Mark had known Indian Summers in Kansas, intense heat mixed with undulating winds—a moving invisible power that could burn flesh. He had never been burned like this; it was a sunburn caught here two days ago from the relentless Kansas sun, while dozing beside a stranger's swimming pool, in Wichita. Sleep kept his clamoring thoughts off of the speeding semi that had smashed his mother's car.

And now, Mark soaked in the stranger's bathtub, the sound of his dead skin pulled slowly in long, wide grafts from his broad shoulders. Just an hour earlier he had asked why he was still here in this house of a stranger. Margot, sister of one of his mother's friends, had told Mark that his mother would be in the hospital for a long time.

"Can I go see her?" he had asked her.

"No, not yet. Your father is coming to get you. He'll be the one to take you to see your mother," she drawled.

That was it. Only matter-of-fact words for an only child, from a stranger who had taken that phone call in her modern, expansive kitchen with her aqua-colored stove, refrigerator and cabinets. He knew it was his father calling when she answered, "Oh, hi Larry!" in that same specious tone of compassion he'd heard when she first saw his sunburn. And, now, his father was coming.

Why? he had asked himself, lying rigid between burning cotton sheets in Margot's guest bedroom, while the song "Maybe," by The Chantels, played low on the living room stereo.

It was then that he decided to write his mother a letter on the notebook paper he'd barely used since starting the 11th grade three weeks before at the new high school. He wrote in bed, hunched close to the table lamp that he'd left on every night since his arrival there.

Dear Mom, I know you are in the hospital, but I don't know what happened to you, or how long you will be there. Dad is coming to take me back to where he lives. I'm sorry that you are hurt. I love you, and say prayers for you. Love Mark

P.S. This letter I pray will find you safe.

He folded the letter and put it under his pillow, resting his head just above it.

There would be no dreams for Mark that night, for he stayed awake picking his burned flesh until morning. During the night, the phone had rung again.

When Margot came to get him for breakfast, she found him dressed, sitting on the end of the bed looking at his packed suitcase and a grocery box filled with more of his clothes and things.

2

"You're all packed!" she smiled.

"When will my dad be here?"

"In a couple hours, hon. He's making a five hour drive. How about some breakfast?"

"I'm not hungry."

"Can I bring you a glass of orange juice?" she asked.

He nodded yes humbly, his short brown hair in motion above his red skin, and she caught her mouth trembling under her hand so he wouldn't see it. At 2:30 a.m., her sister had called to say that Jane had died from her injuries. On her way to get his juice Margot cried for the well-mannered boy who had lost his mother.

Margot was more eager for Larry Freeman to pick him up than Mark was. Since his parents had separated and divorced eight years ago, Mark had seen his father only four or five times, the last time at a family reunion in South Woodbury, across the river from Iowa, in Nebraska.

His sunburn pain should have been excruciating from the touch of his cotton t-shirt on his sensitive skin, yet he couldn't feel its true intensity. He was numb to everything but fear and uncertainty. When his father arrived, Mark saw the expression on his father's usually cheerful face, the two day's beard growth on the older man's cheeks, and his fear and uncertainty rose.

Air Force Master Sergeant Freeman's 1951 Pontiac Chieftain, two-tone sapphire blue above Malibu ivory, was crammed with all of his son's clothes and belongings, along with some of his ex-wife's things he thought Mark might want some day.

Later, he would tell his son that she was gone. Even the thought of breaking the terrible news made his hands tremble on the steering wheel as he took Highway 77 North. Suddenly, Mark asked if they could stop and see his mother before they left Wichita. Larry could only shake his head no; then, imagining no more merciful course of action, he decided to tell his son the truth, instead of putting it off until later.

Cruising on hydra-matic drive at 75, Larry's wiry 5'9" body felt like it weighed 300 pounds on the light gray velour interior. He blinked often, seeing his ex-wife's beautiful white teeth repeated in his son's mouth, and opened the vent system under his steering wheel because the thick, off-square lenses of his brown plastic glasses seemed to have fogged.

Mark could see that his father's eyes were nervous. He looked closely at his father who was staring straight ahead.

Then, Larry spoke softly to his son, his lips barely moving, his eyes going everywhere but to his son's eyes.

"Mark, your mother, she's in heaven, now." He quick-shot a glance at his son, and could see that his words had put fear and confusion into the kid's eyes, the same blue eyes his mother had.

"She died?" Mark returned in a stunned tone. His father nodded yes, his tongue holding back shapeless words and feelings he didn't want to pour onto his son, his only child.

"When did she die?" Mark said.

"Last night, about two in the morning, probably when you were asleep."

Mark didn't tell his father he hadn't slept last night, that he wrote his mother a letter, a short letter that he'd left under the pillow at Margot's. He didn't tell his father how he had imagined handing his mother the letter at her hospital bed, and that she would begin to feel better when she read it.

Mark turned his head away, facing the rolled-down window that flashed the green Kansas prairie. His tears were stopped and held, until his emotions reached his lower lip and spasmed in a hundred places around his mouth. Inside, his belly churned, demanding to know why his mother was taken from him, and so quickly, without a word, or even a vivid memory of the last time he saw her.

As he thought about the last time they were together, he let his head lean onto his father's heavy upholstered door while humid blasts of Kansas air numbed his scalp and wind-dried his tears before his sadly silent father could see them.

Larry turned on the chrome radio dial, thought better of it and quickly turned it off, then told Mark that he was going to pull over so they could talk.

The loss of his own mother when he was a boy had come back for Larry. He had asked himself a thousand times since he left Woodbury for Wichita how the identical tragedy could have happened to his son. The unresolved trauma, old emotions left from twenty-seven years ago were moving again, deep inside his belly, forcing toxic memories to his throat.

That gave him another reason to pull over, the pain in his belly kept getting sharper. On the highway shoulder with traffic zipping past them at 80 mph, Larry cut his spotless Pontiac's engine and spoke to his son softly while clutching the left side of his belly.

"When I was a boy I lost my mother. So I know there's nothing I can say that can take away the terrible way this makes you feel right now. All I can promise you is that it will get better in time."

"The last time I saw her, Dad, she was folding my pajamas in my room. And I asked her why she was doing that, because I was just going to put 'em on. She laughed and said she liked to keep things looking nice. She said she'd always been that way. Then she kissed the top of my head and said she loved me."

They cried together, yet separated by three feet of plush interior.

Paradise

It took a little over five hours to drive to the dinky town of Paradise in Northeast Nebraska, just across the Missouri River from Woodbury, Iowa. Paradise housed 950 people in the 1960 census. Approximately 52 deaths and 39 births since 1960, meant the population remained about the same as it had been five years before.

The only thing Paradise had plenty of was trees, but Mark couldn't see that, based on the view from the highway, until Larry's car turned east toward the heart of Paradise. There stood the Pioneer County Courthouse, oblong, its three stories of brick, certainly the most prominent and largest building in town.

Larry parked on the dirt road facing the west side of the courthouse. Mark got out and stretched his stiff and still-burning body. His mind felt numb from the worst emotional thing that ever happened to him. During their long drive, somewhere near Lincoln, Larry had told Mark how he met his mother at a USO dance on the military base south of Woodbury, the same place he was now stationed. He told Mark that after a week of dating his mother, he snuck into her first floor boarding house window, because the old sourpuss landlady didn't allow any visitors after dark, especially men.

Mile after mile into the endless prairie's horizon,

Mark imagined his parents dancing and having fun and falling in love in the land where he was headed, the place where his parents' people still lived, and where his mother would be buried: in Paradise.

Mark had struggled to recall anything about this part of the country, but found nothing in his memory, for his parents had moved away from Woodbury when he was two years old.

Now, he followed his father down a flight of concrete steps on the west side of the courthouse. The green door at the bottom of the steps was locked when his dad turned the iron doorknob. Larry knocked and they waited in the cool pocket of shade made by the giant oaks and maples that had lined every side of the courthouse for a half century.

"This is where Grandpa Freeman works?"

"Uh huh. Do you remember him?" he asked Mark.

Mark shook his head no. A moment later he could hear footsteps, then the turning of the lock on the other side of the green door.

The boy's eyes began at the floor and moved up as Larry greeted Edwin Freeman, his father's voice echoing in the damp stairwell. Solid, big black work shoes anchored thin 85-year-old legs covered by clean gray trousers. Above the custodian's worn black belt was a cotton short-sleeved green and white checkered shirt that smelled of kerosene and oil, like the red rag hanging from his back pocket. His silver wire-rimmed spectacles were round windows revealing small, pale blue circles of light that were shining down into his great-grandson's own pale blue eyes. The old man's taut German chin thrust from a chiseled head of lean muscle and bone that matched his powerful long arms and imposing hands, giant fingers that tenderly clasped Mark's soft right hand. His bald head had but a few strands of gray/white hair above each ear.

Grandpa Freeman's most remarkable physical characteristic was his incredibly broad shoulders; they gave his head a simian appearance. Those shoulders were known all around the county to have great strength and torque when his powerful arms required lift or pull for the work at hand.

And work he did. He had been a blacksmith during his youth at the turn of the century, pounding and shaping iron and steel by brute force. In fact, the Combination Bridge, the steel bridge that connected Iowa to Nebraska here, was forged by this very man, who was also the first man to ride across the bridge via horse and buggy.

Larry was in awe of his six-foot-tall grandfather, a man who appeared taller just because of his ramrod posture. On their drive to Paradise, Larry reverentially told Mark about how Grandpa and Grandma Freeman raised him after his mother died, and that Mark, too, would live with them in their little house in Paradise, until Larry could obtain suitable base housing for them. But he warned Mark that there was a long waiting list, unless you were married. He told his son that he would continue to live in his private room on base rather than crowd into the same bedroom with his son in Grandpa and Grandma's small two-bedroom house.

Mark and his father followed the elderly janitor into his orderly workshop, a place where silver-colored tools sparkled on nails, aligned from the smallest wrench to the biggest, above a stained workbench that had been under Edwin's control for over three decades. As Grandpa found a third chair for them all to sit, Mark saw a jar of peaches standing beside a faded charcoal gray lunch box.

When the old man talked, it was with brevity and in a husky whisper coming from the back of his wrinkled throat.

"How was your trip?" he directed at Mark.

"Fine," Mark answered.

While Mark's eyes roamed the dark workspace, his father talked, "It was awful hot in Kansas, Grandpa. It cooled down a bit around Beatrice, after we got into Nebraska."

"How'd that fancy car of yours ride?" Grandpa asked, and Mark noticed the old man's dentures creaked.

"Oh, pretty good," Larry replied, glad not to have to discuss the reason for the trip. "It's the smoothest riding car I've ever owned."

"What kinda mileage did ya get?"

"Oh, I s'pose maybe fifteen miles per gallon."

They drove three blocks on the unmarked gravel road that locals knew was Dakota Avenue. The street was lined with older one-story homes that appeared a bit destitute by contrast to the occasional two-story Victorian, or modern ranch style house. Most of the homes were on big lots, which kept neighbors more neighborly.

While driving onto the Freeman dirt driveway Mark asked his dad how old Grampa Freeman was.

"Eighty-five, eighty-six, I'm not sure. Longevity runs in the Freeman family," he added proudly as he parked under the shade of a century-old maple tree that Larry had named Lucy when he lived here.

Five feet ahead of the Pontiac's grill was a low, slant-ceiling garage/workshop where a 1944 maroon Ford was parked. To the left of the garage stood the gingerbread

10

house of Edwin and Leona Freeman, built from scratch by Edwin in 1907, its gold/black tiled exterior and roof part of the third oldest house in Paradise. Edwin had helped build the two older homes in town.

Mark and his dad were filling their hands with Mark's stuff when the back porch screen door smacked shut behind 4'11" Leona May Freeman. Grandma Freeman was half Cherokee and half Irish; her mother, a full-blood Cherokee, survived the Trail of Tears, but died soon after giving birth to Leona May on May Day.

Leona's white cotton apron tied over her floral patterned summer dress was covered with flour and butter stains from baking bread, pies and cookies. Her bowed, arthritic legs were concealed beneath thick, dark brown nylons drawn to her knees above her black half-inch Pilgrim shoes. Her gray hair wound into a bun framed her square-jawed Cherokee countenance.

Grandma didn't say a word. She didn't have to. Her smile was all over her eighty-three year old face. Yes, there were wrinkles, big ones in too many places for Mark to count, but her blue eyes shown with love for her family. She hugged her great-grandson, who towered over her, nearly as tall as his father.

She smelled of good things: lavender clinging to her skin from her evening bath, fresh bread and butter and baking soda, all blended sweetly. The scent of cookies and pies and fresh clean air on the porch would forever be associated in Mark's memory of this moment with the elderly woman who was his father's grandmother.

She backed up a few steps, moving like a penguin, to get a better look at Mark. At first she could see traces of her son Thomas, Larry's father, but then she could see that Mark's physical bearing reminded her of Edwin when he was young.

"I just baked some walnut cookies," she smiled, as Larry hugged his grandmother.

"My favorite!" he declared.

Her laugh came out, a contented sound made by a woman who loved only to work at keeping her home a good place to be. Not many words could convey her happiness, until her laugh told you at once. It was a welcoming sound to hear at the end of the road.

Hurley

Sunday morning. Sixteen-year-old Hurley Gunderson watched for the new kid from his parent's semi-circular front porch. He had seen the new kid arrive yesterday in that cool Pontiac.

The Gunderson's white house with black trim was one of the nicest homes in Paradise, and it was right across the street from the Freeman's house.

John Gunderson, Hurley's father, was the second generation of Gundersons to own and manage Gunderson Monument Company in South Woodbury, Nebraska, across the river from Woodbury, Iowa. Hurley's dad had taken over the company five years ago when his father passed away. Though the monument company was a thriving business in the midst of an elderly population, getting the bulk of headstones for every soul that died in Northeast Nebraska, Hurley knew as well as his father did that there would not be a third generation Gunderson to run the business. Hurley hated the monument business, hated taking orders from grieving customers and having to act so compassionate and understanding—not for Hurley Gunderson. Hurley dreamed about becoming a professional baseball catcher.

The most notable physical characteristic about Hurley was the size of his head, a massive skull with thin brown hair that he slicked back with plenty of Vitalis. Only in the last couple years did his body catch up with the size of his head, filling out with broad shoulders and a neck like a bull.

Now, as Hurley watched the newcomer exit the front door onto the Freeman's porch, he thought the lanky kid might be a pitcher with his long arms and legs, but what was with those shiny black dress shoes?

Mark had slept a long and hard twelve hours in his new bedroom. Thanks to Grandma Freeman pouring Epson salt into his hot bath, his sunburn no longer bothered him. But, as he stood alone on the porch, a sickening sense of loss filled his belly. The thought that he would never again see his mother nearly made him heave up the good breakfast Grandma just made him. He swallowed fast and bolted down the porch steps.

Mark crossed the street before seeing the pale, husky kid with the wide forehead stacking baseball cards on his front porch railing.

"Ya know why they call this Paradise?" Hurley barked at the new kid.

Mark stopped on the sidewalk, waiting for an answer.

"'Cause nobody wants to live in hell!"

Mark grinned at the boy's joke and the way he kept his focus down on those baseball cards.

"You gotta glove?" Hurley asked, still flipping through his collection.

"It's somewhere. Packed in a box."

"You a lefty?"

"Yeah. How'd you know?" Mark asked.

"Your left arm...I can see it's bigger than your right."

Hurley reached down and came up with a fielder's glove and a catcher's mitt with a new ball nested inside. Hurley tossed the fielder's glove to Mark.

"It's for a righty, but it's so worn, you prob'ly can get by wearing it on your right hand."

They played catch, warming up in the front yard. Mark started throwing harder and harder to the squatting catcher, until he let one rip high and wild over Hurley's reach. They watched the ball roll into the neighbor's yard.

"Sorry," Mark said.

Hurley didn't like walking after his ball in the intense sunlight that was squinting his green eyes to slits of pain, and made his big head shine like a hard-boiled egg. When he returned, examining his grass-stained new ball, Hurley grumbled "You shag the next one."

There was no next one to shag, for Mark bore down and kept his control, impressing the catcher more than he let on.

"You want some Kool-Aid?" Hurley said, after a while.

"Yeah."

Mark stepped up to the shaded front door. Something made him stop, without being invited inside, a kind of automatic impulse to be a gentleman, a trait his mother instilled in him.

He could see into the Gunderson's dark front room with its dark fabric curtains and furniture, all arranged in the strict middle-age kind of dark order that had instilled restlessness and a simmering hate into their only child's heart.

From his shaded point of view, Mark could see an oil portrait of Hurley wedged between his seated parents, who looked like grandparents, far too old to have a sixteen-year-old boy.

"Thanks," Mark said when handed a tall plastic glass of lime Kool-Aid, rattling with ice cubes. "My name's Mark."

He waited for his host to say his name as they drank the green, cold, sweet water. Mark finally had to ask.

"Hurley."

"Hurley. I've never heard that name before. Wanna play some more catch, Hurley?"

Hurley poured an ice cube into his mouth and bit into it, chomping it to slush, as Mark followed Hurley's bowed legs to his fenced back yard where they could play catch under the sheltering shade of two magnolia trees.

During Mark's pitches and Hurley's return throws, the boys talked.

"Where'd you come from?"

"Wichita, Kansas."

"Wichita. Never been there. Plan to though. I'm gonna see the biggest cities in every state when I move outta this hick town. I'm gonna play minor league baseball, then the pros, and see every city in the country!"

"I'd have liked that, myself." Mark couldn't meet Hurley's gaze and looked down at his shiny shoes, twisting the baseball in his hand. "But things changed."

"Why'd you move here?" Hurley asked.

Mark's second wild pitch was stopped by the Gunderson's redwood fence. While Hurley retrieved the ball, Mark answered, "My mother died in a car accident."

After more pitches and a long silence, Hurley said, "I wish my parents would die. I'd get their Buick and hit the road."

Hurley sounded like he meant what he said. Suddenly, Mark wanted to get away from the angry boy with the big head and make other friends who didn't wish their parents were dead, or at least kept it to themselves.

"I gotta go," Mark said and handed Hurley his glove.

"You've got a good arm, Wichita."

"Thanks. I'll bet you're a good catcher," Mark drawled.

"I am," Hurley grinned.

Mark was filled with self-disgust; it was a feeling that always came when he failed to assert himself; he didn't like it.

"Well, I'm going to go look around Paradise," he said and walked toward the street.

Hurley watched his new neighbor with the funny Kansas accent cross the street and walk toward the back of the Freeman house. For a moment he studied the boy from Wichita who just lost his mother, and thought: Lost in Paradise.

Mark stood facing Grandpa's garage. His right palm was sore from catching Hurley's throws. He could go right, over to Grandpa's black potato field, or left and to the back of the lot, toward Grandma's neat garden where rhubarb, squash, tomatoes, cucumbers and corn flourished under her care.

Instead, he went straight ahead into the cool darkness of Grandpa's workshop where the sweet/manly, intoxicating smells of gasoline and oil and kerosene kept his nostrils flaring. As his eyes adjusted to the darkness, they went from the grass-caked gas-powered red lawn mower to the silver wrenches and tools sparkling from Grandpa's sense of order all along the dark wooden workbench that spanned the entire right side of the garage.

But he felt ill at ease in his spotless jeans, red nylon shirt and the black dress shoes that he automatically cleaned on the back of his calves. His unconscious need for cleanliness came from a good mother who insisted on keeping things nice and orderly. All at once, he hated that. He thought of Hurley, and his clothes, clean, yet he could kneel and dive onto the ground without care, not the least bit concerned if his pants or shoes were stained, or smeared with grass and dirt. Mark wasn't conscious of his worry about getting dirty, yet he did worry about it, and even now he couldn't remember the color of Hurley's shirt. He only knew that Hurley was free to get dirty.

And now, on this dirt floor with oil and grime in a thousand dark places, the compulsion kept him standing in the middle of it all, safely away with his soft, clean hands inside his front pockets. He thought of his mother's funeral the following day at the Methodist Church in Paradise, of saying goodbye to her lifeless body that just days ago had been so vital, effecting everything she touched.

As he cried, he covered his mouth and sniffed in the fumes around him, and they mixed with the visual images of his beautiful mother, so young at 33 and so much the center of his universe. And now, she was gone...just like that, and he knew it must've happened in one horrific moment of shattered glass, blood, crushed metal and spilled gasoline.

He reminded himself that he never wanted to know the details concerning his mother's accident. His mother's advice: "Think good thoughts...and good things will happen to you. Good things happen to good people."

He pushed shut one nostril with his thumb and snorted a long strand of snot onto the dirt floor. Then, he nearly puked, dry-heaving until his chest and sides ached.

Outside the garage entrance, late September's

autumn air had been dropping a degree by this time of day, every day, and would until winter. Mark decided to pass by Grandma's garden, where he stood and listened to trees that were louder and had another language altogether; and they were colored with leaves more golden and richer in yellow than he remembered in Kansas.

The first sidewalk he reached took him to the courthouse, its three stories of brick resembled a secure fort that guarded all the weather-beaten lower middle-class homes on three sides. This town was far removed from the landscaped upper middle-class Wichita homes that sat surrounded by concrete and manicured lawns.

Not many people were in sight, except for a volunteer fireman hosing the driveway in front of the one-stall fire station, where Edwin Freeman had the distinction of being the town's first volunteer fireman.

Mark stayed on the sidewalk rather than walk on the grass he knew his grandfather maintained. At the front of the courthouse, he turned left toward the only commercial district in Paradise, a few small businesses on this side of the highway: Paradise Drug & Variety, a barber shop, a tavern, and an insurance agent's tiny office.

Inside the Paradise Drug & Variety, Mark discovered a soda fountain with five stools at the counter. The owner, a bald man in his seventies, greeted the boy he'd never seen before.

"What'll ya have?"

"A cherry Coke, please."

The man pumped dark cherry syrup into a tall fountain glass. On the middle counter stool Mark turned slowly 360 degrees. Nothing caught his eye until he saw an open box of tattoo bubble gum. Each flat package contained the same pink gum found in baseball card packages. These came with a tattoo of cartoon characters like Popeye, Superman, Bluto and other cartoon heroes and villains. All you had to do was lick, or wet your skin wherever you wanted the tattoo.

But his mother would never let him "dirty" his body with such a "silly thing" that cost a nickel. Was he now too old for such a silly thing now that she was gone? he wondered.

Outside, after a ten-cent cherry Coke brain freeze, he opened the gum wrapper and looked at the blue and red tattoo of King Kong. He licked the inside of his right wrist and pressed the big ape onto the moisture as he walked slowly to the corner, where he stopped to examine his new tattoo. He tried to put the same tattoo on his left wrist, but it was too faded to make out.

That's when a feeling of unease came over him and he had to lick away the colors on his left wrist. He could tolerate the good tattoo; it was the smeared one that made him run to the courthouse lawn to kneel and pull a fistful of short grass that he rubbed into his spit on his wrist. He rubbed and rubbed until a swirl of colors mixed into a purplish glob of grass and spit just above a blue river of veins that pumped awful words to his brain every minute of every day since his mother's death. It was the same awful memo over and over again: Tuesday, I'm going to my mother's funeral. That's the last time I will ever see my mother in this world. Last time. I must write her a letter.

<u>Beside Rivers</u>

Mark stepped inside the quiet courthouse, up eight marble steps that his grandpa kept shining like some kind of liquid black and white sheet of glass. Only now, as he paused in the vacuous main atrium, did he realize that he was moving farther away from where Grandpa Freeman might be.

Even though it was Sunday, his Grandpa had said there'd be men working, painting the main courtroom on the second floor. Yet Mark heard no sounds other than the light scuffing of his shoes on the pristine floor.

Then, he thought of how Hurley talked about going to all the big cities once he became a big league ball player. And how wonderful that image seemed to Mark, with lots of people around, not like this emptiness in Paradise.

He headed down to the basement, down a flight of stairs that his grandpa had made slip-proof with a layer of pure rubber safety footing found in the alley behind the Cornhusker Tavern next to the dumpster. Edwin Freeman would pick up any piece of trash, or object, just because he abhorred littering. The old man's German work ethic demanded order, especially in the town where he lived. Most things were disposed of, others put to good use.

Mark entered his grandpa's workshop in the boiler room. Edwin was wrapping a long section of twine around

21

his fingers then up to his elbow, making several loops while smiling at his great- grandson.

"You've worked here ever since they built the courthouse, right?"

"That's right."

"And my father worked here sometimes, when he was a kid?"

"That's right. You gonna do something great?" the old janitor smiled.

Mark shrugged his broad shoulders and smiled as he noticed his vision was not quite sharp enough to see into his great-grandpa's eyes.

Edwin put away the twine and handed Mark a rake and a large burlap lawn bag that smelled of grass clippings. He followed the old man out the same door he and his father used when they arrived in town. Under a barren maple, golden orange leaves covered the entire drop zone of the giant tree. Edwin took the rake from Mark and raked leaves toward the trunk, exposing the green/brown grass in a swath all the way to the base of the tree.

Soon Edwin handed the rake to the boy, along with the pair of soiled white cotton work gloves that hung from his back pocket. They fit loose from Grandpa Freeman's massive paws. As Mark raked, Edwin watched and said nothing. There was no pressure to do the job a certain way. It was fun and Mark was lost in Paradise.

That night in his new bedroom, Mark returned to the painful task of unpacking the things his father had picked up from his mother's Wichita apartment. He found the butterscotch-colored shoebox that had held most of his important thoughts and feelings since he was twelve.

Back then, he had heard in school about a boy with

a hair-lip who wrote letters to people in his life who had hurt him, and to people he loved, but could never tell. One day the boy's step-father threatened to burn the boy's collection of letters in the fireplace. The boy snapped, killing his brutal step-dad before his personal letters could be destroyed. At the boy's trial his letters were used as evidence of the terrible abuse he endured at the hands of his step-father, thus getting the boy acquitted and free to live a new life.

That's when Mark began to write about his life, mostly about how he missed his father after his parents divorced. Dozens of his letters recounted Little League baseball games, important plays involving Mark that he described to his absent father before folding the paper and placing it in the shoebox.

He removed the cardboard lid of the shoebox and gazed at the three-inch stack of letters secured by rubber bands. Tonight he would write an important letter, his last letter to his mother, words from his heart. He planned to leave the letter with her body. He would do this—in order to be free, free from living a life unlived, imprisoned by feelings of devastating loss.

It would be a short letter filled with love and happy childhood memories. Just then, he knew he must write a second letter, not to his mother. This would be a letter filled with the terrible rage churning inside him, all the hurt and confusion that God was responsible for.

His eyes were on the framed inscription of The Lord's Prayer above his new bed. He read it quickly, then waited to see if anything changed, to notice if he felt any peace after reading those same words his mother had taught him to say every night before he went to bed. He could write that letter later, when he was more settled.

The First Methodist Church of Paradise had filled with Freemans and Dunns and Pratts. The Dunns were Grandma Freeman's Irish family; the Pratts were his mother's family from East Woodbury across the river in Iowa. His mother's father, Clark, sat in front with Mark and his father; Grandma and Grandpa Freeman sat on Larry's left. Mark did not know any of his mother's people who stared at him from across the aisle after gazing at his mother in her brown business suit now visible within her open coffin.

Larry looked down to his hands, then to his son's hands. He put his hand over Mark's hand where it rested on the boy's thigh and patted it tenderly, as if to say "I love you, and I know what you're going through. And some day you will see that you do not think of her in this painful way."

They rode together in Larry's comfortable Pontiac with Grandpa and Grandma sitting quietly on the back seat. As they followed behind the hearse at ten mph, Larry realized he hadn't really moved on in his life after his own mother's death...until he met Jane. She had been the key to letting go of his mother, and that had been some fifteen years after burying his mother. Emotionally, his divorce from Jane seemed another death, yet somehow harder on him than her actual death. He sensed that today would be his only opportunity to let go of his ex-wife without needing another woman to replace her. Now, he focused on his son across from him and wondered what their divorce must have done to him.

The drive to the cemetery took fifteen minutes though it was only a mile away at the north end of town and not far from the river. The Paradise Cemetery was one of the oldest in the state of Nebraska, located just off the main highway, the only route to South Woodbury. The Freeman plot was close to the highway, separated by a low ditch, and alongside a grassy lane where the passage of tires had worn parallel lines of bare earth.

Standing in the cemetery reminded Larry Freeman that one day he would rest there for eternity with his parents and, now, with his ex-wife. Since Jane's family had no family plot, her father had been content to see his daughter buried with the Freemans, after Larry informed him that Mark's plot was located right next to his mother's. And Larry felt that these details were better off kept away from his son for now.

The coffin was ready for interment after the minister said his final words and they all gathered for the final prayer. Mark looked up to see the bent heads during the prayer; then he noticed another Gunderson Monument headstone in the space that bordered the Freeman plot closest to his mother's grave. The granite headstone read "Rivers."

With his eyes closed and his head down, Mark thought of the two letters he had placed between his dead mother's folded hands when he and his father first entered the church and stood before her open coffin. One letter had been received yesterday from Wichita. It was the letter he wrote the night his mother died and had left under his pillow at Margot's. She had sent the short letter with a nice sympathy card.

The other letter he had finished last night after rewriting it several times. Even now he could see every word on the paper that was now folded and close to his mother's quiet heart:

Dear Mother, I don't think I ever called you "Mother" in my whole life, until now. Maybe that's because I truly don't believe you will know of these words now, or ever. I guess this is written for me, to somehow stop the pain of missing you.

I can see now, and say it now, that I didn't feel as safe living alone with you, after you and Dad divorced. I felt more frightened of the world ahead of me and less certain of my future. Now, I'm even more confused and lost.

People keep telling me that life is about loss; and part of growing is doing the things you are afraid to do. Well Mom...I'm so afraid now...to say goodbye to you...because I know it's for the longest time, for as long as I live, Mom. But during this time I will always remember how much you loved me and cared for me and my every want and need.

I will try to live a good life, Mom. And I will look for the same loving kindness you showed me in the girl I choose to love. She will be sweet, yet tough and independent, able to withstand any storm that comes her way. Just like you, Mom. If I can get through this terrible time without you, maybe I will be stronger and able to face bad times more bravely. If only I have enough courage left, after watching them put you in the ground.

Mom, I will love you always, Mark.

Ruby's Window

If you lived in Paradise you heard about the clean, quiet kid from Kansas with the funny accent who lost his mother, heard that he was Edwin and Leona Freeman's great-grandson. Mark was the buzz of the town.

Wednesday morning, the Paradise Middle & High School principal told Larry Freeman that his son would fit right in with their only 11th grade class, and that thirty-year veteran teacher, Mrs. Kohler, would see that Mark was not given any extra work, even though he was starting a month into the new school year, after only two weeks in town, and with no report card from Wichita.

"Good. He doesn't need any pressure, now," Larry told the sympathetic principal. "He's a shy boy, like I was. He's a great kid."

"I understand, Mr. Freeman. I can assure you that your son is in good hands here."

Mark liked sitting in the back row, except he had trouble reading the blackboard. Like most new kids, he was terrified about attracting attention, especially on his first day in class. Then he was called by name by Mrs. Kohler to stand beside his desk and read out loud for his new teacher and twenty-two gawking faces, spooked faces that were guilty of labeling the new kid "dif'rent," just as their parents had done in gossipy conversations across their dinner tables. Mark's blush rose from within, sure that their minds were casting images of divorce and death and distrust of a stranger in their midst.

When he began to read, Mrs. Kohler knew exactly why she required all of her students to read out loud, even these juniors in high school. Once, most of their parents had stood and read this way. Not to punish or embarrass them, but rather, as a way to conquer introversion, the withholding of a student's vitality and ambition that most Paradise children inherited from past generations.

But not Mark Freeman; he was "dif'rent." The more he read, the more his blush faded, and all that could be heard was his crisp, clear, smooth Wichita drawl, a fresh sound that mesmerized his new gape-jawed peers. It was the voice of the patient plainsman, a slow/lazy, rustic kind of sound that was rural and folksy and rooted five generations deep.

Nearly finished with the paragraph, Mark glanced up and paused in his reading; he saw and felt the affect his voice had on his classmates; and it was a good thing. From that moment on, after he sat down, his life began anew, with a new identity that was only his—this voice of distinction, a brand new sound to all who were strangers to him, except for one.

Hurley sat in the front row with the smart girls. He had listened intently to his new friend from Wichita with the good left arm. He knew Mark's fear, a fear of being alone in the world, something Hurley had always felt most strongly in his own home. So when Mark was finished reading, it was Hurley who started to clap his hands together, making them all join in, including Mrs. Kohler.

Their teacher gazed with surprise and pride at Hurley for being so considerate to his new classmate. Mark smiled at his neighbor for helping him feel welcome in his new town and for being his first friend in Paradise.

On the playground during lunch period, Mark stood off to the side of the lone basketball hoop with its rattling metal net, wanting to play ball with the eight Paradise boys. Hurley was a guard, quick and a dead-eye shot from any distance. Soon, Mark began to hope he didn't get in the game. But after he drove in for an easy score, Hurley called out to Mark, "Hey, Wichita! You're in!"

Hurley pointed to one of his teammates and said, "Beat it." Mark had to play.

The new kid with the nice clothes seemed way too stiff and tenuous, and the soles of his dress shoes skidded, like moving on ice. Hurley dribbled circles around the boys guarding him, barking out orders and plays, for his teammates to move here and there. When Mark finally got the ball from one of Hurley's rocket passes, he yelled "Shoot Wichita!"

Up Mark went, too high, higher than any boy his size should be able to jump, especially in those crummy shoes. Mark's shot was an air-ball, hitting nothing but air and cement, yet Hurley was impressed, and Mark could tell that his new friend was kidding when he barked, "Wichita reads better than he shoots!"

After school, the boys walked the short two blocks home together, stopping on the sidewalk in front of Hurley's house. Though Mark was inches taller than Hurley, it seemed to Mark that if Hurley's legs weren't bowed he'd be just as tall.

"Get some Keds, Wichita. I'd like to see ya jump in good shoes. You play pool, Wichita?"

Hurley had his own private entrance to his room in the Gunderson basement, a vast space with more square footage than the Freeman house and garage put together. The entrance on the east side of the Gunderson house reminded Mark of the entrance to Grandpa's boiler room workshop at the courthouse, except here there were two crabapple trees that appealed to butterflies.

Something brutal happened on the way down the concrete steps. Hurley caught a yellow butterfly bathing in a ray of sunlight. Before Mark could say anything he saw Hurley pull apart its wings and flick the butterfly against the wall as if it were nothing.

Dampness was the first thing that Mark noticed in the dark, humid main room, its ground-level windows curtained and closed. Then he saw the most incredible things any boy could have, especially in Paradise. A regulation pool table and a Ping-Pong table stood side by side with their matching green felt and wood. This room was also used to store the Gunderson Monument business records in dozens of covered boxes lining the walls.

The best toy stood on four burnished chrome legs and offered an explosion of electric colors: red, orange, yellow and green. It was a pinball machine with five inviting silver balls in a row in front of the spring pulley on the right hand side, and two off-white flippers that Hurley had mastered long ago.

"Can you win free games?" Mark asked.

"Yeah. I've gotten it up to twenty-six free games. That's as high as it goes. I did it by puttin' a deck of cards under the front legs to level it out."

Mark looked down to the floor to see if the legs were elevated. Hurley added, "I only did it once to see how far it would go. We'll play it later."

He followed Hurley's pigeon-toed walk into his room, passing a laundry room that smelled of bleach and more dampness. Mark couldn't believe the cluttered mess before his eyes: dirty clothes were scattered everywhere on the floor; two single beds were unmade and littered with more clothes.   His host went over to a dusty stereo and played two of his favorite songs, "I Can't Get No Satisfaction" and "Paint It Black" by the Rolling Stones. As the music blared, Mark sat on one of the beds and pondered the orderly Gunderson house upstairs compared to this place below that looked like a cyclone hit it. He stared at the strewn stacks of baseball cards and an assortment of sporting goods tossed about that belonged to this spoiled kid.

Under the other bed Mark spotted what appeared to be hundreds of true crime and detective magazines, covers that were filled with murder and violence. On the wall above the bed where he sat, Mark read a framed plaque, a quote from Ireland's King Cormac. He had to squint as he read:

"If you are too wise—they will expect too much. If you are too foolish—you will be deceived. If you are too conceited—you will be thought vexatious. If you are too humble—you will be without honor. If you are too talkative—you will not be heeded. If you are too silent—you will not be regarded. If you are too harsh—you will be broken. If you are too feeble—you will be crushed."

Above the music, Mark asked Hurley, "Where did you get this?" pointing to the plaque.

"My dad gave it to me."

After the music stopped, they went into the big room and, for two hours, played pinball, Ping-Pong and pool with Hurley's practiced skills beating Mark soundly in every game. Mark wanted badly to beat Hurley just once, because of the other boy's conceited nature and from enduring his gloating after each win.

Mark left the Gunderson basement the way he entered—humble and without honor, passing the dead, wingless butterfly that had been so harshly broken by his leader, a king in Paradise.

On every Sunday, Larry Freeman drove from his base quarters in Iowa south of Woodbury to spend the day with Mark in Paradise. When his dad called him Wednesday night to see how he was doing, Mark told his dad about the Keds he wanted.

"What size of shoe do you wear?" Larry asked.

"I don't know."

"What? You don't know?" Larry laughed. "Take your shoe off and look!"

"Where do I look?"

"On the inside."

"Nine. It says nine."

"Nine! Good gawd...that's bigger than my feet!" he laughed. "Well, I s'pose I better get ya a half size bigger 'cause you'll grow into 'em soon enough. I'll get a pair at the PX and bring 'em to ya this Sunday."

"Thanks Dad."

But the base PX didn't have Mark's size, so he had to wait one more week.

On October's second Saturday night, Mark's sore feet were looking forward to the next day, when Mark's dad promised he would be bringing the new Keds. Mark was thinking about beating Hurley at basketball, at last, when he heard a light knock on his bedroom window.

When Mark went to his window he saw Hurley standing there wearing a hooded cotton sweatshirt, it was black and sinister looking. Hurley pointed toward the front porch of the Freeman house and walked off in that direction.

The night was the coldest since Mark moved there. October in Paradise: 50 degrees at noon and 36 degrees now. Mark listened to the elder trees in the Freeman yard, a sustained arboreal rattle that came with cold wind that would deepen their autumn colors during this near-freeze. When Hurley stepped inside, Mark could hear leaves that were high above and dancing upon stiff waving branches in the absolute prairie darkness.

"There's a place I wanna show ya, Wichita," Hurley whispered excitedly before stepping into the living room.

Hurley knew the Freeman house better than Mark did, having been invited in often while he tended the paper route he'd had for three years and quit just recently this past summer. Again, he could smell the good home smells that were alien to the sterile home his mother kept. The Freeman house always smelled of good things like the oiled antique wood of their furniture; there was the fresh scent of potted and bedded impatiens and red gerbera daisies lining the front room's window sills; and the fabrics, all washed by hand in Grandma Freeman's lavender lye formula; along with the collectibles behind glass cleaned regularly with vinegar and water. And there was always that salivating aroma of Grandma Freeman's cooking that Hurley could smell from his yard and made his mother's offerings unpalatable: grilled cheese with canned peas, or green beans, or whatever canned vegetable Mrs. Gunderson could warm quickly on her electric stove.

To Mark's surprise, Hurley called out, "Hi

Grandma Freeman and Grandpa Freeman!" when the two peeked in the front room from the kitchen to see who was there.

But this was the first time Hurley had been in Mark's room, a room filled with antique wood furnishings and an old brass bed. From the cedar closet his grandpa made, Mark fetched his black and orange Wichita Braves baseball jacket and slipped it on.

"Cool jacket!" Hurley said.

"Yeah, my mom got it for me."

"Cool."

They exchanged an awkward moment that both dismissed quickly.

They were headed out as Mark slipped on the black dress shoes that sat on newspaper by the front door.

"No Keds yet?" Hurley asked.

"Tomorrow."

Just then, Grandma Freeman entered the front room from the kitchen, her old joints making her sway like a penguin, her black shoes clacking hard on the linoleum floor; she flashed a friendly grin. At this time of the day her dark brown nylons were down and wrinkled on her shins.

"You be in before too late," Grandma told Mark.

"I will, Grandma."

The boys walked past the Freeman garage and headed west, away from the rising moon, skirting Edwin's black potato field, the source of giant white potatoes piled in his cellar.

Hurley talked excitedly, his pale green eyes alive with mischief. He had found a follower in this kid from Wichita, and expected questions.

"Where we going?" Mark inquired.

"To see Ruby. And I mean see. You're not gonna believe your eyes, Wichita!" the ex-paperboy cackled, thrilled to be leading Mark down Paradise Road, surveying a familiar block of homes.

These were the homes of hard-core drinkers, men who fell asleep in front of a television set in a drunken stupor; these were the men who worked the toughest jobs in the world, in Woodbury's massive slaughterhouses. Woodbury was now the king of beef and pork production and the home of the world's largest stockyards, as blazoned on a billboard near the river and proved by the constant stench around the massive holding pens.

Darryl Rubidah drove the gut wagon for Niemann Packers, one of the largest employers in the area. The Rubidah house was the gray one they could now see on the corner. Ruby was Darryl's nineteen-year-old daughter, a tough girl with a tough shape who had taken care of her alcoholic dad's dumpy two-bedroom domain ever since her mother left them when Ruby was twelve. Her real name was Alice; her dad called her Ruby.

"Ruby lives there," Hurley grinned while stopping to gauge the Rubidah house across the street.

"Who's Ruby?"

"You'll see. Come on."

He followed his bow-legged friend up to the side of the house and could see a TV set flickering in the front room with no other lights on inside the house, except for one bedroom window—Ruby's window.

"What are you doing?" Mark whispered.

Hurley hushed Mark with a finger to his smirking lips, then slid over to look into Ruby's unobstructed window. Sexy Ruby lay on her back on her twin bed, in tight jeans and a Cornhusker sweatshirt, wearing thick, white wool socks on her feet. She was lost in the Hank Williams song playing on her radio.

Ruby had fine curly-brown hair and big green eyes that looked wild all the time to Hurley Gunderson. He pulled Mark into the scene and watched for his reaction. Hurley laughed quietly at Mark's fear of being caught. They ducked below her window and over to a stump in Ruby's back yard.

"She's gotta boyfriend who's twice her age," Hurley whispered.

"Let's go," Mark mumbled.

"Wait a minute. Ruby sneaks out about this time every Saturday night with her boyfriend. They go to Hawkins Cemetery and do it."

"Where my mom's buried?"

"No...it's a couple miles from here. It's about a half-hour walk. He should be pickin' her up soon. Come on," he whispered, then added, "One time I followed 'em to the cemetery on my bike and watched 'em do it on the tailgate of the guy's truck. I couldn't see much 'cause they were under a blanket, but they sure made a lot of racket."

Mark didn't say anything, though the image excited him and felt dangerous.

"She's wild, Wichita...wilder that your worst dream," Hurley whispered with such clandestine intensity Mark felt a shiver go down his spine.

"What are you saying?"

"I'm sayin' if ya don't come with me...you'll miss the greatest show on earth, Wichita."

"I don't have a bike."

Hurley's sharp eyes could see that Mark was looking for a way out.

"We're walkin'. I know a shortcut that'll take us

less than twenty minutes to get there. But we gotta go now or we'll be too late. They start right away and I don't wanna miss the beginning of the show."

Hurley's eyes lit up like dull emeralds; there was no doubt in his mind that his friend would come along as he motioned with a neck tug that drew Mark with him, down the dark side of Paradise that led to Hawkins Cemetery on Blue Hill.

Hurley lied. It was more like three miles and a forty-five minute fast walk. The good things about a night walk like this, in bad shoes, and just when the weather was turning cold—the way was all flat and very quiet in the moonlight, with hardly any traffic on a gravel road used mostly by farmers and mourners and local lovers who knew this path to the east side of Blue Hill.

Mark Freeman carried with him a palpable bad feeling about spying on Ruby and her boyfriend. Something about his mother's funeral made this wrong and brought back a vivid memory:

A Wichita summer in 1956. Mark's mother took him to the drive-in twin theatres to see *Gone With The Wind*; the movie wasn't the memory. Whiteness. Blinding whiteness for a boy who did not want to see what his father saw when he divorced Mark's mother. Swinging. Higher and higher on one of six towering iron-legged swings that catapulted a high-kicking apex close to the massive white face of the movie screen. At first his heart would flutter so fast each time he came closer to the whiteness...until he saw only the whiteness for minutes at a time and not just seconds.

He wasn't big enough to go as high as some of the

kids, some even squealing from the thrilling sensation of swinging into a void of whiteness. And if Mark let go: would it be darkness, or whiteness that would take him. Fear of the darkness paralyzed his lungs; he could not scream it out like the other boys, boys whose parents sat together, watching and waiting for their sons' return. They would eat popcorn together, and laugh and cry and yell and scream at each other to "shut up or we're goin' home!"

He couldn't let go. Not like Hurley Gunderson could. Hurley would've been one of those boys that kicked higher and higher and screamed at the top of his lungs, unafraid of black or white, only the zest for letting go and risking himself totally, even in this prairie darkness.

Mark stayed even with Hurley's pace, a quick march that reminded him of the way Civil War soldiers must have marched on the way to Shiloh, on sore feet, and urged on by their leader. And Hurley was the leader, setting their pace for Hawkins Cemetery.

"We're 'bout there, Wichita."

"You said two miles!"

"It'll seem less than that on the way back!" Hurley laughed, a high-pitched devilish squeal that left his throat with a ticklish crescendo that somehow made Mark feel like laughing with him. Not at what Hurley said, but rather the way his laugh was some kind of organic vibrating thing, a particular sound the brain finds so amusing and real.

Hurley enjoyed Mark's laugh, for he knew that his new friend hadn't felt like laughing since he arrived in Paradise. That was all Hurley needed, a start; so he kept on laughing, raising it to a howl just because he felt like it, as they moved like trotting jackals on the dark road that was lit here and there by a distant farmhouse yard light.

This was Hurley's Paradise, a laughable hick town smack-dab in the middle of the Great Plains; and he sure as hell wasn't going to suffer the same life his stiff parents had chosen to live. Sure, his new friend had been dealt a bad hand early in the game, but maybe he could help him forget what God had allowed to happen, and have some fun while stuck in Paradise.

"I can't stay out much later," Mark protested, since his heels were beginning to blister.

"Don't worry...you'll be back before it's too late."

Just off the road, sticking out of the earth about two feet high was a water pipe with running, iron-rich water that mysteriously dribbled year-round from the hills around the cemetery and sparkled in the cold light of the moon. Hurley stopped to get a long drink by cupping his hands under the pipe and slurping from his palms. Mark copied Hurley's technique and drank the cold iron water until his thirst was satiated.

"My feet hurt," Mark complained.

"It's no wonder in those pimp shoes! I don't know why you don't have any good walkin' shoes."

"I outgrew them."

Mark stopped himself from telling Hurley one of his last memories of his mother: how she'd put his old tennis shoes in the trunk of her car before she was killed; she was going to drop them off at the Goodwill drop box when she had a chance.

"Take your shoes and socks off and let the water run on your feet. The minerals and stuff in the water really heals sores fast. I know 'cause my old man has hemorrhoids and he soaks his ass at home in this water. Every couple of weeks he gets a bucketful here. If it works on his hemorrhoids...it's gotta help your feet."

39

Mark let his bare feet slide back and forth on the slick, flat slab of rock as the icy cold water poured over his ankles and onto his heels, seeming to have an immediate effect, cooling the inflamed blistered areas.

Then, Hurley's keen eyes spotted headlights approaching along the road from Paradise.

"That's them, Wichita! Right on time!"

Their eyes moved in unison following the black Ford truck until it made a right turn onto the dirt road that led up to the dead-end at the entrance to Hawkins Cemetery.

"See! I told ya they'd be here. Better put your socks and shoes on. They get started fast!"

Mark's feet felt much better as they stepped lively toward the cemetery's lone entrance. They could see the black truck on the other side, its chrome fender sparkling where the truck was backed up against the fence line.

"Same place they always park," Hurley muttered as he took off down a path that he knew would lead them to a stand of scrub pines directly behind the truck.

To Mark it felt more and more depraved the closer they got to the parked lovers. Even as they moved unnoticed, Hurley's keen eyes saw the dull orange glow of two cigarettes. Soon the distinct sound of jazz music could be heard coming from the truck's radio, and Mark's heart beat faster and faster, for this was the most audacious thing he'd ever done in his life.

In a breathy whisper, he asked, "Hurley, what if they see us?"

Hurley did not answer; he maintained his stealthy pace as if the excitement ahead was all worth the energy expended, a hundred times over.

Suddenly, Hurley stopped in his tracks to listen,

though, they could not see the truck from where they stood. They could hear their own rapid breathing with the music from the truck mixed with the muffled conversation going on behind open window wings on each side of the pickup. Hurley pulled a flat pack of Winston filter cigarettes from his back pocket. He lit one with his back to the truck that was twenty yards away and obscured by a stand of scraggly pines.

He offered Mark a drag but Mark shook his head no, then he watched Hurley suck back the smoke, a satisfied smile on his pale face.

Then Hurley stepped forward and peeked at Ruby and her lover who were kissing passionately, embracing against the passenger-side door. He could see Ruby removing her red sweatshirt, exposing her white bra that glowed against her white skin until she vanished onto the truck's seat with only the burly shoulders and craning head of her lover visible.

The boys from Paradise could hear them easily without moving closer; and this would be as close as they got to these lovers on a night now filled with sounds of Duke Ellington and passion, along with the crunching of leaves underfoot made by two boys brought together by a death 350 miles away.

Hurley was enjoying this more than he was, yet Mark could see that his new friend had taken this invasion of privacy and made it thrilling, an experience to always remember...as long as they didn't get caught. That was Mark's problem: too careful; he knew he was way too careful when it came to anything "not proper."

The boys from Paradise were headed back on good feet. The mystery water from Blue Hill had worked. When

Mark and Hurley stopped to get another drink on the way back, Mark asked Hurley where the water came from.

"There's a few hog farms on the other side of this hill. There's a dinky town called Blue Hill, same as the mountain, 'bout a mile south of here.

Hubbard

From his desk at the back of Mrs. Kohler's classroom Mark looked down at the new Keds his dad delivered yesterday. They were black with white rubber trim and laces; and they were high-tops, a half size too big, but felt about right with an extra pair of socks on. He fantasized about showing Hurley and the others what he could do better than any other boy in this new school.

Just then, he noticed the new girl in class, Hubbard Kay Hawkins. She was a big-boned girl, the tallest girl in class and about as tall as Mark. He thought her glasses looked good on her; they were smart-looking, resting on her freckled face beneath thick red eyebrows that matched the thick, wild, red hair that hung to her shoulders.

Mark couldn't take his eyes off her, gazing at her profile from two rows to her left and one desk behind. She glanced over her shoulder and saw his eyes squinting at her, and knew right off that he would be wearing glasses soon, guessing that he was putting it off just as she had for as long as she could. Hubbard knew more about vision than most people.

One of the reasons she had left the Paradise school system years earlier was sitting in the front row: Hurley Gunderson. In grade school with Hurley, she grew tired of his cruel jokes, especially when daily it seemed Gunderson made fun of her living on a hog farm by pushing in his nose and snorting like a pig. Though it was mean, her classmates laughed at his antics. She had transferred to a bigger school in Warren sixteen miles southwest of Blue Hill.

The county bus took kids from Blue Hill to Warren, but not to Paradise. She'd been living alone with her alcoholic father, Jake, since just after her seventh birthday, when her mother left. Hubbard chose to stay with her father because he was going blind from glaucoma. After their first three years together, he could not drive her to school anymore, so she went to Warren. The one good thing about it was the absence of Hurley Gunderson from her life.

Now, with her father's illness getting worse, she needed to be home more, so she walked to Paradise in thirty minutes instead of the hour each way the bus had taken. Sixteen-year-old Hubbard could drive her dad's old truck, however it needed brakes and a new transmission, and with her father's illness, there was never any money.

It was in Hubbard's genes to use science and math to solve her problems. She got the trait from her paternal grandfather, Hubbard Hawkins, a prosperous hog farmer who doctored his own hogs. The land where Hawkins Cemetery was now located had been signed over to the Blue Hill Township by her Grandpa Hubbard because the Hawkins family was paid twelve hundred dollars a year to lease the land as a cemetery, instead of worthless ground on sloping land. The transaction between Grandpa Hawkins and the township had taken place over his son's strenuous objections. Now, the small amount of money was a blessing.

Jake had named his daughter after his father, because he wanted a boy and had been certain his wife would give him a son to take over the hog farm. His daughter was doing more than cooking, cleaning, ironing, and running their faltering family farm. She was working all hours of the night in her Grandpa's makeshift laboratory/feedhouse trying to find a cure for her father's debilitating disease.

At first, Mark thought Hubbard's off-white linen dress was a dirty-looking thing to wear. But then he caught himself, as he often did, comparing his mother's cleanliness with girls his age. It was wrong. He knew it was wrong from the anxious feeling he got as he scanned his own clothes for lint and specks of things that shouldn't be there. And it felt wrong to discreetly wet his finger and bend to wipe away smudges of the endless Nebraska dirt from his new Keds.

When Mrs. Kohler gave her class a 30-minute reading assignment, Mark sighed. This was time he desperately needed, time to let his thoughts wander, to escape from Paradise, for he had stopped dreaming ever since his mother died.

He missed dreaming. As Dr. Freud had said in the pages of Mark's set of encyclopedias: "Dreams are the best place to go to heal any disease, for the unconscious mind is more powerful than anything on earth."

While the rest of his classmates read their assignment in silence with bowed heads and a minimum of fidgeting, he looked quick at the new girl with the red hair and thought how beautiful she was to be so unselfconscious and mysterious. Then he let his eyes fall to the open book and pretended to read while he recalled the day an encyclopedia salesman rang their doorbell in Wichita:

It was wintertime. Mark's mother welcomed the young encyclopedia salesman into their apartment. The secret of the salesman's success had made him the number one encyclopedia salesman in all of Kansas: he'd sell the kid first, and that would sell the mother.

The kid sat next to his mother on the sofa, a basketball on the floor between his legs. The man said, "Mark, you're a basketball player, right?"

Mark nodded yes.

"Well, you look like you're going to be a six-footer when you're in high school. Am I right?"

His smiling mother chimed in. "Yes. My father is tall."

"I'm going to tell you a secret so powerful, Mark, that if you use just four of these books like I tell you to, you'll be able to jump out of the gym. And jump as high as someone six inches taller than you...and even taller."

Mark and his mother watched the salesman slip off his loafers and stack four of the thick encyclopedias on the floor next to the wall. Then, in his socks he stood on top of the stack on just his toes letting the back of his feet lower then raise up high, stretching his calves as he kept his palm on the wall for balance.

"Do this for fifteen minutes a day, Mark, and I guarantee ya you'll jump like a kangaroo in just six months. The secret is in the calves and the heel cord where the initial thrust of your leap has to be strong. Oh! Not to mention your toes. Your toes will get strong as heck...and that's the place where your jump begins."

He grinned at Mark's mother. "You'll have to make sure he reads 'em. A sound mind in a sound body, like the old saying goes."

Mark watched his mother write the salesman a check for $112.00 and was into his first fifteen minutes before the man hit the bricks again.

Mark had done the exercises faithfully, for fourteen months, every day for fifteen minutes until his mother's accident. But his father left his encyclopedias in Wichita for the Goodwill, since he did not have room for the set in his car.

Hurley would see that his quick shot could not get past Mark's leap in his new Keds. And if he ever got a chance to play on a real team, he would show them all what a few good books could do.

There had been little time to get a feel for his new surroundings. He had been rushed right into this classroom with these new faces, now bent over their reading assignment. Their eyes had gone wide and spooked as they studied him on his first day among them. It was as if they wanted to see his reaction to them, to see what this stranger in their Paradise thought of them.

His mind was now on Wichita, a vibrant city with prosperity everywhere: big supermarkets, bowling alleys with endless lanes, oil men in big cars, ice cream parlors and big movie theaters; yes he remembered all that prosperity and growth around him. And now: here. His consciousness came back to the present with his head turned to the dusty glass of windows closed to keep more dust from coming in.

Everything was worn here: the houses and the unpaved streets; the clothing people wore; even their faces were worn beyond their years. And now, loud outside the window, going down the street he saw a red/worn tractor driven by an old farmer who looked as if he'd driven to hell and back. The man had oil and grime stained into his whole being; his leather brow maintained a stern countenance, a look earned from plowing millions of rows in fields cut into a vast prairie, the same fields year after year, working with the same dirt, dust and endless horizon.

Mark looked up at the clock before casting a quick glance at the red-headed girl with the masculine name. Then again his eyes went down to the same page he hadn't read. He recalled the incredibly graphic dream he'd had the same night his mother bought him the set of encyclopedias. The dream lasted only a minute, yet it held something so true for him that it woke him at four in the morning. He remembered his head lifting from his pillow fast, sitting up on the side of his twin bed.

He had dreamed of seeing a white porcelain toilet shaking and vibrating ominously near a dry canal in the desert. He warned his mother about the toilet, how it was ready to explode. She told him to forget about it, to let it go, and to not tell anybody about it, though it looked like something terrible was about to happen. Soon, the toilet exploded and Mark was standing beside himself unable to stop an incredible river of shit that was too immense. Soon, as dreams go by, adults were all around him, and he felt guilty for not warning them about the vibrating toilet. And he was mad at himself and his mother, because she had told him to ignore it and he had listened to her and obeyed.

When he bolted upright after the dream, he knew immediately what the dream was telling him. It was about his parents divorce. Adults had called him the man of the house now that his father was gone. He had tried to be that, for his mother, because it was expected. And the river of shit was his anger unleashed for not wanting to play that role in his family.

From that moment on, Mark Freeman began to write down his dreams and figure out what they were telling him. Since coming to Paradise, his letters to himself were mostly about why he had stopped dreaming. He wanted an answer.

Just as Hubbard Hawkins wanted an answer. She was wrestling with the idea of moving her father into a Warren retirement home. She knew that her dad was nothing but a wooden Indian when she wasn't around to perk him up. Yet, she could never put him in a home, unless he wanted to go; and he'd never go to a place where he was surrounded by ill and infirm elderly people. He said he'd rather die with his hogs in his hogyard than go to a place like that.

Mark watched Hubbard and saw that she wasn't reading the assignment, either. As if sensing his interest, her head turned just enough to glance at him, embarrassing him. In that moment he knew he'd have to get glasses, for his vision was not sharp enough to see her blue eyes clearly.

Hubbard thought, just because she caught Mark looking at her, she could not let her work on a cure for her father's blindness be interrupted by a new face in a classroom where the lessons and homework were too easy for her and delaying her eventual breakthrough.

Minutes later, Mrs. Kohler called Mark's name to read out loud. Hubbard stopped to listen, letting her hand drop the pencil that had been scribbling formulas to investigate later in her lab. By far, Mark Freeman was the best reader she had ever heard in Paradise, or Warren. The way he used his unique voice, with inflection on important words and dramatic pauses, all made her and the entire class want to hear otherwise uninteresting words that he brought to life.

But then, she saw that smart-ass devil, Hurley Gunderson, looking around the room, noting the faces that seemed impressed with his new friend's ability. She could see Gunderson's big mouth tilted in an impish little grin that mocked them all as prairie hicks, so easily awed. Oh, how she hated that Hurley Gunderson.

During lunch period Hubbard watched Mark jump higher than all the other boys, much higher. In many ways Mark reminded her of Johnny, her pet pig, who had advanced physical abilities, and was very clean and smarter than any of the other swine in her dad's herd. The comparison made her smile.

She could see Mark squinting in the October sun, not wanting to shoot the ball because of his impaired vision. He was just the kind of person she needed to test her vision formula, someone young who hadn't yet been given molded glass crutches in order to see.

The school's brick wall felt cold against her back when she leaned against it and turned her face to the autumn sunshine that fell warm and good on her freckled face. She was thinking of the letter she received Saturday from her cousin Nell in Woodbury, telling her how she wished Hubbard had a telephone so she could call her. Nell had mentioned something in the letter that had been on Hubbard's mind ever since. Nell asked Hubbard if her father died before she could find a cure for his blindness, would she continue her research. It was a fair question and typical of her brusque cousin.

As she leaned against the Paradise school, her denim jacket snagging rough edges along her spine, she pondered whether, if her father did die, she would still be motivated to continue her work.

She stayed with that single thought and the hollow feeling it made in her stomach; then, her blue eyes went over to the boy with the Kansas accent, who was sliding and running and jumping with the other Paradise boys beneath the rusted iron basketball hoop. She saw him jump high: "L-Glycine," she whispered.

It was his leap that made her think of an old formula she had copied from a veterinarian's reference book. It was L-Glycine that jumped out at her. L-Glycine, she remembered, supports a healthy lens by eliminating excess sugars in the eye. She had been afraid to mix it into Johnny's formula, not sure of the reaction to Lycopene and Quercitin.

As she watched Mark jump high for the ball, higher than any of the other players, she could now see herself taking measured chances with several formulas she could try for her father. For the last six months she had feared to do anything. Her father refused to see any more doctors who would only tell him he was going blind.

Hubbard had made her own leap, from a little girl with dreams of pretty dresses and healthy foods prepared in a clean kitchen to the reality of adult strivings, with little sleep, and sustained by vitamin supplements on a hog farm. And if she could not save her father's sight, the V.A. Home in Woodbury would provide three hot meals a day along with the company of other veterans.

She would try it tonight, her formula; and she would give it six months to work. If it worked...fine. If not...she'd try another; she had no way of getting him off the farm without a fight.

Again she followed Mark's moves as he guarded that devil, Gunderson, who was quicker than the new kid from Wichita. Hurley faked his shot; Mark went for the fake and jumped, yet his body kept climbing higher and higher, seeming to hang in mid-air so long that when Hurley did shoot, it still was blocked by Mark's fingertips on the way down.

From this distance, Mark could still see that

Hubbard was there against the school wall watching the game; but his vision, even when he squinted, could not distinguish if she was looking at him. Just then, the bell rang, calling them to their classroom.

"You can sure get up there Wichita!" Hurley barked as they walked to the open double doors where Mrs. Kohler stood with two other teachers.

"If this dinky school had a basketball team," Hurley continued, "I'd want you on it. My old man knows the basketball coach at Warren. If we dust the floor at halftime, he'll let us scrimmage the starters in the gym on Sunday."

"I go to church on Sunday and spend all day with my dad."

"Bummer," Hurley said.

Hubbard watched Mark take his seat, his face flushed from playing basketball. Her eyes dropped to her orange notebook where she logged her formulas for Johnny's feed and her father's medications. She wrote quickly: I'm so bored with my lessons. Without numbers and the hope they bring, I'm lost in Paradise. I must escape from here...to find out who I can become.

<u>Whiskey and Flies</u>

     Luther Blackburn, an elderly, scraggly-faced hog farmer, dropped Hubbard off at her mailbox on Broken Kettle Road. Luther had spotted his nearest neighbor walking down Paradise Road about a mile from her school. She actually preferred this alone time to think about things, however, it had been a while since she talked to Luther, and she wanted to keep him posted about going to school in Paradise.

     No mail. She turned away from the row of five mailboxes that stood together for easy delivery on that side of Blue Hill, about a quarter-mile from her farm. Half the year the mail carrier found unpaved Broken Kettle Road impassable because of mud and snow.

     Hubbard walked the isolated dirt road that led to her farm with her text books cradled to her chest and her paper lunch bag folded and wedged beneath the cheap red plastic belt that she had covered in places with fingernail polish to hide the flaked-away material. She was preoccupied about how her hair seemed too long for her face and had no form. She had noticed her hair in the mirror above the sinks in the girl's restroom at school, as she struggled to pull her brush through wind-blown tangles. Finding fault with her appearance was new to her. She thought about how Mark Freeman was responsible and she smiled. First, she would persuade him to let her help his vision, then, when he could see her more clearly, he'd run for his life. She laughed.

To her right, deep into Clarence Bertrand's corn field where dirty, gold-colored stalks from the recent harvest lay crumpled and twisted in a shriveled mass, row after row, she saw the flock of crows that nested by the river and scavenged table scraps meant for her dad's hogs. Their leader, a burly, darkly sinister male, watched her while she passed with her eyes on his family pecking for corn in the Bertrand field.

Not many trees stood on this side of Blue Hill; however, the oldest and tallest trees were on Hawkins land. They were oaks planted by her great-great-grandfather Hawkins when this rolling land was taken from the Santee in the 1880s.

The township of Blue Hill had less than one hundred fifty people and was a mile to the south of the scooped valley that held Hubbard's family farm. Hubbard was fond of these western folding slopes that turned fog-blue soon after the first freezing sleet covered the hill. Except this distant blue could only be seen from five-miles away and only if you were approaching the hills from the west before the sun rose over them.

Hawkins men did not live long, and they did not produce many offspring. Most of them died in their early 50s from some internal malfunction caused by alcoholism. Lungs, liver, and kidneys were common vital organs to fail Hawkins men.

The Hawkins women lived much longer than their men; and most of them had red hair, while the men went bald young. And none of the Hawkins widows ever remarried, except for one. Hubbard's mother, Alice, married a dentist six months after she divorced Jake. For a second time, Hubbard chose to stay with her father, choosing him over her mother and step-father. Besides not wanting to leave her father alone, Hubbard did not want to leave her newborn pet pig she named Johnny. Johnny was not welcome in Woodbury's exclusive north side.

When her drab, weathered farm came into view, she kept her eyes above it, for the Hawkins farm would always be there. Six hundred yards above were floating giants, the low clouds of autumn—big and white, and moving fast though there was not a trace of wind about her. Something about those invisible winds and all that fleeting whiteness gave her a lift, or rather a push to go to her lab before checking on her dad.

Nearly all the weeds that bothered her eyes all summer had died during last night's twenty-eight degree freeze. She smirked at the dead ragweed lining the Hawkins fence line, vicious blooms that made a quarter of every year miserable for her. Next summer she would be ready to take the anti-allergy formula she perfected just a month ago. She named it "Fearless"; she had put every known pollen in Eastern Nebraska in her formula, and mixed it with pure honey bottled in Woodbury. Six tablespoons a day, and Fearless took thirty days to build up immunity in every one hundred pounds of body weight. She'd be ready for next summer's pollen with two gallons of golden Fearless sealed and waiting in her lab, a feedhouse the size of her bedroom, except it had two windows and a higher ceiling.

Her lab was sixty yards back of their simple, one-story, house and thirty feet from the barn where a hundred head of white American Landrace were penned with nine-year-old Johnny. Her pet came snorting out of the herd when he saw Hubbard standing by the iron gate.

"There's my boy! You miss me, baby?...huh? Come

on...I wanna check your vision."

Johnny snorted as he exited the open gate, then waited beside her until she closed it. Johnny's trim sixty pounds of lean pork muscle and bones walked briskly beside her with an air of importance that the other swine ignored.

Jake Hawkins allowed his daughter to keep only one pig for her experiments, which in turn kept Johnny safe from the slaughterhouse. The combination padlock she dialed kept her dad from stumbling in drunk and messing with the formulas in her lab. When she entered the lab with Johnny she left the door open and raised each window sash to let in air laden with the scents of pig shit and mud, two things she was used to.

Johnny sat beside her bow back side chair while she held his snout with one hand and shined a pen light into the pig's brown eyes to gauge the health of blood vessels of his eyes and eyelids.

"They look better," she smiled and kissed his tough brow when finished.

She dreaded going inside the house. She sat back in her chair, exhaled deeply, eying the six dozen glass vials, all of them labeled with white tape, on top of her worktable. She stared at the stainless steel German-made Sartorium scale she used for weighing milligrams and grains. She had bought it used with her birthday money from her dad and considered it one of her most prized possessions, now covered with a plastic bread bag and twist-tied for dust proofing. There were dozens of hardcover books on shelves, books about herbs and drugs for humans and animals she'd been given by Doc Jensen, a veterinarian in Blue Hill.

After a quick scratch at the back of Johnny's ear she

was up and out the door, not locking it behind them. They walked to the back screen door that was usually open for fresh air at this time of day, since the wind usually blew toward the barn. The door was closed. She made Johnny wait outside by giving him a light brushing back with her foot. When her father was home, he always threw a fit if she allowed Johnny into the house.

Immediately, she smelled the sour, second-hand odor of consumed whiskey saturating the interior of the house, a fetid smell made from a thousand snoring breaths. As she passed the bathroom she saw that the window by the toilet was open and that the season's last houseflies were numerous and slower from the cooler weather. She knew Jake had left the window open after heaving up blood and whiskey still floating in the unflushed bowl. She vacillated whether to let him sleep it off, or get him up now so he wouldn't keep her awake all night with his pathetic moanings and wailings, and banging into everything in his way.

When Hubbard stepped into her father's dark room to wake him, she heard none of the usual snoring that went with his drinking episodes. Flies crawled around his lower lip, black flies dining on the spilt whiskey drops that had run down his stubbled gray chin. His blue eyes were slit open and too vacant to be focused on anything still on earth. She knew he was gone, but she checked his throat and both wrists for a pulse. Nothing.

Hubbard stood at his bedside looking at the dead face of a man she had never really seen live. She couldn't cry. There was nothing she'd miss about him. Always, when she had cried, she had lamented being stuck here with a man who hated himself and all life around him.

After she chased away the flies on his face and

pulled Jake's muslin bedding over his head, she wondered if he had been like this last night, long dead before she left the house for school that morning. She wondered if he had been dying while she spent a couple hours in her lab before going to bed.

Last night, she had been daydreaming about visiting Nell, in Woodbury, seeing herself trying on her wealthy cousin's clothes and letting Nell fix her hair into something stylish and pretty. She had planned on going into the city on the first of the month, when her dad's $412.00 disability check came. Her dad always handed her his signed check to cash at the bank in Blue Hill, then he gave her $100 of it to last her for the month, for things she wanted to buy.

A little of her money went for second-hand lab equipment she'd buy from Doc Jensen for next-to-nothing. Some of her money went for minerals, vitamins and herbs the friendly vet sold her at cost from his regular mail-order supplier in Omaha.

Now, she wished she had a telephone so she could call the Warren ambulance to come and take Jake out of his soiled bed. She felt a moment's panic. How would she ever be able to live here now, she wondered. She would never want to raise hogs for slaughter; that had been her father's operation. And what about Johnny? Johnny could never go with her to Woodbury to her mother's house, or to Nell's rich neighborhood.

Her pet was squealing to come inside. She opened the door for him as her mind raced, searching for a possible way she could keep Johnny. Each question she considered was answered, especially the biggest one: Jake Hawkins wanted to be buried with his hogs, not in Hawkins Cemetery.

That night she shoveled a grave four feet below the hogyard. Under the full October moon her father's 5'9" skinny corpse, wrapped in his muslin sheet, was dumped out of the wheelbarrow into his eternal resting place, landing face down as if kissing the world goodbye while in supplication.

Shoveling the cold Nebraska earth into the grave, Hubbard knew she hadn't broken any laws yet. That would happen on the first of every month when she cashed Jake's government disability check. Shovelful after shovelful, she played over and over in her head the past times she had cashed her father's checks in the Bank of Blue Hill, seeing clearly his scrawled signature endorsed on the back of every check. Yes, for Johnny's sake, that would be her crime: cashing the checks of a dead man.

"It's worth it," she told herself, while Johnny stood snorting and rooting in the cold pile of dirt that slowly filled the new grave; soon it would be trampled flat by the hooves of Jake's beloved hogs now asleep in the barn.

Nap Town

The 1st of November and December came 'round fast and furious for Hubbard. Each time, the two-mile round trip walk to the Bank of Blue Hill seemed to take longer than the entire month between checks. Not a soul talked to her; not one curious mind pulled at her to question her father's whereabouts.

Now, this first Saturday in December, she waited at the frost-covered row of mailboxes on Broken Kettle Road for her Aunt Helen and cousin Nell to pick her up for Christmas shopping in the city, and to sojourn until Sunday in the parallel universe of the rich and clean, who took for granted telephones, cars, good food, fashionable clothes and nice things.

She felt good that Johnny could stay in the house now and while she was at school. Since Johnny was smarter than any dog, he had been housebroken in just two days, now trained to do his business in the bathroom on a bed of straw piled four inches high on flattened cardboard. Besides that, he only ate small portions of the energy food formula she'd had kept him on since he was four years old. She smiled at the notion she had left on the radio for Johnny to listen to. Johnny loved music, especially country.

Then she saw the shining chrome of her aunt's new Buick moving toward her down Broken Kettle Road. A familiar feeling of shame came over her when she saw the stylish new winter coats her aunt and cousin wore so naturally, as if they deserved to wear nice things. She looked down at her father's Navy coat that covered most of her thighs, then to her black rayon slacks. She'd let the hem down twice in the last two winters. She blushed as she inspected the lime-green plastic half-inch heels she bought at the Blue Hill Methodist Church's clothing sale last spring.

Pride assaulted her, activating an irksome twitching around her mouth, a place on her face that always revealed her raw self-consciousness. Much as she would love to have better clothes, she reminded herself that she would buy only new glasses today, since her old prescription caused her to misread small print in her lab studies, and it was nearly impossible without a magnifying glass to see her scales's weights and measures. Not because her vision was getting worse; on the contrary, it was improving, thanks to her vision formula she'd been taking for six weeks.

She sat in the middle of the back seat, luxuriating in the car's plush interior, enjoying the opportunity to see both her aunt and Nell.

"How are you, Hubbard Kay?" Helen inquired from the front passenger seat.

"Fine, thanks," she smiled.

"Mother, she wants to be called Hubbard, not Hubbard Kay! I've told you a thousand times!" Nell implored in her confident, deep voice, before grinning at her cousin via the rear-view mirror.

"Oh, that's okay...I don't care what you call me," Hubbard smiled back at her sixteen-year-old cousin who was also a high school junior.

As Nell left Broken Kettle Road and turned onto the

main highway she asked, referring to Jake, "How's Big Daddy?"

"He's fine," Hubbard said as she removed her glasses and cleaned them with a plain white hanky that had belonged to her father.

Pretty Nell, her full lips covered with red lipstick, went into her usual diatribe. "I don't know how you live out here Hub. You could live with us or your mother anytime you want. It's a mystery to me why you'd keep yourself stuck way out here in the middle of nowhere. We could be going to school together...graduate together...see each other every day. And Hub, you could join the swim team, and we could spend every Saturday shopping and doing whatever we wanted."

Hubbard put her heavy plastic frames back on and turned her head to look at the western sky just before the Buick made the turn onto the road that led to Paradise. The first snowfall bloated the clouds deep into the Nebraska horizon. She was thinking how a stop at the stockyards could be made. She didn't know how she was going to get Nell to take her there. She hoped that soon Johnny would be the only animal on her place. But, yes, snow was coming and everything would work out. She smiled inwardly as Nell and her mother rambled on about clothes and men and jewelry, things that these Hawkins women from the city would surely always have.

At Downtown Optical, the optician explained that an exam, lenses and frames would run close to a hundred dollars. After getting the wings on her old frames tightened for free, Hubbard decided that she would begin doubling up on her formula and improve her vision naturally without a dependency on a new prescription. She told the surprised optician, "No thanks. I don't need any crutches." With the hundred bucks she saved on glasses she could buy some new clothes and shoes at Nell's favorite store. Then, she had to convince the two women to transport her to the Livestock Exchange where farmers assembled in droves to check on ever-changing market prices for their livestock.

Three hours later, Helen and Nell sat waiting in their idling Buick outside the Livestock Exchange in the heart of the world's largest stockyards. Hubbard had promised them that the errand for her father wouldn't take too long. She pushed through the glass front doors and approached a middle-aged man sitting at a desk in the Cattleman's Credit Union; he looked up from his futures magazine and saw the tall red-headed young woman smiling at him.

"Hi! I have a hundred hogs...say two hundred fifty pounds per head...and I want a livestock truck to pick 'em up at my place near Blue Hill, Nebraska. What would be a fair price to have someone pick up a hundred head and haul 'em to the yards here from Blue Hill?"

The man blinked fast before answering. "I've heard ten percent of the gross weight for current market value goes to the livestock transporters, but some have a minimum charge."

"Then the livestock transporter will come out to my place, haul 'em here for a percentage of the gross weight?"

"That's right."

"How do I get paid?" she asked bluntly.

"I believe the transporter gets paid by the yards and takes the commission out of that check, then they send you the difference."

"Is there a livestock transporter near here?"

"Quite a few. The stockyard's main office is down the street a block or so." He pointed. "They'd know phone

63

numbers of transporters and can answer all your questions."

"Thank you," she smiled, then headed for the front door.

Through the heavy glass doors she could see the Hawkins women carrying on an animated conversation while they waited in the Buick. She did not want to ask them to make another stop, so she turned and walked in the opposite direction, toward the back door, following a circuitous path through milling farmers and ranchers. The men were clothed in overalls and jeans, boots and overboots below a collage of dull colored vests, plaid shirts and baseball caps that advertised a brand of feed, a fertilizer, a local bar, or cafe.

Outside the back door it seemed colder and her breath fogged as she beheld the world's largest holding pens, a maze of tall wood fence enclosures with manual gates, acres of squared space. Twenty thousand head of cattle were crammed together, motionless, snorting clouds from wet/black nostrils, bawling their pathetic guttural death knell, a wailing cry regurgitated from a cavernous stomach, saying, "We will be slaughtered here! Every ounce of us used to feed and make products for the two-legged ones who profit from our deaths!"

Hubbard hastened downhill to a cement sidewalk bordered by a four-foot-tall fence in front of a canal full of animal sewage, a river of ever-flowing waste that never froze over even on the coldest days of winter. This route lead to Nap Town directly behind the Stockyards Building, where the man in the Exchange had said she could find information about livestock transporters.

Her memory was clear about the day eight years earlier, just before Jake's vision started going bad, when he brought her to the huge stockyards and she watched as he unloaded eleven hogs from his pickup. He'd told his little girl how a bawling calf that was injured was called a "downer." He said the yards foreman would order the calf dragged by ropes onto the conveyor belt moving through the gas chamber called Nap Town.

Jake told Hubbard how cruel death was for the cattle and hogs that were not quite unconscious from the gas before the butchers from Nap Town slit their throats. Jake Hawkins knew this first-hand because he had been one of those men assigned to wield their blades, waiting at the other end of the conveyor belt while a steel harness was attached to the animal's hind legs and it was hoisted in the air by chains. Six men held knives, and one was Jake Hawkins.

He told Hubbard that he worked there some ten years before she was born, when he was young and needed money after being discharged from the service.

Now, as she neared the massive holding pens she held the image of her father's face as he told her about that downer calf the last day he worked at Nap Town. It seemed so real now to Hubbard that she could feel the emotion of her father's words welling in her throat and freezing on her eyelashes as she blinked back to the day she stood beside him here.

Jake's strong arms had raised her above the fence line while he pointed to the dark area far back in the shadows of the holding pens where the ominous black hole known as Nap Town was located. He'd said, "I'd rather be buried with my hogs, than work here another day."

"That's exactly what I told my supervisor," Jake informed little Hubbard. "I was complainin' about how some of the calves were still awake when we cut their throats. All at once, this calf was down at the entrance to the belt on the other side. I could hear it bawlin' and the yardsmen cussin' to get it out of the way 'cause it was cloggin' up the entrance. This poor calf had a broken leg and was gettin' stepped on real bad by the herd. The yard supervisor kinda smiled at me and told me to attach a chain to its leg and pull it through the belt."

"What'd you do, Dad?"

"Well, at first I couldn't do nothin'. And the boss kept yellin' at me to attach that chain to the calf, I saw the pain and terror in that animal's eyes. So, I pulled out one of my knives and slit its throat right there. I walked away and never went back."

When Hubbard returned to the present, she still looked into the darkness that led to Nap Town. She remembered thinking at that time how brutal it was for her dad to kill that calf. And then she remembered a dream she'd had a few days later. In the dream, her father had rescued the calf from a torturous death. In reality, even an eight-year-old girl could see he was drinking away the fact that he never did anything about the hundreds of other downers dragged into Nap Town.

And all through the years after he'd run away, she could tell that whenever he took his hogs to the yards, he was hoping never to hear or see another downer. All because he was unwilling to fight a system that paid him $412.00 a month for the bad back he claimed he got from slipping and falling in the blood spilled on the Nap Town kill floor.

As she walked away, headed for the Stockyards Building, she remembered her father's stuff still in storage against the back wall of her lab. Rolled into the musty old hammock that he used in summers before his back began giving him too much pain, were the black rubber apron and hip boots he wore home that last day at Nap Town.

Something about the images of Nap Town, his apron and hip boots, and that musty old hammock abandoned in a corner of her laboratory inspired her, now, to continue her research on her vision formula. Suddenly hopeful, she felt that something good was within her reach.

At the entrance to the Stockyards Building, she stopped and whispered a sudden revelation, "The hammock...the swing."

She could see clearly the intangible ingredient she'd left out of her vision formula: relaxation.

Inside the warm building, wrapped in heat that fogged her useless glasses, she envisioned crystalline pages from books she'd checked out at the Warren Library, black and white photos of Chinese students doing daily exercises that would relax their eyes between their studies. It was the swing, the motion of the hammock in her mind that had given her the key to clarity—her own perfect vision. Now, she was certain.

Christmas in Paradise

Christmas morning in Paradise. The smell of pine from the tinseled six-foot-tall Christmas tree standing in the front room window drifted to Mark's bedroom. He awoke thinking of his dad who would be coming later for dinner; they would open presents then.

Grandma's nested patchwork quilts kept Mark so warm his feet perspired. The Freeman antique sleigh bed with its soft mattress was by far the most comfortable bed he'd ever slept in.

Here, in the blue/silver darkness of a winter morning, he felt reluctant to leave this cozy place. But, the guilty pull to get up and go to his mother's grave was growing stronger. Yet it was Grandma's good, early cooking smells that made him want to get up and tackle the day. And he could hear his grandpa come into the kitchen and knew the old man had already shoveled last night's snowfall from the driveway and a path from the back porch door to the garage.

As he sat up in bed, there was a familiar tapping on his window. He got up and tip-toed on the cold linoleum in his white briefs and t-shirt. He raised the window shade and saw Hurley holding the present he'd gotten from his parents. Ice skates. They were tied at the laces and draped around Hurley's neck. He wore a brown wool ski mask, raised and covering the top of his huge skull.

"Come watch me skate!"

That sounded better than going to a grave on Christmas Day.

Seated beside the hot floor furnace in a half-rocker upholstered with one of Grandma's simple floral patterns, Grandpa was reading his King James Bible. When Mark came out of his room in jeans and bare feet to let Hurley in, Grandpa said, "Better get some socks on those feet."

"I will, Grandpa."

It really surprised Mark to see his guest remove his wool mask respectfully when he entered the front room from the porch. To Hurley the gesture meant more than respect. For this was the old man who had let little Hurley sit with him on the driver's seat of the town's new fire engine. Hurley had been five then, yet always remembered the incredibly loud siren and the huge truck that seemed so much bigger than life.

"Merry Christmas, Grandpa Freeman," Hurley waved.

"Merry Christmas, Hurley."

"Merry Christmas, Grandpa," Mark said.

"Merry Christmas. You goin' skatin'?"

"I don't have skates," Mark said.

Grandpa got up from his chair and headed for the back of the house.

Hurley followed Mark into his room where Mark got dressed fast, putting socks on then a warm sweater. Soon, Grandpa came into Mark's room with a pair of old, worn brown skates that had belonged to Larry when he was Mark's age. Grandpa told him not to try on the skates in the house, that the boys could go out to the garage to see if they fit; also telling them that he'd had the old wood stove

69

going in the garage since 5:30 this morning, so it was warm in there.

"And no smokin'," he directed at Hurley.

Grandpa Freeman knew that Hurley smoked below an open basement window at night after his parents went to bed. Quite often for a boy his age, the old man thought and even had talked about it in bed last night with his wife.

Grandma Freeman never said much about her neighbors, good or bad. If there was a problem, she'd pray about it, give it to God. That's what she did when her husband first told her about Mark runnin' with Hurley. They both knew that Hurley smoked and was a tough kid known for getting in trouble in Paradise.

In the Freeman garage, Mark discovered that the old skates were too small for him.

"I can't wear these."

"Bring 'em for looks then. There's gonna be some girls from the Boys and Girls Home skatin' at the park," Hurley grinned.

"What's a Boys and Girls Home?"

"A place for kids who run away from home...orphans and girls who got in trouble."

"Trouble?"

"Had a kid! Are you that naive, Wichita?"

Paradise Park was a square block of massive oak trees. Every winter, the Water Department opened a fire hydrant and filled half the park with three inches of water that quickly froze into an oval-shaped skating rink.

Dolly and Dee had become fast friends at fourteen, after each one gave a baby to the state for adoption. They smoked together, away from the other twenty-plus girls skating under the eyes of two female supervisors on this

Christmas Day outing.

Hurley spotted the two girls smoking and made his move, with Mark looking over his shoulder during the whole scene. They were plain girls with no attractive features...unless you were Hurley Gunderson.

The girls were making fun of Paradise when the boys walked over to them and stood near a block-long snowbank made by a county snowplow.

"There's prob'ly more pigs than people here," Dolly laughed.

"Yeah! And we prefer it that way!" Hurley smiled, lit up one of his cigarettes and smoked with the giggling girls. Hurley stayed right with the girls while Mark said nothing.

"You girls are from the Boys and Girls Home, aren't ya?"

"That's right," Dolly smiled.

"Where's the boys?" Hurley grinned.

"They keep us separated," Dolly laughed then handed her lit cigarette to her friend to share.

"Why do they do that?" Hurley sounded curious.

The girls hot-boxed their cigarette and laughed as this aggressive boy from Paradise answered his own question. "'Fraid you might get in trouble?"

"Who's your friend?" Dolly asked Hurley.

"This is Mark. Say somethin', Wichita."

"Wichita?" Dolly asked.

"Yeah, he's from Wichita, Kansas...ain't ya?"

"Yeah."

Mark kept his hands in his pockets, his eyes low, with his dad's skates draped over his shoulder as Hurley flirted with Dolly. He couldn't believe the things Hurley was saying to that girl, and right in front of him and her friend. Even her tough friend, Dee, was taken back by Hurley's crude approach to Dolly.

"Hey, I got a great idea. Let's go warm your hands up behind those bushes," Hurley winked at Dolly.

Mark and Dee were shocked to see the girl follow him over to the bushes, giggling as if this might be fun. Dee shook her head in disbelief, for it was clear to her that this guy meant business. All Dee said to Mark before she walked away was, "Whatever."

Now alone, Mark stood, breathing onto his palms by raising each glove at the wrist, pretending nothing unusual was going on just forty feet behind them.

It was obvious to Mark that Hurley was getting more aggressive with Dolly; he turned and saw her sitting on Hurley's coat spread on the frozen ground. Mark could hear Hurley peppering the girl with his fast talk about how it would be safe and easy without any way of getting caught.

It sounded, to Mark, like begging was coming from both of them, except Hurley was begging for more and Dolly was half-pleading for him to stop. Mark saw Hurley tugging down her pants.

"Hurley, come on!" Mark called.

His words had no effect; Hurley was totally lost in his lust and going to take the girl in broad daylight at a public skating rink.

Dolly wasn't putting up much of a fight, only telling Hurley to stop. That's when Mark stepped into the bushes and lied, saying that a teacher was coming. Mark held his breath, because the look in Gunderson's eyes was something like seeing the devil himself. When Hurley got off the girl, she pulled up her pants quickly before he could see that there wasn't any teacher in sight. His thing was still out of his pants and red from the freezing cold.

As Hurley buttoned his pants, he complained, "Wichita, there's nobody comin'!"

Dolly hurried away.

"I could've had her!" he protested to Mark.

"You're crazy. That's rape, Hurley. You could go to jail for that."

Hurley laughed at the thought. Then Mark walked away, not wanting to be around Hurley in case the girl called the cops, and because Hurley was a mean kid out of control.

Mark walked faster and faster, glad to be away from Hurley and the rough girls from Woodbury. The old skates' laces were scratching his neck, so he lifted the laces onto his coat collar and began retracing his first few months in Paradise while his overboots made the cold crushing sound of compressed snow between road and rubber.

He knew he had become more cynical by hanging with Hurley. While he walked, time and again his mind grumbled about being stuck in Paradise, dumped onto Grandma and Grandpa's laps with nothing fun to do like there had been in Wichita. Then it hit him, the reality of being here and walking to his mother's grave. She was really gone. And he wondered how many Christmas Days he would spend here, before he could decide on his own where he would live his life.

Step after step he vowed to be less cynical, and to think of each step he took from now on as one step closer to leaving Paradise, to a better life, a life not determined by people who shared your family name.

Hubbard stood outside her back door gazing at the

old barn and hog yard. She was thinking how this was her father's first Christmas in Paradise.

Johnny was now the only animal left on Hawkins ground. Hubbard had been paid $3300 after shipping expenses for Jake's hogs. And she had made good on her plan to remove anything inside the house that reminded her of her father.

Now, Johnny and her research would take over the house, and that suited her fine. Even her father's musty hammock that held her dad's Nap Town apron and boots had been sent to the dump. It had been a great day when she precariously drove her dad's old pickup, bad brakes and leaky transmission and all, to the dump north of Blue Hill. It took five trips to get rid of every piece of furniture, clothing or thing related to Jake, except for his bedroom set.

Yes, his things were out of her sight. Her improving sight. Since her visit to Nap Town, she'd doubled her intake of her vision formula and could tell that her vision had strengthened in just a couple of weeks.

There was no way to test Johnny's eyes, but they certainly looked healthier to her; and, her white pig was much happier living in the house with her, out of the cold barn that she had planned on burning to the ground, but changed her mind, when she realized her neighbors were sure to call the fire department and ask hundreds of questions. No one would miss Jake as long as everything remained very quiet on the Hawkins farm.

Christmas cards to all their relatives were signed by her from Jake and Hubbard. She was certain that no visitors would ever come by. Jake's reputation as a cynical drunk kept everybody away.

Now, at least, she could fill the spartan interior of the house with the sounds of Christmas and country music, keeping it on loud all day for Johnny when she was at school. And she could wear the new navy blue dress she bought in Woodbury with Nell and Helen. She would wear it to school on the first day back from Christmas break.

With over $5000 in savings in the Bank of Blue Hill she could afford to get a telephone in January and still pay her electric bill every month. Her new unlisted phone number would be in her father's name and only given to Helen, Nell, and her mother, so there would be no surprise visits by any of them. She would then be able to call Doc Jensen in Blue Hill to order ingredients for her formulas, instead of having to stop after buying groceries at the A & P, or after she cashed her dad's disability check.

So far, so good, she told herself several times a day, especially at school when the negative thoughts about concealing her father's death would creep into her mind during study time, and stay with her until she was engaged with math problems that she managed with ease.

Reading was easier for her now without glasses. Gone was the usual blur; and it was the same with Mrs. Kohler's hurried writing on the blackboard. Of course, at times she would wear her old glasses that were now taped on both wings at the frame hinge in order to make them stay secure on her freckled nose.

On the playground she overheard that Mark had turned seventeen in October, near the date of her own birthday; and she heard Hurley bragging to Wichita how he was gonna be the starting catcher for the Paradise baseball team.

"But you're not eighteen," Mark had replied.

"You can be seventeen an' play," Hurley said.

"Then I can play?"

She remembered how happy and surprised Mark

seemed when he found out he could play for the only sports team in Paradise.

Now, she stepped back inside her house where the radio played Christmas music as Johnny rested on his side, his lean body stretched long on the polished walnut floor that she had exposed at Thanksgiving. Then, she had removed all the rugs in the front room and both bedrooms. She kept her father's bedroom as it had been in case anybody stopped by.

Nobody cared if Jake Hawkins was alive or dead. Still, she knew that soon she would have to stop cashing his disability checks and let the law know he was dead.

"But what will I do?" she asked herself in the bathroom mirror. "I can't live with my mother...and I'm too young to get a job."

That's when her thoughts changed to abject terror. From the bathroom window she watched Aunt Helen's Buick pull into her drive and swing around the house to park by the back door. Nell had been riding on the back seat, her own mother on the front passenger seat.

Quickly, Hubbard carried Johnny into her father's room and closed the door. She scurried back, bringing his new kitty litter box from the bathroom. She ran to her record player and turned off the music, since her mother would know that Jake wouldn't stand for it in the house.

Nell's hard knock on the back door startled Hubbard. She couldn't remember the last time anybody knocked on her door. When she opened the door, Helen and Hubbard's mother, Alice, stood smiling behind Nell, all holding wrapped Christmas presents, including a tin holiday canister of cookies. Hubbard had to invite them inside.

"If you had a phone we could call first," Nell declared without any sense of invasion.

"I'm getting a phone soon."

"That'll be good," Alice smiled. "Where's your father?" She frowned.

"He's sleeping."

"Merry Christmas," Helen whispered with a smile.

Nell gave Hubbard a hug and handed her a wrapped present, "It's that blouse you wanted."

Suddenly, Johnny squealed to get out of the bedroom and rattled the door. Hubbard blushed from the fuss he was making. Jake would never have allowed the pig in the house. So, as the three guests stood staring at Hubbard with gifts in hand, Hubbard decided that Christmas Day was a good time to confess.

"Mom, remember when Dad wrote that will and you tore it up, because it said he wanted to be buried in his hogyard?"

Alice nodded yes as the women watched Hubbard open the bedroom door and saw Johnny come running out, his toenails scraping the floor.

"Mom, Dad died in his bed a couple months ago...and, well...I buried him in the hogyard without tellin' anybody."

"Why would you do such a thing?" her mother gasped.

"To keep gettin' his checks."

"You've been cashing his disability checks?"

At her daughter's positive nod, Alice howled, "Hubbard Kay Hawkins, that money has to be paid back!"

Hubbard put her gift down on one of the two folding chairs standing alone on the bare wood floor, as Johnny nudged her calf. She reached down and scratched behind his ears.

"I was afraid to stop the checks."

"Well, Hubbard Kay, you're in big trouble. You have to know that. You can't just bury someone and not tell the authorities. You have to have a death certificate. Otherwise, how do they know you didn't kill..."

"Mom! He died in his bed. He was drunk, he had a heart attack, I'm sure."

Alice shook her head in disgust.

"Mom, I thought they'd make me live with you and I'd have to give up Johnny!"

"You're worried about that frigin' pig?" Nell laughed in disbelief.

"Nell...don't start," Hubbard warned.

"You have to tell the law," her aunt said.

"Look, I don't care if I'm in trouble..."

"Well, you should care!" Nell blurted out.

Hubbard watched her mother pace around the spartan front room until she stopped and said, "We'll have to post bail."

"Not on Christmas Day," Helen said.

Nell stood stunned by this bizarre news and how her cousin would be known as a criminal. She was selfishly absorbed in what her high society northside friends would think about such behavior.

"Will this be on the news and in the paper?" Nell wanted to know.

"Quit thinking about yourself!" Hubbard snapped.

The next morning, Hubbard and Johnny stood in Luther's hogyard with him and his grunting herd of hogs. Johnny wore a yellow collar around his neck that Hubbard had covered with fluorescent paint. She'd told the old farmer everything, saying she had no idea how long she'd be gone. Luther agreed to care for her pet while she was away. When she tried to give Luther some money, he refused it. She was more concerned about Johnny than for herself; she worried about taking him off his formulas, but didn't want Johnny on them if she wasn't there to monitor his condition.

She kissed and hugged her pet goodbye, got into her dad's old truck with its bad brakes and leaky transmission and drove the quarter-mile downhill to her house where her family soon would pick her up.

Luther closed Johnny within his new home, and thought about the girl's problem, and how he didn't think it such a terrible thing that she buried Jake on his land; in fact, he wondered if it really was a crime at all. Then he recalled Jake Hawkins telling him how he wanted to be buried with his hogs because he preferred their company.

When her female relatives from Woodbury arrived, Hubbard was leaving the hogyard after placing a feed shovel over her father's grave.

The Visitor

After Hubbard's confession, Nell made the whole scene in the sheriff's office on the 3rd floor of the Paradise Courthouse as difficult as possible. Nell acted as her cousin's voice while Sheriff Hickey fingerprinted Hubbard and told her that she'd have to be held there until the judge got back from vacation in Montana.

"And when's that?" Nell demanded.

"January 3rd."

"January 3rd! Christ...that's next year! You can't keep her here! So her father's dead. He wanted to be buried on his farm! Is that a crime? Her mother can prove that. And we've got the twelve hundred thirty-six dollars she cashed. She turned herself in, Sheriff! It's not like she's a dangerous criminal ya have to lock up! She's only seventeen!"

"So, I have to go to jail for nine days?" Hubbard inquired.

"I'm afraid at least that long," the sheriff said.

Then Alice asked the sheriff why there wasn't a substitute judge when the judge goes out of town.

"We don't get much crime 'round here," he answered.

"So, you're going to lock up a young girl with criminals?" Helen said.

"No, no...there's nobody else we're holding. Now, she'll get three good meals a day from Leona Freeman's stove, so she'll prob'ly put on a few pounds here," he chuckled.

Nell wasn't the least amused, but Hubbard was thinking about the nice kid from Wichita who could read well. He was a Freeman.

"What about the publicity?" Nell snapped.

"Now, there won't be any publicity 'cept for local gossip. She'll most likely end up in Warren House."

"Warren House?" Nell fired back.

"It's a home where young girls live."

"For how long?" Nell demanded.

"How ever long the judge says."

"Well, our attorney says we can visit her and have a right to see where she's locked up," Nell said firmly.

The sheriff unlocked the cell door for his new prisoner; the three women from Woodbury stepped inside the cell with Hubbard. They stood together in the first cell of six cells on the 3rd floor.

"At least the toilet has a stall around it," Nell observed cynically.

Hubbard sat down on the twin-sized bed that was low and flush against the far wall, beneath the one barred window. She opened the window to let a little cold air into the 20' by 20' cell.

Standing just outside her cell door, the sheriff told her, "Ya get a good breeze from the west in this one." He smiled at the women.

Then Hubbard asked why Mrs. Freeman provided meals for the jail.

"Her husband's the janitor. She's been doin' it for

as long as I can remember. Like I said, we don't get many visitors here.

Hubbard's relatives stayed long after she'd changed into the brown jumpsuit worn by Paradise inmates. Before they left, Nell snatched Hubbard's glasses and told her, "I'm getting you new frames. These are horrible, and you won't need them while you're in here."

After a tearful goodbye from her three visitors, who promised to visit tomorrow, Hubbard finished the catered meal her relatives had brought her during the long afternoon, turkey and lettuce sandwiches with butter, one of her favorites. She passed on ordering dinner when the friendly old sheriff asked her. Sheriff Hickey told Hubbard to give him a little notice when she wanted a meal delivered, and to use the button by the cell door to ring him in his office.

She organized the lab books that she brought from the house, and thought it was nice how the sheriff told her he'd get any books she wanted from the Paradise library.

That same night, at the Freeman dinner table, Grandpa began telling Grandma about the Hawkins girl from Blue Hill who skipped her meals in the Paradise jail.

"Hubbard Hawkins?" Mark exclaimed. "She's in my class. What did she do?"

Grandpa Freeman didn't know, but he told Mark that he could deliver meals to his classmate until school vacation was over.

Earlier, Hubbard had watched the women from Woodbury drive away. Then, she had busied herself with her books until sundown. She kept her mind busy and off thoughts of Johnny and her future.

Tonight Hubbard decided to help herself relax by taking some kava with a little water. She discovered the natural relaxant last summer, and smuggled it into her cell in her soap dish. Johnny liked kava, too.

After taking just a few drops of kava it was easier for her to relax her stressed muscles, which in turn helped her mind relax during her first night behind bars. She found the bed more comfortable than her bed at home. And she had ordered breakfast for tomorrow.

Soon after lights went out at ten, she knew it was more than the kava making her smile this first night in Paradise.

It was taking Mark too long to fall asleep because he was looking forward to seeing Hubbard tomorrow. Before sleep came, he thought about how, before today, he had never spoken to the tall redheaded girl with the taped glasses; and now he was going to deliver three meals a day to her in jail. He thought, too, of those words that Grandpa had plainly stated about the Hawkins girl going to Warren House, a place for girls in trouble.

Hubbard had set her alarm clock for seven. The clock, a gift from her mother, had accompanied yesterday's sandwiches. There was no problem now between Hubbard and her mother; Alice was just happy that her only child was free from her former husband, "a despicable drunk," she had called him.

Now, at 7:52 in the morning, Hubbard sat at the tiny writing table against the wall across from her bed, where she would eat her first meal prepared by Mrs. Freeman.

She thought of that old man who was strong and had

good posture, the man who was the janitor in the courthouse. He had led her 3rd grade class through an incredible tour at the Paradise Fire Station that was across the street on the other side of the courthouse.

Mark carried the heavy, covered plate down the steps to the basement door at the courthouse. Grandpa Freeman saw Mark coming and opened the door for him, then led the way up four flights of narrow back steps that passed by the jail and ended at the courthouse roof.

Grandpa unlocked the door at the far end of the cell area. Mark followed him to Hubbard's open cell door. She sat at the small table wearing a cinnamon-red silk blouse that illuminated her blue eyes and complimented her striking, thick red hair. She smiled. He'd never seen her without her glasses on.

The custodian kept walking, through the main entry door and toward the sheriff's office, leaving Mark alone with his classmate.

Mark entered Hubbard's cell gingerly and placed her breakfast tray on the table/writing desk, his arms aching from its weight. She sat there looking down at the covered plate.

"Smells good," she smiled up at Mark.

"Biscuits with sausage gravy, with potatoes and toast," Mark said.

She lifted off the heavy lid and marveled at the best meal she'd seen in years, though she would not eat any of the tiny pieces of sausage.

"There's silverware in the napkin. My grandpa's getting you some orange juice from the fridge here."

"Thanks," she smiled.

"Where are your glasses?" he asked.

"My cousin's getting new frames for me."

"I'm supposed to get glasses. My dad said I can get a pair free at the Air Force base where he's stationed."

"You don't need glasses...if you're willing to make your vision improve without glasses."

"What do you mean?" Mark blinked as she took a small bite of her hot breakfast.

"I have a pet pig I've been treating for vision enhancement. Then I started taking the formula."

He watched her take another bite; he was eager to hear more, but his grandpa returned with her juice, placing it down near her plate.

"Thank you, Mr. Freeman."

"You're welcome. What is your name dear?"

"Hubbard Hawkins."

"Oh, yes. I know of your people," he smiled. "Well, Mark, you'll see her again at noon, huh."

She watched them leave the way they came in, after saying goodbye. Now she felt lonely, even more lonely than on her farm. Mark seemed to be interested in her vision formula; she thought about that as she enjoyed her breakfast.

Later, at half past eleven, the three Woodbury women arrived at her cell with news from Helen's attorney that Hubbard would probably have to spend some time living at Warren House in Warren, Nebraska, sixteen miles southwest of Paradise.

They couldn't tell her a thing about Warren House she hadn't already heard before. In fact, her father, in one of his depressed moods, had driven her by the girls home in his truck and told her that she could live there if she ever wanted to.

Her visitors saw that the prospect of moving to Warren House did not upset her at all.

"At least you'll be off that pig place," Nell declared, as the other women waited for Hubbard's reaction, which never came.

"Doesn't that color look great on her?" Nell asked, pointing to Hubbard's new blouse.

"Yes, yes," they agreed.

"How come you're wearing it in here?" Nell wondered.

She could feel her blush burn against the cool fabric, and hoped Nell wouldn't pursue the topic. She wanted to change the subject to breach another that was more important to her. As she sat on her bed they stood before her holding their purses as if they couldn't stay long.

"I started my period this morning and I don't have anything..."

Nell waved her hand in the air as if she would handle the problem. "Is there a store around here?" Nell asked.

"Around the corner on Main, on the other side of the courthouse," Hubbard pointed.

Nell hurried out.

Mark felt it was a mistake to have told Hurley about Hubbard Hawkins. Hurley just tagged along, in two more inches of snowfall, yakking away as Mark carried Hubbard's lunch, another covered plate that was now wrapped inside an old buckskin jacket that Grandpa said would insulate Grandma's cooking.

Hurley peeked around the hood of his winter coat before bending to form a snowball that he stuffed down the front of Mark's sweater.

"You bastard, Hurley!"

Mark struggled with his hands full as the cold snow slid down his chest and belly and he endured Hurley's jackal laugh.

"Take this!" Mark demanded.

"No way! She's your prisoner," Hurley laughed and refused to take the covered plate.

Eventually Hurley did take the hot plate so Mark could shake out the snow from his raised sweater at his waist. Afterwards, again toting Hubbard's meal, Mark told Hurley that he didn't think his grandpa would let Hurley go upstairs.

"He will. Grandpa Freeman likes me."

"How come you call him Grandpa Freeman?"

"Everybody does, Wichita."

"Still, I don't think he'll let ya."

"Ah, c'mon, Wichita! I just wanna see the jail...see what it's like. I don't wanna mess with your girlfriend."

"She's not my girlfriend."

"You talk about her like she is."

"I just want to talk to her and you'll want to go," Mark complained.

"No, I won't. I'll just go get me a Coke, or somethin'."

Mark explained to his grandpa that Hurley wanted to see the jail. Mark was surprised when the old man handed him the key to the cell area, taking it from his key ring without saying a word, or coming along with them.

When Mark entered Hubbard's cell with her lunch, Nell was just returning from the drugstore. Helen and Alice were seated on folding chairs near the prisoner's bed and Hubbard was at her table. Suddenly, Mark found himself surrounded by four women. He stood shyly holding the tray while Hubbard introduced the delivery boy and told the women how he was in the same class with her at school.

Nell spotted the bow-legged Hurley lurking at the other end of the cell area.

"Who's that?" Nell pointed, referring to Hurley.

"That's my friend, Hurley Gunderson. He's in our class, too."

"What's Gunderson doin' here?" Hubbard demanded, as if disturbed by his presence.

"He just wanted to see what it's like up here."

"He's leaving now...with me," Mark said. He put her plate down. "I'll see ya later," Mark said with contrition.

"Don't bring Gunderson here again...please."

"I won't."

Mark hurried out of the cell embarrassed, but had to return for her empty breakfast plate.

Hurley followed Mark down the courthouse stairs after Mark locked the door behind them.

"That was cool, Wichita!"

"She doesn't want you up there."

"She said that?"

"Yeah. I don't think she likes you."

"She doesn't even know me!" he protested.

"Oh, well."

"I've never said two words to Hawkins!"

Mark was surprised again when his grandpa told him that he could keep the key until he went back to school.

All the way to return the empty plate to Grandma Freeman, then back to the counter stools at Paradise Drug and Variety, Mark felt proud to be entrusted with Grandpa's key; he only half-listened to his friend harping about Hawkins: "Her glasses are six inches thick"; "she prob'ly killed her old man for his government checks"; "I heard she sleeps with pigs."

Cherry Coke

It was dark as night at 5:30 p.m. At six, Mark would deliver Hubbard's first catered dinner from the Freeman kitchen. From the window above Grandma's kitchen sink he watched the trees standing within the half-circle of illumination cast by the flood light on the back porch. Howling wind flung the gray-brown, barren branches in a thousand directions, as the drifting snow grew in some places and exposed bare ground in others.

Grandma stood behind Mark at her farmhouse table ladling her delicious chicken and dumplings awash in her yellow/thick gravy onto the prisoner's plate. A good helping of her garden green beans and hot apple pie were sealed under the lid, as Mark went out to the porch, pulled on and buckled his black overboots before donning his coat, ski mask and gloves.

"Be careful out there, Mark. Nobody's cleared the sidewalks or streets...so it's awful slippery," his grandma warned.

From the table he lifted the buckskin-wrapped container and cradled it to his chest while Grandma opened the door for him. She hastened back to her warm kitchen and over to the window, where she watched her great-grandson make his way slowly through the winter storm. She knew that her husband would be watching for him and return home with him.

The diminishing figure of her grandson struggling through the wind-blown snow as he crossed the backyard brought back a memory to Leona May. She was five years old and among the second wave of her people on the Trail of Tears. There wasn't as much snow as this—but it had been cold. The memory seemed so real as she stood in her heated kitchen, she rubbed her fingers together to warm them. Then she smiled.

She was half Cherokee; she figured that Mark's lineage must be a sixteenth. She told herself that this walk to the courthouse would be good for his character, would test his survival skills. And she knew full-well that her full-blooded German husband was as much of a survivor as any man she'd known. To Leona May Freeman, a survivor was someone who kept working and living well, not complaining about the past, or worrying about the future. Her absolute faith in God assured her that Mark would be returned safely; and Lord knows, the boy's had enough to bear, she prayed.

Grandpa Freeman heard Mark open the door to the basement stairwell that he had just cleared, scraping snow to the side of each step, giving Mark a free path into the warm courthouse basement.

Mark stomped the snow from his boots and peeled off his ski mask and gloves. When he asked if he could visit with Hubbard a bit before returning home, the old man said,"Take your time. I'll be here, waitin' to lock up behind us."

When Hubbard heard Mark unlock the back door, she walked over to her open cell door and watched him bending down to pick up her meal while holding the door open with his backside. She still wore her new blouse as she hurried to sit at the table in her cell.

"Hi!" he smiled.

"Hi! I wasn't sure you'd make it here in this weather."

Upon placing her meal before her, he asked if she'd be coming back to class at school.

"I don't know. My mom says I'll prob'ly have to live in Warren House getting home-schooled after the judge sees me."

"Warren's not too far from Paradise," he said.

Hubbard lifted the cover from her plate. "Chicken and dumplings!" she exclaimed.

"My grandma's a great cook."

"I'll say," she agreed as she began to eat, yet she turned to him on her chair as if she wanted him to stay.

"Tell me about this vision thing," he said.

"It's a formula I started to put together using marigolds. They have a natural antioxidant that helps maintain proper eye lens density. It's kind of complicated with many other natural ingredients," she said while enjoying her meal.

"Can I try your formula? I have to squint to see the blackboard and when I read."

She already knew that was true. Before she could answer him, he asked her if she wanted anything to drink.

"Oh, no thanks...my mom brought me some juices," she pointed.

"How do you take this formula?" he asked.

"I mix it in juice or I sprinkle it on my food. Do you want to try it?"

She got up and found a small sealed jar in a tall

grocery bag, handed it to Mark. "Take a half-teaspoon three times a day. It's enough to last you a month," she said.

"Will my vision get better?"

"Your eyes will be healthier. Time will tell if it helps your vision."

He put the jar inside his coat pocket and packed up her used plate.

"I'll start on it tonight. See ya tomorrow morning," he smiled.

"See ya."

On his way to the door at the other end of the cellblock she called out to him from her cell doorway. "Mark!"

"Yeah?" He turned.

"You might sneeze a few times right after you take it. I did. But it'll go away."

"Okay. Oh...Hubbard?"

"Yeah."

"Why don't you like Hurley Gunderson?"

"He's mean...I just don't like him."

New Years Eve. On this last day of 1965, the women from Woodbury braved the winter weather and brought the inmate a party hat shaped like a silver cone and a Chinese paper horn that curled out when blown.

That morning during her breakfast delivery, Mark had told Hubbard he would bring a cherry Coke with her evening meal to celebrate the new year. So the visitors listened in amusement to Hubbard's excited talk about her classmate who was bringing her a cherry Coke that night.

Nell was appalled that some boy would take a formula that her cousin had used on her pig. Then, Nell surprised Hubbard by giving her a portable radio, saying, "It has an adapter. It works with or without batteries. The sheriff told me it was okay for you to have it. Of course, it was after he looked inside it to see if I was smuggling in "contraband," he called it.

Alice and Helen laughed at the way Nell flipped back her square-cut, shoulder-length, white-blonde hair and lowered her voice to emphasize the word "contraband."

"I can take it with me to Warren House," the prisoner smiled.

"It's all so remarkable how well you are taking this," Alice told her daughter.

"Kava," Hubbard smiled.

"Oh, no, another one of her special formulas!" Nell teased.

The cousins noticed the concern on the women's faces and exploded into raucous laughter that echoed throughout the cellblock.

An hour before that evening's mealtime she could see from her cell window that the wind and snow had stopped suddenly, imparting an eerie soundlessness to Paradise.

When Mark entered her cell with her meal she knew that he had forgotten to bring her cherry Coke.

"Oh, I forgot your cherry Coke. I'm sorry."

"That's okay."

"I can't stay long. My grandpa wants to go home now. Maybe he'll let me bring you your cherry Coke later tonight."

"You don't have to."

"How else would you get one?" he said while packing up the empty plate.

"Have you been taking the formula?" she wondered.

"Three times a day. No sneezing."

"Good."

Not long after he left Hubbard felt lonely. And that's a good thing, she told herself, because she was feeling something besides kava, her formula, and her approaching hearing with the judge and probably Warren House.

She went back to the window and saw Mark and his grandpa walking home. She thought about how she and Mark were alike. Both had been delivered to strange places after the death of the parent they were living with. His father was living his life outside of Paradise, as was her mother. And both would end up in homes chosen by higher authorities and run by determined people.

She put on her new, thin plastic, red-framed glasses for only the second time since Nell brought them to her two days earlier. At the window she stared at her reflection in the glass. She looked into her eyes and imagined seeing her side of Blue Hill, the hills covered with whiteness. Then she smiled at the image of her Johnny asleep and safe in a warm barn. At least he wasn't alone. Perhaps some day she would get her dad's old truck fixed and drive around the city with Nell...and Johnny. She laughed.

Then a melancholy doomed feeling came over her that there was a place she never wanted to return to on the western side of Blue Hill. That kind of life was filled with solitude and certain friendless nights more lonely than this cell could ever be. Here, she ate better meals by far and had more company in one day that she enjoyed than in three months on Hawkins ground.

"And I met a boy I really like," she smiled.

Images of Paradise and Blue Hill locals labeling her as the girl who buried her father in a hogyard so she could cash his government checks, would be around her as long as she lived here, no matter what she ever did that was positive and good. That's why she knew she needed Mark's softness, to round off the tough independent nature that she inherited from her dad, and was all around her in Paradise, Blue Hill, and certain to dwell in Warren House.

Mark wasn't from this world of pig farmers and packing house laborers; he had to know that his kind would never fit in here, or even want to, if he had any sense at all. But then, she thought, he may want to be a big fish in a little pond like Paradise, where dirty little fish like Hurley Gunderson could prosper by leading those like Mark Freeman into corruption and evil.

By the time Mark carried home the empty plate, he had talked the easy-going custodian into letting him have the key to the courthouse basement door so he could surprise Hubbard with a cherry Coke before the new year.

Grandpa had said to be sure to return the key to him afterward. When they reached the backyard of the Freeman property, Mark asked his grandpa what he knew about Hubbard's family.

"Oh, they kept pretty much to themselves, as far as I know. Those hills have always had a Hawkins livin' on 'em. I know they liked whiskey."

"Whiskey?"

"The Hawkins men were hard drinkers."

After supper that night, his grandpa asked Mark what the stuff was that he mixed in his juice.

"It's a vision formula that will improve my eyesight."

The bespectacled couple were thinking alike when Grandma Freeman said, "Your father can get you some glasses at the base for free."

"I know, but I don't want to wear glasses, if I don't have to."

"Eat carrots," Leona said.

"I don't like carrots that much."

"I see ya squintin' at your homework. That can't be good for learnin'," his grandma insisted.

At 8:30 that night, he followed his grandpa's big tracks in the moonlight, until he reached the shoveled courthouse sidewalk. The snow was hard and crunchy under his boots as he cut across the huge courthouse lawn to the other sidewalk that bordered the courthouse. Then, he crossed the street to the one-stall fire station. At the corner on Main where the highway ran through Paradise, he discovered the "closed" sign in the drugstore's front window.

His heart beat with this second failure to get Hubbard's cherry Coke, until he had the idea to continue down Main to the Paradise Tavern where winter-dirty cars crowded the space out front.

The bartender in the dark tavern was missing a front tooth; he was tipsy/friendly when he gladly made Mark a carry-out Coke with his fountain gun then added two maraschino cherries before sealing the lid. He told Mark it was on the house and wished him a Happy New Year.

Back to the courthouse, retracing his steps, Mark let himself in the basement door, not finding a light switch once inside. He locked the door behind him and found his way to the 3rd floor cellblock door, groping in total darkness without spilling a drop of Hubbard's cherry Coke.

She was surprised to see him walking toward her down the cellblock hallway.

"You brought it!"

"Happy New Year," he smiled as he handed her the drink and explained the makeshift formula. She laughed and handed one of the cherries to him by its stem. After they each ate a cherry she told Mark that she would supply him with her vision formula if he would walk her pig, Johnny, once a week while she was in Warren House.

Before he could answer, she was giving him easy directions to Luther's farm, telling him to cut through Hawkins Cemetery on the eastern side of Blue Hill.

"I suppose I could walk him on Saturdays," Mark mumbled, reasoning to himself that good vision for the upcoming baseball season was worth it.

She offered him a drink of her cherry Coke but he declined, since his mother had admonished him for drinking from the same cup of a friend.

"You make any New Year resolutions?" she asked.

"No."

"I did. Wanna know what they are?"

He nodded, as they stood side-by-side in the empty hallway.

"I'm gonna learn how to cook. No pork though," she laughed.

"My grandma could teach you. But she gets up too early for you to see her making breakfast," he drawled.

"Your accent isn't as strong as it used to be," she noted. "You're startin' to talk like the rest of us."

"I guess it's wearin' off," he laughed.

She glimpsed him walking home from her window while she finished her cherry Coke.

"He's a sweetheart," she whispered dreamily and watched until he vanished from her view.

As If God Knew

On Saturday, April 5th, Hubbard began her fourth month at Warren House, a place that would be her home for about a year. The Pioneer County Judge sentenced her to house arrest there until her eighteenth birthday for defrauding the government, and, of course, she had to pay back the monies received. No charges were brought against her for burying her father on her property, since Hubbard's neighbor Luther and her mother testified that Jake Hawkins often said that he wanted to be buried with his hogs.

The judge had granted Hubbard forty-eight hours to handle her affairs before moving to Warren House; and she had been in her mother's custody during this transition period.

Her last two days of freedom were spent alone with Johnny on Blue Hill. She emptied her antique double dresser and danced in its Swedish oval mirror as she played country music on her little record player. She dawdled over her packing and took long walks with Johnny. Visiting Doc Jensen in Blue Hill in order to put together a good supply of her vision formula for herself and Mark, she found out that there was no way the vet could board her pet for a long period of time. So, she bought a fluorescent yellow dog collar for Johnny.

The day the Woodbury women delivered Hubbard

and her things to Warren House, there was no sense of punishment during the process. Mrs. Flood, the Warren House director, told Hubbard and her family that after three months of good conduct, once a week she would be given a pass for three hours; unsupervised, she could shop in Warren, go to the library, attend a movie at the lone Warren theater, or walk around the quaint, clean town of seven thousand industrious people—a place that seemed a million miles away from the gossip in Paradise and Blue Hill.

Three months flew by for Hubbard. Ninety days of structured living was not difficult for her. She maintained good grades, performed her cleaning chores and kitchen duties with a good attitude; she was friendly to all the girls, but got close to none. None of the girls shared any of her interests, or were as focused about pursuing them.

She received her first three-hour pass on a Wednesday, which would be her day of the week from then on. Her mother picked her up and drove her over to Luther's place so she could walk Johnny before they went to Woodbury and had lunch with Nell and Aunt Helen.

On Saturday, after thirty minutes of brisk walking, Mark reached Hawkins Cemetery wishing he had a bike, though a bike wouldn't make it any further, he knew, than where he now stood at the crest on the eastern side of Blue Hill.

Rough gullies ran downhill on the western slope in a hundred directions, crossing and then recrossing each other as if made by giant tractor tires, leaving ruts and grooves that could not be traveled, unless on foot. Dampness from a late-night spring rain caked mud up each side of his Keds as Mark followed his own tracks made on previous Saturdays, since the spring's first thaw in late March.

In just a few hours he would be on Paradise Field trying out with Hurley for positions on the Paradise Panthers baseball team on this first day of practice.

Hubbard's vision formula was working. He became conscious of improvement about a month ago when reading the moving red and white license plates on his Saturday trek to walk Johnny. Then, he noticed that each Saturday he saw new things around him without squinting, just as now he was able to read the blackboard in class and his text books without the usual blurring of letters.

Deeper into the western slope of Blue Hill he could now see Luther's mud-splattered farm that had its own distinct look and was surrounded by new-green pastures where fenced reddish-brown cattle grazed listlessly, here and there, in cool breezes that carried intense odors of sweet, rich soil and animal dung mixed with the young spring grasses that swiped and cleaned his shoes with each slicing step.

Only one Saturday in February Mark had not walked here; his dad had spent the whole weekend in Paradise and drove him to Luther's farm in his Pontiac. Nearly every day since his father's extended visit, Mark recalled the simple words his dad had spoken during one particular late-night talk while sharing Mark's antique bed.

As the faint scent of Old Spice wafted above the bedding, he'd asked about the first time his father met his mother. Mark still remembered his dad's words exactly.

"I met her at a party on base. She was sitting at a table with a girlfriend and I asked her to dance. We danced the whole night without stopping. I gave her a ride home...kissed her good night...and asked her to go on a Sunday drive with me the next day."

Those words were important to Mark, because he

had never seen his parents happy together; he promised himself that he would not repeat their kind of relationship, one that ended in separation and divorce.

Johnny's streamlined body could always be seen waiting outside at Luther's hogyard gate, when his walker arrived. And most times, as now, Mark saw the old farmer in his faded-green overalls tending to the chores that kept his operation afloat, a sea of deep mud bordered by rotting fences containing over a hundred grunting swine.

Sometimes the old farmer would wave at Mark, his yellow, jagged teeth welcoming the kid from Paradise.

"Howdy, Mark!"

"Hi, Luther!"

"The Prince of Pigs is waiting!" the old man grinned as his wobbly-thin legs moved from task to task.

Upon retrieving the ten-foot-long piece of rope used as a leash tied to the pig's yellow collar, Mark could tell that during Hubbard's visit on Wednesday Johnny's white short hairs had seen the business end of a steel brush and had been scraped clean down to his pink hide.

Johnny stood staring at Mark, his wet pink snout above a wide grin that said he was happy for the coming exercise. Off they went on a slack leash, down the dirt lane to Broken Kettle Road, side-by-side, and soon passed the simple Hawkins house where Johnny always wanted to stop on the muddy road and his small brown eyes stared at his old home.

They continued down the road until they reached the Hawkins mailbox, whereupon, most Saturdays, they would turn around and trace the half mile back to Luther's. But now, as Johnny's spliced curly-q tail swished and he sniffed the road, Mark's old cowardly feeling of paralysis came upon him, and he could not leave the letter that he wrote to Hubbard last night in her mailbox.

He knew she checked her mail every Wednesday on her three-hour pass. She had sent him a postcard with a hog on the front; on the back, she had written in small letters how she would be at the farm from nine 'til noon. She told him not to walk Johnny any further than her mailbox, because it was not a good idea to walk the pig more than a mile. "And the walk should be under twenty minutes...not that long to walk for good vision...ha! ha! Hubbard."

Tonight he'd put another letter unsent into his shoebox, he thought. And save it. And save it.

Next Wednesday. The letter Hubbard had wanted to write was with her now, inside the back pocket of her blue dungarees, as Luther drove his old truck out of the Warren town limit. Her blue flares and matching blue cotton shirt were to be worn when girls were out on their weekly pass.

Luther wouldn't bring Johnny along in his truck; he said he didn't like hauling a pig around town, he'd told Hubbard on the phone and repeated now, "One pig'll fall on the turns. It's not like haulin' a load to the yards," he smiled.

"I know. I'd rather go home and see him anyway."

"What's it like in that place?" Luther asked.

"Oh, it's okay. I eat better and I guess it's good to be around girls my age. I share my room with a girl called Sherry."

"That's why I go into town, to get away from the hogs. Boy, I sure wouldn't spend my free time visitin' no pig," he laughed.

"It's good that Mark walks him on Saturday," she changed the subject.

"Yeah. They both seem to like it. But I sure as hell don't know why that boy walks from Paradise and back, just to walk a pig. Seems a long ways to go and a lot of trouble, if ya ask me."

Hubbard just smiled and turned her head to her passenger window as the old farmer drove east and the treeless hills of Northeast Nebraska rolled under them with undulating smoothness that afforded frequent shortened vistas of cloned earth under a baby blue sky dappled with clear-white puffy clouds that appeared motionless.

Because her period began last night, she felt like shoving her elbow into Luther's skeletal face when he lit his walnut-scented tobacco in the old cherry wood pipe he plucked from his ashtray. It's his truck, she told herself, while coping with the idea that she could spend every Wednesday looking forward to just this.

By the time they arrived at their turn onto Broken Kettle Road she had softened her attitude toward Luther, an affable hog farmer who was of the same breed as her father; they were men who raised animals for slaughter. They were men who felt even less than the very hogs they delivered to Nap Town. Both men lived solitary lives after failing in marriage. Both spent their profits on drink and tobacco; yet she knew that it was their daily regimen of lard and animal fat from the very animals they raised to kill that would eventually choke off every drop of blood moving through clogged arteries to a petrified heart.

Yet somehow she felt compassion for the crusty old codger who had filled his truck's cab with sausage burps and smoke, even though her innate aversion to his kind kept her distant from him, just as she was around her own father.

At the row of mailboxes she told Luther that she would get her mail when she walked Johnny. Alone; she wanted to be alone when she opened the letter she hoped Mark had left for her. Alone; she wanted to be alone when she left her letter for him, the same letter that was now wrinkled and sealed and forever to be unchanged now that she had rewritten it five times during the late hours on her bed long after her roommate began snoring like one of Luther's pigs.

Driving up the hill she could see her drab house to the left. Now it stood on her land. And her land no longer held her father's dead body after being exhumed and examined by the county coroner. Exonerated, Jake's daughter agreed from her Paradise cell that cremation and unclaimed ashes were good enough for a life unlived.

"Luther, I want you to have my dad's bed, or give it to someone who wants it. Just have it outta the house before I move back in. Okay?"

"Okay. His truck needs a lot of work. When I started it up the other day it was missin' pretty bad."

"I'll get it fixed later...or have it hauled to the junkyard."

Johnny squealed with delight when he saw his momma coming. After kissing his snout and hugging his lean body, Hubbard secured the rope around his yellow collar and walked him slowly down the hill by her place, passing the green shoots of spring's lush grasses and weeds, their tops beginning to tilt toward the muddy road in patches of verdant greens and yellow-browns. They reminded her to be sure and grab a jar of her allergy formula that she'd stored in her lab.

She hated her hair now; it needed to be cut, styled like she had wanted at that northside salon where Nell and Aunt Helen went. She ran her free hand through the thick red waves of her course hair, as she talked to Johnny.

"You like it when Mark walks you?"

Johnny's grunting while walking sounded like a positive response as she continued, "I'll keep comin' to see ya every Wednesday 'til I'm home."

Another grunt brought a smile to her freckled face as she breathed in deeply the April air so alive with the sweet earth smells of new growth and open skies.

Just then, Johnny tugged on his leash to turn right onto the Hawkins dirt drive, but she yanked him along, continuing toward the Hawkins mailbox.

"We're not goin' back to that place to live for a long time," she said firmly, as if telling a spoiled child. "I may sell everything when I get out. So get used to that idea," she laughed.

She felt anxious, her palms moist as she and her pet neared the row of crooked mismatched mailboxes that were, in most cases, the only communication with the outside world for Blue Hill residents who were few and far between.

At the mailbox she tied Johnny to the hickory board behind her box so she could focus on her mail without worrying about Johnny wallowing in the nearby ditch. She laughed at the sight of her trembling fingers as they opened the aluminum box. It was full of a week's mail that Mark must have decided she would pick up today. Twice she flipped through her stack of mail held against her chest. Nothing from him. He hadn't opened the box after all.

Dazed from dashed hopes, she realized that now she could not leave her letter here for him to find on Saturday. She left the letter in her pocket as she headed Johnny back up Broken Kettle Road, unconscious of everything around her. A thousand thoughts told her the same thing: "He doesn't care; he's not really interested in me; he doesn't think I'm pretty."

This time she followed Johnny's pull onto her dirt drive, becoming saddened at the sight of familiar things she hadn't missed since her incarceration. She thought of the hand-written will her mother had found in Jake's sock drawer that left his only child his land, the house and his truck; and there was the proof in his scrawl that he wished to be buried without a funeral under his animals.

At first oblivious to the direction Johnny led her, she was now aware that they stood before the closed weatherbeaten door to her lab, her sanctuary from her dying father. The padlock had been cut away by the sheriff. When she pushed open the door she let go of Johnny's leash and followed the rope's end into the empty little space that sparkled from dust beams of sunlight falling through the open door.

She watched Johnny lay down on the rough oak floor that had been smoothed in places from their shared endless hours spent there. Her mind drifted to Warren House, thinking of all the dirty pots and pans she had to scrub every day three times a day with her rough/red hands. They were chores she had done for Mark vicariously, because of her hope that he cared for her and liked her enough to write to her today, as he wrote in their classroom with such sincerity.

Sentimental Mrs. Kohler had read his words to the class for all her students to hear with rapt attention and wonder. He wrote about his first autumn in Paradise and the teacher had posted his essay on the bulletin board with a big red-penciled "A+" at the top beside his name for all his peers to see:

"I never truly saw the morning until I moved to Paradise, Nebraska. It was as if I began my life here when I discovered these new colors and things that surrounded me when my father brought me here to live in his boyhood town. I did not even know how to spell autumn until I saw it here with my own eyes. But now, autumn means colored trees and good smells coming from my grandma's kitchen; and it means the feelings of love I feel inside the home of my great-grandparents.

"They were scented colors that I could see and smell every new morning of my first autumn in Paradise. My grandpa says that a meal should have lots of colors made from God's food grown under His sun; and he said that His yellow light turns tomatoes red, cucumbers green, potatoes brown, and onions white. And he says that, if God is given thanks for this food he's blessed us with, we will carry the light of His love that will sustain us for all of His seasons.

"Yes, my first autumn in Paradise has opened my eyes to color, and best of all, these things have shown me that I am not alone. Because I was mad at God for taking my mother from me. Then I realized that to be mad at Him means that I must believe in Him.

"Being here in Paradise under my grandparent's roof of loving colors, has given me the courage and faith to trust in Him again and to forgive myself for being so frightened of my new life in Paradise. It was as if God knew I was coming here."

Hubbard recalled how Mrs. Kohler cried openly after reading Mark's words. And Hubbard could see all of the faces turned to his face that was blushing from unwanted attention. She saw then that he was a stranger among them who could never be one of them.

She could not send her letter, the letter she now held

in her hands below her waist. They were words telling him how she looked forward to being free again and returning to school where perhaps they would graduate together. She had written about how much she enjoyed his writing when Mrs. Kohler read it out loud in class. And she said she'd love to get a letter from the best writer in Paradise, a letter that he could leave in her mailbox on Saturday. Your friend, Hubbard. P.S. Hope to hear from you soon! And thanks for keeping Johnny in shape!

She returned her letter to her back pocket and then saw what she had always missed right in front of her nose. It was Johnny; he was stretched out on the floor of her lab, his brown eyes disconsolate and waiting for her to lie beside him—and cry with him again—because every time before she had played with him afterward. A pig crys without tears, like any animal. For a thousand times, as now, she had lain down with him, rubbed his belly and sobbed out her loneliness as the caretaker for a miserable alcoholic who had nothing positive to say about anything...ever.

Now, her red fingers rubbed his pink belly while tears poured from her blue eyes and splashed onto her long red lashes that closed tighter and tighter until all her salty toxins were released down her face and neck with the drops of pent-up sorrow now dark stains on the feedhouse floor that her grandfather built long before she was born.

It was Johnny who raised his head first, his tiny brown eyes checking to see if her eyes were open and showing him things he had seen better than her father, a father drowning in denial about his life unlived.

Hubbard spoke to Johnny. "I won't let livin' there and away from you get me down. I choose not to suffer. I'll come out of that place a stronger person. And never again will I let anybody run my life and control who I am. I promise, when I get out we'll be together...no matter where that is."

She paused, remembering the oppressive voice of her father saying always, "I can't afford it."
She had grown so tired of hearing those words over and over again, even his unspoken ever-constant ways of saying it, in grunts and groans and ways his face could say no to every little thing she dreamed of wanting or having. "I can't afford it."

Even the thought of wanting, then asking for an extra nickel for a second carton of cold milk from the school milk machine was drowned in that raspy voice of a broken man behind the lit cigarette saying, "I can't afford it."

Now, Hubbard sat up, her flared jeans cuffs scraping the uneven floor; she turned Johnny's face to hers and held it there as she spoke into his eyes, "I will live here. He cannot control me now. This is my home...my land...and I can afford to fix it up the way I want it to be. I can afford it!" she laughed.

She hopped up, grabbed a jar of her allergy formula and ran outside with Johnny running after her. She laughed all the way to the back door of her house where she found the key that her mother left for her under the rubber doormat.

After school, after fielding ground balls in Hurley's back yard, Mark stepped into his cool bedroom that Grandma always made ready for him. He kept his shoebox of unsent letters in the dark closet. They were mostly words written to his father while they were separated; and of late a stack was growing of folded letters written to his mother since moving to Paradise. At the top of the stack was the letter he'd written to Hubbard, the one he could not leave in her mailbox. The envelope was addressed simply "To Hubbard." He opened the letter inside and read it with deliberation, outloud, in a whisper.

Dear Hubbard, It was one cold Saturday this March when I was walking Johnny by your farm and I followed his lead to your house. He went straight to that little building near the hogyard that looked like an old doll house, a place where you must have played. The door was unlocked so we went inside the little room. I left the door open for more light even though it was windy and cold outside. I saw Johnny lie down on the floor, grunting with his eyes open. At first I thought he was tired, or not feeling well. Believe it or not, I thought that he was crying, missing you, his sad brown eyes reminding me of caged puppies in a pet store. I asked him if he missed you and he grunted yes. It was so clear to me, Hubbard, that Johnny understood me, so I got down on the floor with him and scratched him behind his ear, telling him that I know what it's like to miss someone you love. I found myself crying harder and harder after telling Johnny that. I guess the privacy made me want to cry, I don't know. Anyway, I felt so much better afterwards, I thought I could see better, better than before I went into that tiny room. My walk back to Paradise was filled with more things to see than I've ever noticed before. I guess what I wanted to say to you, Hubbard Hawkins, is thanks for being my friend and sharing your wonderful vision formula with me. I truly hope that everything works out for the best, as my grandpa says it does. So, if not for you being on the 3rd floor of my grandpa's courthouse, I would probably be wearing glasses by now and missing so many things right in front of me. Hope you are doing well. Your friend, Mark. P.S. It's as if God knew.

Wichita Kid

By May, Mark knew that he could hit. After the
second week of practice with the Paradise Panthers, every
player and coach knew that the left-handed kid from
Wichita would be at the top of their batting order and play
first base.

Hurley had a very strong throw to second base and
would be their starting catcher. The whole team started
calling him "Gunner" soon after Hurley threw out speedster
Terry Breedlove trying to steal second base. Mark had been
warming up, swinging two bats together in the on-deck
circle when Hurley nailed Breedlove from his knees.

"Good arm, Gunner!" Mark yelled.

Hurley raised his mask and smiled when his friend
stepped up to bat on the left side of the plate.

"Yeah. Wichita...you try to steal on me and you'll
get gunned down, too!"

Mark pressed his batting helmet down to fit snug
and faced Ted Slocum on the mound, the Panther's #1 ace.
The right-handed beanpole fired a fastball a notch off the
outside corner of the plate, yet Mark's long reach had no
problem drilling it for a double into right-centerfield.

Mark was hitting the ball so well because he was
seeing so much better. He no longer squinted to see
anything.

After practice on the day before their June 1st opener against the Blue Hill Bluebirds, Gunner and Wichita talked as they walked home carrying their gloves, their steel spikes draped over their shoulders.

"I have to get my driver's license now," Mark replied after Hurley asked him if he wanted to watch the Yankees on his parents' new color TV.

"You got wheels?" Hurley remarked, as if insinuating something cynical.

"No."

"Well, join the club, Wichita. I've had my license for three months and ya know how many times my parents let me drive? Twice! Once to the store with my mom! And the other time they let me drive around the frigin' block three times while they stood on the front porch and watched me like some damn baby. I'm gettin' my own wheels first chance I get."

Mark laughed at his friend's frustration and said, "My dad'll never let me drive his Pontiac. And my grandparents only use their car to go to church and the store."

"Then what good does it do to get a license?" Hurley railed.

"Some day I'll drive. I just wanna get it. Besides, how many kids our age wait to get a license until they have their own car?"

"I'm gonna get my own wheels. That's for damn sure. Hey, maybe Hawkins'll sell that old truck you said's parked at her place."

"She'll prob'ly drive it when she gets out of Warren House."

"When is she gettin' outta there?" Hurley asked.

"I don't know."

"Don't ya ever talk to her?"

"No, she only gets to leave for three hours on Wednesdays."

"I'll betcha she'd sell that truck right off for a couple hundred bucks. Why don't ya call her? Better yet, write her a letter. You're a good writer. Girls love to get letters."

"I do write her letters," Mark said.

"Did she write back?"

"I never sent 'em," Mark confessed.

"Why not?"

"Didn't want to."

"What good does it do to write 'em if ya don't send 'em? It's a big waste of time, if ya ask me," Hurley pronounced.

"I enjoy writing them," Mark stated firmly.

"Oh, I see! You're afraid of being rejected!" Hurley laughed, causing Mark's face to burn.

"Drop dead, Hurley."

"Afraid to strike out, Wichita?" Hurley asked in mocking laughter that made Mark clench his jaw, unable to speak.

Mark veered off, away from Hurley, taking a shortcut to the courthouse as it began to sprinkle from scudding patches of dark clouds. He knew Hurley was right; and he realized that losing his mother was at the root of his fear of being rejected by Hubbard. A thousand things that he could never tell her in person he'd said in his letters. Just last night he'd written another letter to Hubbard about how much he missed her. He'd been writing about his mother when he wrote:

It's a terrible thing when God takes. My dad says

it's always for a reason, some big plan, he said, and it's not for us to know why. My dad doesn't go to church, but I believe he knows what he's talking about when it comes to knowing God. He lost his mother when he was young. So he knows more than I do about it.

Anyway, since summer is here, I can stop by some Wednesday and see you, maybe even learn how to drive your truck and take you back to Warren. Luther told me he doesn't mind picking you up 'cause you pay for the gas and gave him all that feed after you sold your dad's hogs. I'm going to get my driver's license real soon, and it would be so cool if you could teach me how to drive a stick shift.

I guess I'm trying to get some time with you before someone else takes you away from me and shows you how special he thinks you are. You know so many cool things about animals and nature and the science of your formulas. To be around you when you're just living your life sounds like fun and so different from my world of words and sports and playing games with Hurley Gunderson.

Well, Hubbard, I better get some sleep. My first game is in a couple days and we sure want to beat those Bluebirds from Blue Hill. See ya soon, I hope. Your friend, Mark.

He entered the county clerk's office in the courthouse and took a seat on one of the hard chairs the county made people wait on and made them wish they were out of there. The elderly woman behind the counter was busy helping someone find tax records. It looked to Mark that he was in for a long wait.

Mark's thoughts drifted to another letter he wrote, one addressed to God. He wrote the letter to God after his mother's funeral, a letter that he believed would never be read. It was an angry letter written by an angry boy who felt injured and lost in Paradise.

He had read it again last night, after he'd chickened out once again, deciding not to give Hubbard the letter he wrote to her. He'd taken the sealed envelope from the shoebox containing all the other letters he'd never sent and slit it open. It read:

Dear God, In church, the minister said it was your divine plan to take my mother from this world in order to be with you in heaven. Why did you not care that I need her with me? I know that if I hate you for taking her, it means that I still believe you exist. Ever since I lost her, I feel more scared than I've ever been. It's a feeling I can only explain by saying this has hurt me. I cannot imagine losing anyone more important to me than her. How dare you do this to me so young, knowing full-well that losing her will decide who I am, who I become, and who I choose to love for the rest of my life? I am not your little boy to boss around any more. If fear is part of your plan for me, just know I will fight this fear you have instilled in me. Mark Freeman, in Paradise, Nebraska.

The Panthers' first game was played under the lights at Paradise Field. Larry Freeman was seated in the bleachers with Grandpa Freeman. Grandma Freeman's arthritis was bothering her too much for her to attend the game.

All eight teams in the league had voted to have half their games at night under the lights for two reasons: humidity, and more beer would be sold at the concession stands. Blue Hill, Paradise, Warren, Walthill, Emerson, Pender, Ponca, and the expected repeat champion, South

Woodbury, made up the eight teams in the Northeast Nebraska League.

South Woodbury's population was ten times bigger than any of the other towns. Just across the river from Woodbury, South Woodbury's pool of players was good because they competed with athletes in Woodbury schools in football, basketball, and track. Yet the number one reason South Woodbury was expected to repeat was their star pitcher, Greg Landers, back for his last year as a seventeen-year-old. Greg was being scouted by two pro teams, the Cubs and White Sox.

As Ted Slocum warmed up on the mound with Hurley, Mark was throwing hard grounders from first base to his three infielders.

From their bleacher seats, some 150 supporters from Paradise and visiting Blue Hill gabbed and laughed while the younger boys darted here and there waiting for the game to begin.

Edwin Freeman's jaw was slack as he waved hello with a big smile; it seemed like everyone knew and liked Mr. Freeman.

Catcher Hurley Gunderson taunted the lead-off Blue Hill batter when he stepped up to the plate. "Arnie Stagg...Sandbag...battin' for the Bluebirds, hell, I remember when ya got caught beatin' off while sandbaggin' by the river!"

"Up yer ass, Gunderson," the batter returned.

Slocum delivered the first pitch and the batter swung and missed.

Hurley laughed. "Sandbag's not used to playin' with a big bat!"

After Sandbag struck out swinging, Hurley cackled so loud even some of the spectators could hear across the fence in back of home plate. Veteran umpire, Prunes Davis, behind the plate, who got his name for farting during games, laughed at Hurley's trash talk.

Bottom of the first inning, Grandpa Freeman and Larry applauded when lefty Mark stepped up to the plate to bat with the lead-off man on first base. Mark could see the ball so clearly it appeared to be slowing down for him. He swung at the first pitch and hit the ball to deep right-centerfield for a double. The Wichita Kid went 3-for-4 with two doubles and a single, with three RBIs, and he scored two of the Panthers' eight runs in the 8 to 2 victory over Blue Hill.

After the game, the three Freemans and Hurley sat at a picnic table outside the Paradise Dairy Queen near Larry's parked Pontiac, eating ice cream. Larry praised Hurley on his batting.

"Two singles," Hurley said, reserved in front of the Freeman men.

"You guys'll be right there with South Woodbury, if ya keep playin' like ya did tonight," Larry said.

It felt good to Mark to have his dad and grandpa there after a victory. Grandpa was sitting so straight in his green and white checkered short-sleeve shirt and olive green pants, sipping his iced tea with such a contented look on his face; his mere presence infused a sense of respect into the hearts of the others, especially Hurley. Mark had never seen his cocky friend so quiet and well-mannered, even in front of adults.

Grandpa Freeman said to Hurley, "How's your mother and father, Hurley?"

"Fine, sir. They're workin' a lot." Hurley's mother worked as a bookkeeper for her husband's monument company in South Woodbury.

"How come they didn't come to the game?" Mark asked his friend.

"They've been busy with a bunch of funerals. Those boys who drowned in the river, they had their funerals today. I wouldn't swim in that river with all them whirlpools."

"I used to swim across it and back every day in the summer when I was your age," Grandpa Freeman smiled.

"Really? You ever get caught in a whirlpool?" Hurley asked him.

"Not any big ones. They'll getcha if you're tired, or if you're not a strong swimmer."

He turned to Mark. "Your great-grandma was a better swimmer than most men in her day."

"Really?" Mark said, wide-eyed.

"She was a good diver, too," Larry interjected. "Didn't she dive off the Combination Bridge?" he asked the old man.

Grandpa Freeman laughed without sound except for his creaking dentures, then he said, "She jumped off it. I never saw her dive off it."

Larry laughed, saying to his son, "I wouldn't put it past Grandma, she's still pretty spunky."

When they got up to leave, Mark's dad surprised his son. "You can drive us home, Wichita Kid."

Wednesday morning after the Panthers' second victory, Mark woke to the sound of a dove cooing its soft melody outside his open bedroom window. Last night, his father had promised to buy him a car when he graduated from high school. That was still a whole year away. The thought of waiting that long for a car gave him the courage to hop out of bed with the bold idea he thought of during the long drive back to Paradise from Ponca after last night's game. Both father and son had been in a good mood, because Mark had gone 3-for-3 with three singles that helped beat the Pirates 6 to 4.

Mark spread open the beige muslin curtains at his window to see if Hurley was on his porch across the street. Then, he decided he'd better go alone, since Hubbard didn't particularly like Hurley. The antique soft-ticking clock on his dresser read 8:05. If he washed his face, brushed his teeth and got dressed fast, he thought he could be there before Luther brought Hubbard to Johnny. Besides, he was running low on her formula and that was his good reason for being there.

He beat Hubbard there because he ran half the way to Luther's farm. Mark had Johnny leashed and grunting to walk when the roar of Luther's old truck rolled onto his muddy drive.

Mark's heart was racing with Johnny's when he saw Hubbard's surprised face behind Luther's dirty, cracked windshield. He thought she looked good without her glasses on.

When she got out of the truck Hubbard became self-conscious, worried about how she looked with uncombed, fly-away hair, and she thought her thighs looked too fat in her flared dungarees.

"This ain't Saturday!" Luther barked good naturedly.

Mark approached with the aid of Johnny's excited pull. "I'm almost out of formula," he said.

Hubbard smiled at him. "I'll bring some next Saturday and leave it in the mailbox for you...if I didn't see you."

"Okay," he said, then looked up at the sky and frowned as it began to rain lightly on them.

While Luther tended his chores, they walked Johnny, Hubbard taking the rope attached to Johnny's yellow collar.

"We need the rain," she turned her face up to the cloudy gray sky and smiled.

When he'd thought of seeing Hubbard, he hadn't planned on talking about the weather. After an awkward pause, Mark told her that his baseball team was playing the Warren Warriors the next Saturday, adding, "Too bad they only let you out on Wednesdays."

"Warren Warriors?" she laughed. "Try sayin' that fast a few times."

They laughed at the tongue twister that tripped both of them.

"It would be fun to go to a game," she lamented. "Oh! I get out of Warren House when school starts this fall!"

"Really?"

"Yeah, but I have to live with my mom in Woodbury. They won't let me live alone here."

"Why not?"

"They think I'll bury someone else, I don't know," she laughed.

As they neared the Hawkins drive, the house appeared older and dirtier and looked smaller and more drab to her now, after seeing some of the nicer homes in Warren. Still, they followed Johnny's habitual pull onto the Hawkins property.

"You prob'ly think I'm weird for buryin' my dad here."

"That's what he wanted, right?"

"Yeah, but now I think it was a weird thing to do. I think it's best I go to school in Woodbury. I don't want to spend my senior year bein' gawked at in Paradise."

"Yeah. What about Johnny?"

"Luther will keep him. I can't drive my truck 'til I

get out." Hubbard held her hand out, catching the last drops of the brief rainfall. There hadn't been enough to even dampen their shoulders.

"That's what I wanted to ask you," Mark drawled. "I have my license now and I was wondering if you could teach me how to drive a stick shift."

Jake's old Ford truck's black paint was nearly worn to its metallic skin. Hubbard inspected the tires like an old pro and told Mark he'd have to get behind the wheel by using the passenger-side door. After he got in, she put Johnny on the seat, too. The inside of the truck smelled of mildew and oil. The shredded leather seat felt musty/damp and was more curled on the driver's side. The ashtray was filled with her dad's cigarette butts.

Hubbard got in, opened the rusty glove box and found a key that she inserted into the ignition. Pieces of moldy insulation padding hung from the roof in several places directly over Johnny who sat on his haunches between them, sniffing the old interior.

"It has a new battery, so it should start," she laughed. "Push in the clutch, that's the pedal on the left."

She put the floor shifter in neutral and turned the ignition until it sputtered. The exhaust spewed white smoke while the truck rattled in idle. Hubbard shifted into first gear for him.

"This is first gear. Ya have to always start out in first gear. This is second...and...third," she demonstrated. Now, you do it."

Mark shifted into first gear.

"Good, now second."

He shifted to third gear, let out the clutch a bit and the engine stalled.

"No, that was third. Down here is second," she

showed him. "Clutch in," she laughed as she turned the ignition. "Down and over is reverse. Try reverse. Good! Now, let out the clutch slowly."

The truck jerked back in reverse and stalled. Hubbard laughed as if it was a big joke. Mark's heart raced fast and he pretended to laugh, nearly overwhelmed by feelings of self-criticism.

Hawkins land was not for crops; it rolled and banked from the very hills it was made. Mark drove slowly along the old gray barnwood fence that, in places, leaned at 45 degree angles. Up the hill, Blue Hill, on a narrow uneven lane littered with aged corncobs, spillage that had fed the Hawkins swine. The debris in the road made their bodies jitter and quake as if they were passengers on a covered wagon pulled by three-legged mules. Hubbard kept shouting above the engine.

"Downshift! Put it in first gear! Give it gas!" All of it mixed with her beautifully-loud laugh.

For some one hundred yards, that seemed to Mark to take forever amidst stall after stall, they finally reached the top of Blue Hill. Mark's adrenaline was all used up; Hubbard's belly ached from laughing after the truck stalled atop the highest point on her land. They turned together to look out the cracked rear window at the barren land overrun with poverty grass and weeds, and small separated stands of cottonwood. Sunshine was to their backs as they climbed out via the passenger door and stood side by side near the rusty tailgate beholding the isolated beauty of the prairie starkness.

"It's always been like this here...ever since I can remember," she said softly.

A burst of hot wind from the west appeared to hold back their words, then she laughed, "Still want to drive a stick?"

"I'm not as excited about it as I was," he admitted and laughed with her. "I wish you could go to my game in Warren."

"I'd like to. Maybe I could get a pass. But I think my mom has to go with me."

"We're undefeated."

"I can give you your formula at the game, if I go, or like I said, I can leave it in the mailbox on Wednesday."

"Okay."

When he looked at her, he could see white light emanating from her blue eyes. He had to ask her, "How come my eyes don't have the same light that yours do?"

"My dad used to say the same thing when I was little."

Hubbard scanned the Hawkins buildings and all her unmanaged land left barren of cash crops since her grandfather died. Regrets and past neglect were not going to ever live in her life again. She changed the subject.

"If I had enough money, I'd tear down everything down there and build a little yellow house up here...with a greenhouse, so I could grow herbs for my formulas...and grow vegetables for me and Johnny."

She looked back to see Johnny staring at her from the truck's front seat.

"Is yellow your favorite color?"

"Johnny's"

"How do you know that?"

"I know."

"You looking forward to living in the city?"

"It's better than Warren House. When I graduate I can move back here, if I want...if I don't sell the place."

"If you sell, you can't have that yellow house here."

125

"I might need money, if I want to go to college, or buy a car...lots of things. My mom's husband has money, but I don't want to owe anybody anything...ever."

"Why's that?"

She pushed her thick red hair behind her ears and looked right into Mark's eyes. "When you owe money, you're not free. I'm free. How 'bout you?"

"What?"

"Are you free?"

Something about the way she put those words resonated like a dull bell in his ears, a sound that struck profound chords of emotional truth and induced a sudden crimson blush.

She could see plainly that he was struggling to form words after he self-consciously turned away from her toward her land. She waited, then she asked him softly from across the tailgate, "Mark, what is it?"

He wanted to strike out, to say "at least I'm not in Warren House." And that's what bothered him. He could not say what he truly felt. Instead, his chin trembled and he turned from her, as he swallowed old feelings he'd been using for energy, energy that made him the Wichita Kid, the boy from Paradise who could hit the hell out of a baseball. And yes, he was always that poor kid from Wichita who lost his mother and now lived with Edwin and Leona Freeman.

Wichita. Every time he was called Wichita he thought of his mother: at the plate, in the dugout, at first base, around Hurley and in school, and even his father called him Wichita Kid. A thousand times a day he was reminded of losing her to that final resting place in the Paradise Cemetery among his father's family, all people who never knew her, never met her.

Hubbard Kay Hawkins from Blue Hill, can you somehow help me heal this deep bruise on my heart, so I do not have to go there alone? That is what he could not voice to her now. No debt he owed would free him, but rather, it was the wound to his heart from losing his mother that bound him and kept him from being free in body and mind.

He couldn't do it. He couldn't scream out his pain and risk losing this friend, this girl who had saved him from being just another average player who rarely got noticed, and never had a chance to make it in the big leagues. All because he wore glasses. Glass around the eyes was dangerous in this era of 100 mph fastballs, sliding and collisions, and glasses just plain looked bad in a weak kind of way; they were magnified glass barriers to players who could never make it all the way to the top.

He finally looked up at her. "I wanted to thank you for your formula. It's really helped me see the ball better. And it's easier to read and see the blackboard. I know you could help a bunch of people like me with it, Hubbard."

"Doc Jensen says I shouldn't give it to people, 'cause if something goes wrong, I'd be in trouble. Johnny's okay on it though." She looked back at Johnny still sitting on the truck's seat.

"What could go wrong?" Mark asked.

"I don't know. All I know is it's workin' for you, me and Johnny. Doc says I gotta get a patent on it and find an investor, or company who wants to get it approved to sell it to the public. It takes millions, he said."

"Hurley said you should give it to the umpires," Mark laughed.

Hubbard smiled and asked, "Want to drive down the hill?"

After they got back into the truck with Mark behind

the wheel, Hubbard told Mark that he didn't need to start the engine, they could coast back down if he put the truck in neutral.

The truck began to roll backwards as Mark craned his head to the rear window, steering as the truck picked up speed. When he went to use the brake, the pedal went all the way to the floor with no resistance at all.

"There's no brakes!" he cried out to Hubbard. Johnny's front hooves slid over onto Mark's lap as the truck gained more speed on the rough ride, rolling and pitching back and forth over rut after rut.

"Steer it that way!" she yelled and pointed to the slope on her side where the weeds grew tall and would slow the truck's speed.

After what seemed an eternity to Mark, the truck finally slowed, then stopped lengthwise on the sloping ground that surrounded the Hawkins land. Hubbard was laughing so hard when she pulled up the emergency brake that she had to get out of the truck. Both of their hearts were racing fast from the perilous ride down the Hawkins part of Blue Hill.

Hubbard got behind the wheel and drove the truck slowly in first gear back to where it had been parked before the driving lesson began.

"Still wanna drive a stick shift?" she laughed.

"No way!" he grinned at her.

First Kiss

Saturday evening, under the lights at Warren Field, Nell parked her new burnt-orange Plymouth convertible on the dusty parking lot. The white top was down. Hubbard had gotten a pass to go to the game with her rich cousin, but she had to be back at Warren House by ten. The director had allowed Nell to escort Hubbard to the game without checking the fake ID that proved Nell was 21.

Nell looked over 21 in her tight, black sailing pants, her white silk blouse and low heels. As Nell teased her blonde hair in the convertible's rear-view mirror, Hubbard became self-conscious about wearing her Warren House dungarees, t-shirt and tennis shoes. Nell looked so much more attractive than she did tonight, it bothered the girl from Blue Hill more than she let on. Even though there was no hostile competition between the girls, Hubbard felt glum as she followed her stylish cousin into their seats in the visitor's section.

Then the home team took the field to begin the game.

"You see your boyfriend, Hubby?"

"He's not my boyfriend...Nellie. Don't call me Hubby."

Nell agreed with a laugh, because she hated to be called Nellie.

129

"What's his friend's name?" Nell asked.

"Hurley Gunderson. He's a loud mouth. You might like him."

Nell punched her cousin's arm, but returned cynically, "If he's cute, I don't care."

In the Paradise dugout, Hurley, who batted eighth, was wearing his catcher's protective gear except for his mask. Mark, batting second, warmed up, swinging two bats near the on-deck circle. Hurley saw Hubbard and Nell near the end of the bleachers in the second row behind Mark. The brash catcher stood up and called out to his friend in teasing mockery, "Hey, Wichita! Look who's here!"

Mark and the entire Paradise bench turned to look at the two girls. Hubbard waved to Mark.

"Mark's cute," Nell said. "Which one's Hurley?"

"The one with the big mouth starin' at ya."

Nell waved at Hurley and said to her cousin, "He's cute, too."

Hubbard rolled her eyes.

Hurley was in Mark's ear, inside the on-deck circle, as the Paradise lead-off batter stepped up to the batter's box.

"Wichita, who is that sexy blonde thing with Hawkins?"

"I don't know."

"She's a fox. You better hit today, Wichita."

"Go away Hurley."

Hurley turned back to the girls whereupon Nell smiled at Hurley.

Hurley told Mark, "Introduce me after the game. We can all hang out together."

Mark turned to see his dad and grandpa in the bleachers. Then, for an instant his eye caught Hubbard's and she smiled at him.

Frank Belzone, the Warren pitcher, was good, and had a reputation for brushing back the top of the lineup in the first inning to intimidate them. His right-handed fastball hit 95 mph and moved all over the place. After his inside fastball had scared the hell outta the lead-off man, Belzone fired three strikes in a row that sent the Paradise batter back to the bench with a big K. When Mark stepped up to the plate he could hear Hubbard and his dad cheering for him to get a hit.

The first pitch to Mark was inside and fast. The second pitch, Mark fouled off. Next pitch: WHACK! A base hit drilled past the pitcher's head into center field. While standing on first base Mark could see Hubbard cheering excitedly for him, which made number 8's heart race even faster than it had on Blue Hill.

Bottom of the fifth inning, Hurley was catching behind the plate. The Panthers were leading 3 to 2 when the Warren pitcher, Belzone, came up to bat. Hurley called for time out and sauntered to the pitcher's mound with Mark joining them from first base. Hurley had that crooked smirk on his small mouth when he told the lanky pitcher, "Knock 'im down. I want this guy to get a little taste of his game."

"Hurley, you can't hit a guy on purpose!" Mark protested.

"Stay outta this, Wichita. I'm callin' this game."

The next pitch was a fastball at Belzone's head that sent the batter flat on his back, but missed hitting him. Hurley laughed.

"You like gettin' dusted off, Belzone? It's comin' again, so watch it!"

That's when the coach came to the plate from his coaching box at third base to protest to the umpire.

"That was intentional! He told his pitcher to hit my batter! An intentional brush-off is an automatic ejection for the pitcher!"

"Aw, sit down! Let 'em play!" Larry Freeman yelled from the bleachers with his hands cupped around his mouth.

Meanwhile, Nell became more and more eager to meet the brazen catcher, number 13, who kept looking at her and waving from his dugout.

"We can get some wine, Hub, and drive out in the country," Nell suggested.

"I have to be back."

"Not until ten. We'll have time."

Nell used her compact mirror to freshen her passion red lipstick; she offered some to Hubbard who declined, saying it made her look like a clown.

Hurley kept bugging Mark in the dugout about leaving with the girls after the game.

"My dad's gonna take us to the D.Q."

"Dairy Queen? C'mon, Wichita! Give me a break, will ya! We got two beauty queens hot to trot for us here! Wake up, for Christ's sake!"

Right after the game Hurley made his move. He was cockier than usual after hitting the winning double to keep the Panthers undefeated. Mark jogged a step behind him and willing to let Gunner do all the talking.

"Hi, girls!" Hurley smiled and eyed Nell up and down. "You wanna party with us, you gotta have some wheels."

"We have wheels," Nell laughed.

While Mark checked with his dad to see if he could ride home with friends, Nell was laughing at the big fuss

Hurley was making over her car.

"These are your wheels? Wow! A ragtop! You must be rich!"

Hubbard raised her eyes skyward and shook her head as Hurley walked around the entire car, strutting like a rooster inspecting a new hen.

Nell seemed to like everything about Hurley. He was bold and knew how to talk to this particular rich girl: with confidence. Hubbard couldn't hear what Hurley was saying to Nell; she guessed they were talking about buying beer or wine, since her cousin showed him her fake I.D.

Before Nell strolled inside the Warren liquor store, Hubbard convinced the two Panthers to take off their uniform shirts so they couldn't be recognized in the open convertible.

Later, Fats Domino sang from the car radio, two miles out of Warren on a dirt road with nothing but fences and cornfields and zero traffic. Nell parked her car on the shoulder with the Plymouth's right side covering prairie grass. Mark wouldn't open his beer until they parked, while Hurley was on his second beer and belching, accompanied by Nell's raucous laughter at his crudeness. Nell and Hubbard shared a bottle of wine, passing it back and forth, since they had no cups.

After another loud beer belch from Hurley who lay sprawled on the convertible's front seat, Hubbard jeered, "Gunderson, would you quit that, please!"

"Sorry, Hawkins, but a man's gotta do what's natural when he's havin' a cold beer."

"Yeah, act like a pig," Nell laughed, then realized she'd said something offensive about pigs, because Hubbard climbed out of the back seat and walked away from the parked car.

"Sorry, Hub," Nell called out.

"Sorry 'bout what?" Hurley asked.

Nell explained to Hurley, "I compared you to a pig, and she doesn't like that, 'cause she keeps one as a pet."

"Go after her, Wichita," Hurley said.

Mark got out of the car and handed his friend his full can of beer. "You drink it, I don't want it."

He caught up with Hubbard in the middle of the road under a sliver of moon.

"Hey, Hurley's kind of crude."

"Kind of?" she scoffed, as they walked along together.

"Your cousin seems to like him."

"Nell's standards are low."

"Yeah," Mark chuckled.

After a long pause. "I'll leave the formula in my mailbox for ya to get Wednesday."

"Okay."

"I didn't want to get any liquor tonight. That was Nell's idea," she told him.

"They can drink it. I don't like the taste of it much. Does Nell drink a lot?"

"She likes it. Her mother gives her wine all the time."

"We'd get kicked off the team, if our coach found out."

"Oh, I'm sorry, Mark. I would've told her not to get any."

"That's okay. It's no big deal."

"You really are a good baseball player."

"Thanks. Thanks to you I see the ball really good," he drawled. "What time do you have to be back?"

"Before ten. We should leave pretty soon."

"I'm glad you came to the game"

"Me too," she said.

When they returned to the car, Hurley and Nell were making out and not slowing down any, when Mark and Hubbard climbed back into the car.

"We should go now, Nell," Hubbard told her.

Hurley turned, his grinning mouth smeared with red lipstick, and said to Hubbard, "Not until you give Wichita a victory kiss."

Nell giggled, adding, "Yeah, Hub, give Wichita a victory kiss."

Mark looked very uncomfortable, making Hubbard think neither of them had kissed on a date before.

"If I kiss him, we can go?" Hubbard asked, watching the sloppy kissing up front.

"That's right," Hurley grinned again.

"She doesn't have to, Hurley." Mark insisted. "She's gotta get back, or she'll get in trouble."

"Oh, for Christ's sake, you two! One kiss won't kill ya! Wichita's a virgin!"

"Shut up, Hurley."

Hubbard smiled at Mark, as if to say she might like to kiss him, after all. Mark turned his face to her and made a clumsy move with his shoulder, wiping his mouth, before shrugging, as if saying he didn't mind. She moved closer to him. Nell and Hurley watched as they kissed.

"Wahoo! First kiss!" Hurley howled.

"Shut up, Hurley," Mark repeated.

Hubbard sat close to Mark on the drive to Warren House. Hurley drank all the beer by himself and made bold plans with Nell to go to the drive-in movie in her car next Friday night in Woodbury.

Mark kissed Hubbard good night and told her he'd see her Wednesday. He watched her hurry to the Warren House front door and returned her wave before she went inside. He saw that the clock on the dashboard read 9:52 as the convertible drove away.

<u>Wednesday</u>

Very early Wednesday, at two in the morning, Mark finished writing a love letter to the girl who had been on his mind since he last saw her. He read the letter once more before going to bed, and he would read it again before he went to Blue Hill.

Dear Hubbard, I've thought about you often since Saturday night. I'm glad Hurley was with us because I don't believe I would've kissed you if not for his big mouth. For once I'm grateful he has such a big mouth, because I cannot imagine seeing you from now on without kissing you.

I got back safe to Paradise after dropping you off. I saw Hurley and Nell kissing in her car in front of his house even after I took my bath. It looks like they really like each other. Hurley talks about Nell all the time and wishes we could go to the drive-in with them this Friday. I wish you could go, too, because now I would not need Hurley's help to kiss you...and I'm anxious to prove it to you.

Before last Saturday, all I ever thought about was baseball and the next game coming up. Maybe that's why I'm doing so well. Now, all I can think about is you and how I look forward to seeing you on Wednesday. Tomorrow I will wake up and spring out of bed knowing that every step I take brings me closer to Blue Hill and the beautiful girl

Hubbard Hawkins. It is thrilling to be alive now. Love, Mark.

Grandma's breakfast wasn't what bothered his stomach as Mark walked fast, leaving Paradise. Blue Hill's east side shimmered emerald green from morning dew and glittering sunshine.

"Chicken-hearted" is what he'd called himself this morning when he awoke and read the letter again, before adding it to his shoebox collection in his bedroom closet. He was sick of the cowardly feeling; it was draining his energy.

"What are you afraid of, Mark Freeman?" he petitioned himself on this walk. "If not for Hurley I would never have kissed her, or taken this chance of having my very first girlfriend."

How she could replace his need to excel in baseball, and so fast, was the mystery that kept his stride long and double-quick. Yet none of his letters could he dare let her read.

During breakfast, after Grandpa had gone to work, Mark had confessed to his grandma about the letters he couldn't send to Hubbard.

"Autumn letters" Grandma had called them. "They're letters written from the heart that aren't meant to be read."

He could still hear his grandma's words.

"You'd rather not know if she feels the same way as you do, rather than risk finding out that she doesn't."

"That's exactly right!" he exclaimed.

Leona Freeman wiped her rough hands on her apron, already stained with flour, butter and egg whites from making banana/walnut French toast. Then those same rough hands patted his head; she looked into his eyes from behind her thin, silver, wire-rimmed glasses and said, "In my day, boys like you were famous for their autumn letters. Before I met your grandpa I had a beau who sent me letters at school and sometimes left them in places outside my home where I would find them. He never wrote anything that my father wouldn't want to read. But he told me about the letters he wrote to me that he didn't have the courage to send. Oh, how that made me want to read them even more," she laughed.

The two sat in companionable silence, and she watched with satisfaction while Mark devoured his breakfast. After a while, she continued.

"Autumn letters are like prayers; nobody on earth knows about them, except you and God."

"I wrote a letter to my mom when she died. Is that an autumn letter?"

"Yes, I'd say it is."

"But I did want her to read it. I didn't know she had died."

"Same thing. The letter was unread. There are all sorts of autumn letters."

"Grandma, I feel like a big chicken for not giving the letters to Hubbard."

"Don't be so hard on yourself. There's plenty of things in life that are real hard on a person. Just think of those letters as written prayers, or wishes maybe, that are not meant to be read by anyone."

"Yeah, they are like prayers. But Grandma, I always feel like a coward...like I never have any power over my destiny."

"Just enjoy your youth," she laughed.

Mark's pace quickened toward Blue Hill. He

pushed off each stride forward from his big toe and swung his arms higher, gliding over the gravel road until he reached the unmarked turn that led uphill to Hawkins Cemetery.

Now, he wondered why the cemetery named for Hubbard's people was not where her father had been buried. Why in his hogyard and not here? Was there some secret reason? he wondered.

Then, from a hundred yards away, he could see flowers, and see that they were open and artful in deep blue. The flowers had been there the last two Saturdays, clinging to the Hawkins Cemetery's western fence line.

He had seen the flowers again every Sunday, when he drove to the nine o'clock morning service at Paradise Methodist Church with Grandpa and Grandma in their old Ford. The Freemans usually sat in the front row so Grandma could hear the minister's soft voice. And the flowers were there on the podium, standing in a vase in front of the minister's lectern. Mark could not take his eyes off the brilliant violet-blue of the trumpet-shaped flowers exploding above their lush green stems. The more his eyes relaxed, the more he began to truly see them. Each flower had thin, pinkish-purple lines inside each star-shaped bulb—the morning star in all its glory.

Mark did not know the flower's name at the time. It wasn't until coffee and sweet rolls in the parish hall that he overheard one of the ladies mention "those glorious morning glories."

Now, he began to run toward that line of blue, a blue that made this place Blue Hill more than anything else. To find the perfect morning glory for Hubbard would erase his autumn letters and say everything he wanted to say.

Flowers obscured the cemetery's western fence line, thousands of morning glories in bloom on twining vines. He scouted for the right one until he realized they were nearly all the same size, open and funnel-shaped perfectly. He plucked one with enough green stem to carry it without touching the delicate flower. When he smelled it, the flower closed around his nostrils and would've stayed there, if he wished.

An angry bee, high on sweet pollen, buzzed around his face, so he continued on up and over to the trail that overlooked the Hawkins side of Blue Hill. Though he was his undefeated team's best hitter and led the league with a .437 batting average, legs that feared no pitcher's fastball or menacing curveball became weak from the image of offering the flower to Hubbard.

Down the hill, number 8 stumbled. He knew he was out of his element and getting closer to exposing precious bits of self-esteem that his great-grandparents and baseball had instilled in his heart since arriving in Paradise.

Never in his young life had he been so terrified, with big butterflies in his stomach that seemed to be telling him to drop the beautiful blue flower, because it would bring danger and a new kind of heartache so devastating it might somehow ruin his dreams to play in the big leagues.

His stride shortened with each step, each one less sure than the one before. Thanks to Hubbard's formula, from this distance he could see that Luther's truck was gone. Yes, he was early, as he had hoped, yet he could tell by the warming sun behind him that she would arrive soon.

To forget the flower in his hand, he placed its stem inside his waistband, letting the dew-moistened flower ride against his belly under his white t-shirt. Then he stopped to clean the rubber toes of his dusty Keds, swiping them in the wet grass just before reaching Luther's place.

It seemed as if Johnny had smelled the friend who

walked him faithfully every Saturday, because the white pig was standing alone and grunting behind the rusty gate, his wet pink snout sniffing the air. But this was Wednesday, Hubbard's day, and the pig watched Mark curiously, as if he knew that this was not Mark's day to be there.

"Yeah, you're right, Johnny," Mark smiled down at the pig while letting him out.

While he attached the rope to Johnny's mud-splattered yellow collar, Mark heard the roar of Luther's truck coming up Broken Kettle Road. Quickly he put the morning glory under Johnny's collar behind his head on top of the pig's bristled neck. Now, the abject fear he had felt, diminished some, yet he stood frozen and smiling, while his mind yelled "COWARD."

Mark returned Luther's wave. Hubbard's red hair looked good, shiny and brushed to a thick radiant cascade that touched her shoulders. She stepped out of the truck wearing the same flared jeans as always, and a pink t-shirt that had white stenciled words on the front: "Pigs are Beautiful."

"Hi!" she smiled.

"Hi!"

She showed him a paper bag that she held. "Your formula."

"Great."

Then, she bent to hug Johnny and fussed joyously over the flower under Johnny's collar.

"It's beautiful."

"It's a morning glory."

"Did you get it from the cemetery?"

He nodded yes, then asked how she knew.

"There's a whole bunch of them there this time of year."

He stopped himself from telling Hubbard that he hadn't planned on giving the flower to the pig, but to her, yet somehow she acted and looked as if he'd done both.

He watched her clean Johnny's collar by wetting her fingertips from a nearby water spigot. Then, they walked, with Hubbard leading Johnny by the leash.

"I saw in the paper your team is undefeated."

"Yeah."

"You don't sound too excited about it," she laughed.

"It's only a game," he smiled.

"Life's a game."

"And it's not a fair game."

"That's so true," she agreed as they followed Johnny's pull onto the Hawkins drive.

"When I was walking by the cemetery, I wondered why your father wasn't buried there. I mean...a lot of the Hawkins family must be buried there, if it was their land."

"That's why. My dad hated his father and grandfather. He wanted nothing to do with them. I know they turned him mean and soured him. My dad liked orderin' my mom around like his father did to him. My mom stopped taking his crap one day and left him."

"And you stayed?"

"Yeah, but he wasn't that mean to me. He never bossed me around much."

They stood near the back door of her house; she reached under a rotted rubber doormat and picked up her house key. That's when he asked her why she stayed so long here taking care of him.

"I thought he'd die sooner, if I left, too. And I was afraid to live in the city."

"Woodbury?"

"Yeah. I knew if I got away from here, I'd see

another world that would make me hate him. Have you ever hated your mom or dad?"

She held back from unlocking the door until he answered, "No." But then he said, "I was mad at God for letting my mother die."

"I used to be angry, too...for my parents splitting and me living out here. Then I realized that my anger only hurt me."

"What did you do?"

"I let it go."

"I can hit a baseball because I'm mad at it. I pretend it's something coming at me that can hurt me if I don't smack it away. Like it's this world trying to mess with me," he drawled.

"To strike you out."

"Yeah...so I smack it away from me."

"That's so interesting...for you to know that, Mark."

Inside the house, all three of them went from room to room.

"This is my room," Hubbard stood beside an open door.

Only a bed and a mirrored blonde dresser remained, along with a few keepsakes on top of the dresser. He noticed her room did not look like a girl's room, or at least the way he remembered his mother's room, with feminine furnishings, colors and soft things that reveal a feminine touch.

When she opened the door to her father's empty room there still remained the stale smell of old tobacco smoke seeping from the walls.

"This was my dad's room. You can tell he smoked in bed. I always thought he'd burn himself up in bed. You wouldn't believe how many times I came in here and found him asleep with a lit cigarette in his hand, or one burning through the sheets. I'll paint the whole place inside and out after I move back here."

In the barren front room that adjoined the kitchen, the old kitchen table held a portable record player. She blew dust from its needle. From inside the paper sack she brought with her she handed Mark his formula sealed in a plastic bag.

"That should last you a couple months."

"Thanks."

He watched her remove from the bag a handful of 45 records in paper sleeves.

"Some of these are mine and some I borrowed from my roommate."

She offered the records to Mark. "See if you like any of these." she said.

They sat down and she watched him go through the stack of records, reciting each title out loud along with a curt comment that, for some reason, embarrassed her a little.

"'Downtown'...no; 'A Lover's Concerto'...yeah; '(I Can't Get No) Satisfaction'...sounds like Hurley and Nell; 'Come See About Me'...good dance song; 'Help'...don't like the Beatles; 'Love Potion Number Nine'...no way; 'This Diamond Ring'...forget it; 'Yesterday'...too depressing; 'Goin' Out of My Head'...like it; 'Tired of Waiting for You'...like it."

He handed her his four picks, "You can play something else, if you want."

"No, I want to play what you want."

She stacked his selections on the adapter that allowed the record player to hold 45s instead of the old fashioned 78s, then punched the power button. Little Anthony's recording of "Goin' Out of My Head" crackled and played as they both watched the record spin on the turntable.

She looked at Mark several times during the first song, but he kept his eyes down, or off to the side, away from her. In fact, he displayed such a shyness toward her that she lost her sense of felicity and began to wonder what he was thinking. Between songs she said, "I guess Hurley and Nell are goin' to the drive-in Friday. Do you know what's playin'?"

He shook his head no. "I don't think they know either, or care much." He smiled.

Hubbard laughed as The Kinks' song, "Tired of Waiting for You" began. She wanted to keep talking, but again he withdrew into himself. She wondered if he was trying to tell her something by picking that song, then dismissed the thought as silly. Johnny, still wearing his morning glory, ambled over to Mark and Mark scratched him behind his ears.

"That's his favorite spot," she smiled.

"I know."

"He needs a bath," she said above the music.

"You give him baths?"

"Yeah...about every three months. He hasn't had one since I left. I'll use the hose on him when we go outside. Did you know Johnny can dance? His fav'rite song is 'Johnny Angel'."

Hubbard stood up and Johnny followed her to the middle of the empty front room. The Supremes' recording of "Come See About Me" began and Johnny did dance, his front hooves moving up and down while facing his partner who danced unselfconsciously, then playfully invited Mark to join them.

He got to his feet on weak legs and moved over to dance across from her, with Johnny bobbing between them. Mark kept his eyes down, on Johnny, his body as rigid as the pig's. When Mark did look up to her, she met his eyes and smiled at his self consciousness.

When the song ended, Mark bent down and patted Johnny's flank. Hubbard walked over and opened the large front room window to let in fresh air. The Toys' recording of "A Lover's Concerto" was a romantic, slow song. Still kneeling beside Johnny and before his nerves could warn him to stop dancing, she came over and stood in front of him. Smiling down at him, she told him that she really loved the song.

She could see his fingers trembling on Johnny's rough hide in this sweet kind of palsy; something made her reach for them, to take his hand so he would dance with her. He stood. Then Johnny's hooves pattered off to the bathroom to relieve himself after all his exercise.

Hubbard stepped close to Mark and put her arms around his back. They rocked and shuffled their feet to the uplifting torch song, moving slowly, her face flush with his and gently resting on his broad shoulder. His body shuddered and quaked when he wrapped his long arms around her upper back creating a connection of nervous energy between them. He noticed the delicious strawberry fragrance of her shampoo when her eyes closed.

The quick love song ended too fast for them, yet they continued dancing. He waited for the courage to come that would let him kiss her and thought of the words he had written to her last night in the message at the top of his growing collection of autumn letters. None of those words he could tell her now.

She lifted her head from his shoulder and gazed at him with merciful light-bearing blue eyes, to tell him she wanted him to kiss her. He did. A long kiss that opened his eyes to hers that flared with the same silver twinkling light he first noticed when she wasn't wearing her glasses.

Again he kissed her full lips; this time he hugged her tighter, pressing her breasts to his chest, and just as he gained the confidence he so desperately craved, pig flatulations resounded from the bathroom and made them laugh until tears came to their eyes.

Wanting more time with her, he told Hubbard he wanted to ride back to Warren House with her, that he could hitch a ride back with Luther, or someone else. She smiled and kissed him quick.

"Okay."

They sat on the bare wood floor in her front room facing each other with Johnny resting his head on Hubbard's lap.

"I wish I didn't have to go to school in Woodbury this fall."

"Will you go to Central?" he asked.

She nodded yes.

"Wow, what a change from Paradise."

"I know."

"I heard that Central is the city's biggest high school with over three thousand students."

"It's bigger than Paradise and Blue Hill's entire population," she laughed.

"Hurley's parents are getting him a car for his senior year. He can drive me to Woodbury some weekends, maybe, if he still likes Nell."

"Yeah."

"You seem sad about something," he said.

"I don't know. Goin' to that big school and livin' with my mom and her husband. I'm not really excited about leaving this place and Johnny."

"You can visit him. I can still walk him on Saturdays."

"No, I don't expect you to keep walkin' him after I get out."

"I don't mind."

"I know...but it's not easy to walk here from Paradise, especially in the winter. I'll keep ya supplied with the formula and, Mark, you don't have to come here every Saturday. I'll come out on weekends. It's my responsibility."

Johnny got his hide hosed when they left the house. On their walk to the Hawkins mailbox, they held hands for the first time and Mark carried her sack of records. They talked about meeting next Wednesday, but then Mark remembered he had an afternoon game against the Emerson Eagles.

"Maybe the next Wednesday," she said.

They walked slower on the way back to Luther's. She kept looking at the Timex on her wrist as if counting the minutes they had left.

Then Mark said, "Something just made me remember this strange dream I had last night. I was pitching in this game. And each baseball I threw was falling apart, or losing its roundness in mid-air. I kept asking these kids in the bleachers if they had a baseball, but each new ball I got would fall apart and explode if the batter hit it...like it was an apple, or a potato. It seemed as if nothing would go right for me. It was so frustrating. I always have these frustrating dreams about sports."

"That's interesting. I dream more...or at least I remember them easier since I moved away from here. But I really look forward to sleep, because I usually have good dreams that don't scare me."

She knelt down on the road and felt Johnny's skin after his shower to see how it was drying.

"I've got to dry him off more."

She peeled her t-shirt over her head and knelt beside the pig in her bra. Mark felt himself blushing and did not know if he should look at Hubbard, or not. But she seemed unconcerned. After turning her shirt inside out she started to wipe the pig's underbelly with it, then his throat, explaining to Mark how pigs were like people, they could get pneumonia.

After drying Johnny, she reversed the shirt again and wore it inside out and dirty.

"Now Luther will think I had your shirt off," Mark joked.

"I doubt he'd even notice," she laughed. "Did you know Luther goes to the Blue Hill Tavern after he drops me off?"

At the bend in the road before reaching Luther's place, Mark stopped to kiss Hubbard, saying first, "This one has to last two weeks."

He stepped up to her smiling blue eyes and felt closer to her than he'd ever felt with anyone else.

Lake U-Wanna

Nell canceled her Friday night date with Hurley and told him she'd go out with him the following Friday.

Now, on Sunday, Hurley showed no sign of disappointment. Both he and Mark were clad in cut-off shorts and t-shirts, toting rolled bath towels on a hot, four-mile hike on the flat gravel road northwest of Paradise.

Hurley's pockets rattled with coins saved from the paper route he quit shortly before Mark moved to Paradise. The paper route accounted for Hurley's knowledge of every inch of Paradise and most every person in town. For three years he had delivered on foot the Sunday morning Woodbury Journal to some 150 customers. Saturday nights he'd collect for his route and was hardly ever duped by deadbeats. He picked the night before delivery day to collect because most of his customers got paid on Fridays, so they still had some cash, and a lot of them were half-popped from whiskey and beer and more likely to tip their gregarious paper boy.

Mark couldn't have picked a better guy to show him the ropes around his new stomping grounds. Besides that, Mark was a follower, and a good one. Since Hurley was an aggressive leader, most other Paradise boys had been told, or learned to stay clear of the cocky Gunderson kid. Mark and Hurley were a perfect match.

Though Mark stayed with his brash friend's bow-legged stride, it was clearly Hurley leading the way.

"It's a hidden gem," Hurley exclaimed, "an oasis...named Lake U-Wanna!"

"That's a funny name for a lake," Mark said.

"You're not gonna believe the place, Wichita!"

"You said it's never crowded. How come?"

"I didn't say never crowded. I said hardly ever."

"Okay, how come it's hardly ever crowded?"

"'Cause it's surrounded by a junkyard and there's a lot of weeds in the lake. And sometimes it smells."

"Smells? Smells like what?"

"Like shit."

"Oh, great! No wonder it's hardly ever crowded."

"My dad says it's some kind of gas made from weeds in stagnant water."

"And you swim in it?"

"When I get hot enough!"

"Gawd, Hurley...it sounds like a swamp to me," Mark drawled.

"You'll sing a diff'rent tune when you see Ruby layin' out on the high-dive platform in her pink bathin' suit. I swear you can see everything from the end of the divin' board. I damn near passed out from divin' so much.

Dozens of vehicles must have passed them on their walk, and nearly every single driver honked or waved at the ex-paperboy. And Hurley was so intensely alert and observant, he knew who they were before they finished waving or honking.

"That's Harlan Biggs! Hi, Harlan!" Hurley waved back, then he added some cynical or lewd comment about the person.

"Yeah. Harlan! You homo! Harlan lives in a big

house all alone. And I don't want to come in and have any hot chocolate...Har...lan!"

Another honk and returned wave to a passing vehicle.

"Howdy, Mr. Dowdy! Don't get so frigin' rowdy! He beats his wife and kids, 'cause he hates his job at the power plant! He spends eight hours a day sittin' in a chair starin' at gauges that never move!"

Another passerby.

"That's Jubal Stang! He's a fat old fart that lives by the river. Jubal has the gout. What the hell's gout, for Christ's sake, Jubal?"

They turned down a dirt lane, the entrance to Lake U-Wanna, an unmarked route with two dry cornfields on both sides of the lane. The corn was too high to see anything, and Mark could smell an awful stench.

"We must be getting close, huh?" Mark said, his lips nibbling each other from the powerful stink.

"Yeah, but that's not the lake. That's a frigin' skunk!" Hurley laughed.

Hurley watched for his friend's first impression when they turned into the picnic area with tables scattered here and there. Straight ahead was a cement block concession stand with wet, sandy footprints all about the concrete walkway where a dozen or so kids in bathing suits waited in line for hot dogs, candy and pop.

Inside a hut across from the concession stand, a jukebox with exterior speakers boomed Ray Charles singing "Hit the Road, Jack."

This is by far the best place I've seen in Paradise, Mark thought, as he stood at the railing overlooking the green/brown lake dotted with islands of weeds outside the

153

swimming area. A patch of sandy gravel, maybe seventy yards long and thirty wide, must have been hauled in to make the beach area. Fifty yards out into the water was the platform where kids dived off one side from the high board and, in the other direction, off the low board, with a little room in between for sunbathing on the carpet covering. He could hear kids squealing with jubilation in and out of the water.

Hurley stood behind the men's restroom with Bud Steimstra smoking a marijuana joint. Bud's father owned the park; Bud was a big, red-faced German who never liked Gunderson, until now, when Hurley surprised him by coming over to him.

"I thought I smelled weed when I was pissin'. You gonna smoke that by yourself?" Hurley grinned before taking the offering.

Shelly Daum and Alice King, classmates of Mark and Hurley, stood near the jukebox hut in matching one-piece black bathing suits. The girls were chatting away, their full figures stretching the limits of their bathing suits, top to bottom, as their heartthrob, Bobby Vinton, sang "Mr. Lonely." Mark turned from his view at the railing and watched Hurley enter the music hut where he shook the jukebox until the song skipped off, the vinyl scratching sound squealing out of the loud speakers. When Hurley sauntered out of the hut the girls confronted him.

"Hey, Gunderson! You owe us a dime!"

"Bobby Vinton sucks," Hurley smirked and strolled over to Mark.

They walked down four levels of sandy, concrete steps to the only beach in Northeast Nebraska. Hurley nudged his friend's side. Mark followed Hurley's devilish eyes over to a shapely girl in a pink bathing suit. Ruby, the girl they had spied on at Hawkins Cemetery, lay on her back on a black beach towel, wearing sunglasses and rubbing on baby oil mixed with iodine. Hurley and Mark walked over and spread out their towels five feet from her, with Hurley taking the lead.

"Hi, Ruby!"

"Oh, hi, Hurley," she nearly smiled.

"How's the water?" Again he nudged Mark to look at her body.

"I haven't been in," she answered.

Mark looked tan compared to Hurley's bleached-white muscular legs. Both boys peeled their shirts and removed their shoes and socks and lay down, restive on towels covering annoying bits of gravel and tiny stones. When Hurley turned on his side to stare at Ruby, a bunch of change fell out of his pocket onto his towel.

"Can I buy ya a pop, Ruby?"

It seemed to Mark that she'd never answer Hurley as she pursed her lips and thought about what she wanted.

"A Dr. Pepper with lots of ice sounds good," she smiled.

Hurley shot up and hot-danced on the sand toward the steps, calling back, "What about you, Wichita?"

"A Coke please!"

Mark caught a quick smile from Ruby, as she applied oil to the back of her legs before flopping onto her stomach. He wanted to say something to the older girl, but he was chicken. Before long, she asked him if he got his cute accent from Wichita, Kansas.

"Yeah," he said, making the drawl even more apparent.

"I've never been to Wichita. What's it like?"

He thought about his answer under the sweltering glare of the early afternoon sun while squinting at Ruby's long, smooth, glistening legs.

"Well, it's a big city with lots of things to do."

"Oh, yeah? Like what?"

"There's lots of movie theaters. Lots of places to eat. And the people are busy making money. Oh, and there's lots of new schools and a big college," he drawled.

"That sounds like a fun place to live. Do you live there now?"

"In Paradise."

"Oh, gawd...what a change!" she laughed. "Did ya move here with your parents?"

"My dad. I mean...my dad moved me here. He lives in Woodbury, on the base."

"What about your mom?"

"She died in a car accident."

"Oh, I'm so sorry," she said with genuine compassion, as she sat up and crossed her legs under her. "I lost my mom, too. She died from pneumonia when I was twelve."

"I'm sorry."

Then, Ruby leaned to him as if she wanted to tell him something special. "The first year is the hardest...then you don't think about it as much. Time really does heal all wounds...believe me."

Just then, Hurley returned with three pops standing in a slotted container, his pocket change jingling from hot-footing over to his towel.

He handed Ruby her pop with a straw.

"Thank you, Hurley," she smiled.

"You're welcome, Miss Ruby."

"Thanks, Hurley," Mark said, as they all sipped

their cold pop.

"Ruby, are you still goin' with that guy from South Woodbury?"

"Rex? Yeah, we go out now and then."

"My dad says he's married," Hurley grinned.

"Not for long. He's gettin' a divorce. You can tell your old man that," she said testily.

"He got any kids?"

"Two boys."

"Uh, huh," Hurley said.

Ruby lay back down on her towel keeping the bottom of her cold cup on her stomach as if she'd said enough.

"Hey, Wichita," Hurley challenged, "after we finish our pop let's go dive off the high-dive."

"I don't dive off the high-dive, I jump."

"Whatever, you pussy," Hurley cackled.

Mark blushed, shamed by his friend's foul language, which only made Hurley go on with more crude words.

"You're still a virgin, ain't ya, Wichita?"

"Shut up," Mark's blush deepened.

"Hey, Ruby! You wanna dive, or jump with us off the high-dive?"

"I don't wanna get wet now," she said.

"Suit yourself. C'mon, Wichita."

The boys from Paradise dashed over the hot sand and into the cold waveless water. Hurley dived in after running and screaming for as far and as long as he could, while Mark waded in gingerly, test-splashing the cold water onto his thighs, with Hurley's contemptuous words still burning his sensitive skin.

Hurley swam like a seal, fluid and sure, whereas Mark braced for and flinched from the cold splashes from other kids around him. He resisted the urge to just dive in, as if to follow fast meant he was truly the pussy he had been called.

Mark turned back to see Ruby sitting up and watching his apprehension. Just then, the thought of his mother swept over him, and the feeling of loss made his vision blur as he remembered watching her dive gracefully from a low diving board at a Wichita public swimming pool. He could see that her perfect dive made very little splash behind her. And now, she was gone, never to surface again.

Gasping short breaths, Mark moved deeper, where the cold muddy lake bottom oozed under and between his toes until his feet slipped and he fell forward with gulps of water choking him as he surfaced.

Having climbed the platform's rungs, Hurley was next in line to dive off the high board. Gunner's muscular legs propelled him high as he yelled like a banshee all the way headfirst into the water.

Mark Freeman was no Hurley Gunderson. He wished he could be free like Hurley, and free right now from dreading having to jump into the water and hearing the derisive slurs that were sure to come when he surfaced.

"What a pussy!" Hurley laughed.

"I'm not a pussy. Shut up and don't call me that!"

Hurley didn't bother Mark again at the lake. Not because he feared Mark's anger, but because he so liked having someone he could lead around his territory, like a tough mongrel dog who could teach this new pup how to hunt and prowl and live life with unbridled freedom.

And Mark knew that more crude Hurley-talk was coming on their walk back to Paradise.

"Did you see those Ruby melons, Wichita? Wow! What a bod, huh? I told ya, didn't I?"

Changes and Mind Games

Summer of '66 ended. The Paradise Panthers finished second in the league, after losing to South Woodbury twice; the last defeat was for the league championship in Paradise.

Mark led the league in hitting with a .417 average. He had the Panthers' only hits in the final game, two singles, against South Woodbury's ace pitcher, Greg Landers, a Native American right-hander with a wicked curveball that only the Wichita Kid had been able to hit.

Hurley had a chance to tie the game, with two outs and the tying run on second base, in the bottom of the last inning. He struck out swinging. The Paradise crowd sat in stunned silence as Gunner angrily broke his bat over his thigh like a pretzel, fingered the pitcher and yelled cuss words at the umpire, threatening to cut off his head and shit in his neck. Hurley hated losing.

And Hurley was in love with Nell. His delayed date with her at the drive-in seemed to change him. The morning after his first date with Nell he woke his friend across the street by tapping excitedly on Mark's bedroom window. Once inside, he told Mark everything, whispering in the fog of morning as Mark blinked from under his covers.

"You wouldn't believe it, Wichita. That Nell is one cool chick. She brought a cooler in the trunk of her ragtop, loaded with ice-cold beer. We kept the top down for about an hour during the first movie."

"What movie?" Mark yawned.

Hurley laughed and smacked the side of his own head. "Ya know, I don't have a clue what any of the movies were. We talked and laughed through the first one. Then, we started makin' out. And the best part, Wichita...after she put the top up...she took her top down and we climbed onto the back seat. And man, Wichita, what a body that girl has! You would not believe that body! Boy, did I have my hands full, if ya know what I mean," he cackled.

"Next Sunday, she wants me to ride along with her to Omaha. She's gonna buy some new clothes for school. Man, Wichita, looks like I got the best end of those two chicks."

"What do you mean?"

"Well, let's face it, Hawkins ain't rich and she don't drive no ragtop. And she's not exactly gonna win any beauty contests."

"You are stupid, Hurley. Hubbard is beautiful. Have you ever really looked at her? No. You're always too busy looking at a girl's tits!"

"Hey, don't get sore, Wichita. I didn't mean anything by it. Hawkins is okay. She's Nell's cousin. I have to like her."

But there were changes in Hurley that Mark hadn't noticed until their senior year began in September. Nell had bought Hurley some new clothes when they went to Omaha. Gunderson was the only boy in his class to wear Madras and pin-striped, buttoned-down shirts with locker loops like the Beach Boys wore in California. And he cut down on his swearing because Nell said it showed a person's ignorance and lack of refinement.

The most obvious change for Hurley was the gray '56 Ford his parents bought him. The car seemed to give him a certain sense of responsibility that Mark could see had resulted in his friend getting out more, away from his stultifying home environment.

The Paradise Class of 1967 now respected Mark as a first rate baseball player, instead of just being the boy with the Kansas accent who could read and write well. Their new teacher was Mr. Sanders, a jovial, middle-aged, corpulent man with a penchant for creative writing, which Mark liked and made him glad their school was yet too small for multiple classes, as in Woodbury.

Solitary Saturday walks with Johnny were over for Mark once Hubbard told him she'd be spending weekends at her house on Blue Hill. Johnny still spent the week with Luther's herd, since Hubbard felt that company was better for her pet than solitude, even though Luther's health appeared to be declining after a mild stroke in August.

Time and again Mark found himself thinking about Hubbard during the long days of Indian summer that were still hot and very dry in Nebraska, with ceaseless winds outside the open classroom window that blew lingering waves of restlessness and the gloomy feeling of prairie isolation about him.

Like most Americans, he too calendarized everything, such as this first anniversary of his mother's death. And like most, Mark could feel the blues of suffering coming today, yet he refused to go there. Instead, he chose to wonder how Hubbard liked her new life in the city, in massive Woodbury Central High. He pictured her at the dark four-story stone castle on a hill that educated the city's youth in more ways than an expansive liberal curriculum intended to prepare the way to college for the more fortunate and eclectic student body.

Hubbard and Nell shared three of their six classes, sitting across from each other in each one. All Nell talked about was Hurley Gunderson and his "gross-looking car" she felt embarrassed to ride in, because it sounded like a fart machine on wheels. She would go on and on about their last date, parked in Stone Park, sparing no details about their wild intimacy on Hurley's back seat. When Nell asked her quiet cousin about Mark and supposed they should double-date sometime, Hubbard just smiled and said, "Maybe sometime."

Never in a million years would Hubbard reveal to Nell the notebook on her desk that was filled with daily love letters to the boy in Paradise she was falling in love with, every hour of every day. She wrote the letters in study hall because her studies were too easy for her. Every letter began the same:

Hi Mark! I'm in study hall and thinking about you for the whole hour. It is so good to be out of Warren House and in new surroundings where nobody knows me, except Nell. Haven't made any new friends yet. Nell is my only friend and, as usual, she talks about Gunderson. I don't see what she sees in that knucklehead. I find myself thinking about you when she talks about him. Most times I think about our times together on Blue Hill when we'd walk Johnny and talk about things. I really miss those few hours we had together, and I can't help but think I'm stupid for not having you walk Johnny on Saturdays. I'm selfish I guess. This coming Saturday I'd love to see you at my place on Blue Hill, and kiss your sweet lips again and again while we dance to "A Lover's Concerto" with nobody else in the whole world to bother us, or tell us how we should be. Just you and me, sweetie, and of course Johnny. (Here she drew a smiley face) *Miss you. Love, Hubbard.*

On Friday, the boys from Paradise would be taking their city girls to Woodbury Central's big football game against cross town rival East High. Thursday night, Hurley stopped over to the Freeman house where Mark was polishing his white dress shoes on his bedroom floor over an open newspaper. The boys were planning on wearing their flashy, white slip-ons on their date, risking embarrassing image-conscious Nell.

"I should've brought my shoes over for you to polish," Hurley grinned and sat on Mark's bed.

"Do your own shoes!" Mark snapped.

"Look who's grouchy!" Hurley teased Mark, then ticked him off by deliberately putting his fingerprint on the drying left shoe.

"Hurley, you dipshit!"

"I'm sorry. Look, I need a favor, Wichita. A big time favor."

Mark dabbed the spot Hurley made on his shoe and ignored him.

"I'm serious, Wichita."

"Look, I don't want you to call me Wichita anymore. It makes me think of my mom."

"Okay...Mark. Nell's got my head all messed up. Nell's not sweet all the time like your Hubbard is. I mean...I've been with her a bunch of times, parkin', messin' 'round and stuff...ya see...but she never lets me go all the way like I want."

"I've heard you tell guys in school Nell does

anything you want."

"That's just talk."

"You mean ego bragging," Mark said, looking down at his polishing.

"Yeah, whatever. They like it when I make up stuff. But I'm not like you, Wich...Mark. I've been all the way with girls before and it's drivin' me nuts when she says no all the time."

"Maybe she's not ready. Or doesn't want to get pregnant and she's scared..."

"Oh, I got news for ya. I'd be her third guy. I tell her third time's a charm. I spend money on her. I steal money from my parents so I can take her to fancy places she's used to. Then she gets me all hot and bothered and stops me cold like tits on an Eskimo."

"What do you want me to do?" Mark asked.

"Write Nell a love letter from me. I mean...I'll copy what you write so it's in my handwritin'."

"No way! Write your own letter, stupid!"

"Mark, everyone knows you're the best writer in the whole school! I can't write near as good!"

"Well," Mark corrected.

"Whatever. You're letter could get me lucky with Nell."

"That wouldn't be right."

"Right! Who's talkin' about right! I want to keep this girl...and a hick like me don't stand a chance with a rich girl like Nell. You'll see her house tomorrow and know what I'm talkin' about. C'mon Mark...please. I've got forty bucks for tomorrow night. I'll give ya twenty bucks if ya write me a letter for Nell."

Mark needed money, and he knew that Hurley counted on that and was manipulating him to get his way.

Then Mark thought about how easy it would be to write the letter by pretending he was writing to Hubbard.

"Okay. But I want the twenty bucks before I even write one word."

"What...you don't trust me?"

"You said it."

"Okay. I'll go get it now. Be right back."

Hurley left Mark's room in a hurry, but then returned because he forgot something.

"Wich...Mark, can I bring my shoes over and polish 'em?"

Mark could hear Hurley's running feet cross the street. Quickly, Mark went to his closet to his collection of letters in the shoebox. At the top of the pile he grabbed his most recent letter to Hubbard written right after their last time together on Blue Hill. There were lines that he knew could help Gunner win Nell's heart.

Minutes later, Hurley sat on the floor rubbing polish onto his white shoes, smiling and listening to the sound of Mark's pen moving across paper just above his head on the bed. The twenty-dollar bill was fisted in Mark's right hand as he wrote up a storm with his left, determined to finish the letter quick so Hurley could go home and copy it.

When Hurley's white shoes had dried on his old employer's newspaper, Mark asked Hurley what name Nell called him.

"What do ya mean?" Hurley asked.

"I'm done with your letter...and when you sign it...does she call you Hurley?"

Hurley grinned and told him, "She calls me The boy from Paradise."

After Mark handed Hurley the letter, Hurley said, "Don't tell Hawkins you wrote this, 'cause she'll blab it to Nell and they'll both laugh in my face."

"I won't," Mark said.

"Promise me," Hurley insisted with intensity.

"I promise!"

"Did ya make it sound like me?" Hurley asked.

"Yeah, but nice."

Double Dating

Hurley was right. Nell's house was imposing, a brick mansion with four solid white pillars in front and a circular driveway where three new cars were parked, including Nell's convertible. Mark could see plainly that Nell's neighborhood belonged to Woodbury's wealthiest, situated to the west of Bandshell Park, named for the structure where the city's symphony orchestra played during the summer. Neither of the boys from Paradise knew that Nell's father, Donald Evers, owned the biggest fertilizer plant in the region, and thus was the symphony's largest benefactor. Nell had told her date that her dad sold fertilizer.

Upon getting out of Hurley's just washed Ford, they stood and stared at Nell's home, feeling silly now in their matching white shoes.

"Must be a lot of money in shit. Her dad sells fertilizer," Hurley mumbled. "I always feel like a big hick when I come here."

"You are a big hick," Mark laughed.

"Up yours!" Hurley snarled.

The boys surveyed the massive landscaped estate surrounded by manicured hedges and tall oak trees.

"Would ya look at this layout, Wichita. Jesus, I hope your letter works."

"Just be yourself."

"Easy for you to say."

The boys from Paradise looked at each other and burst into laughter. Hurley wore a white tricot polyester long-sleeved shirt with black polyester rayon bell bottoms touching the tops of his white pointed-toe slip-ons. Mark had on a red and white polyester shirt with a zipped-down chest and front pocket; his denim flares with corduroy front pockets covered all but the tops of his white shoes.

The girls came out of the front door together before their dates could ring the doorbell. Hubbard looked better than Mark had ever seen her. Even Hurley gave her the once-over with his quick little green eyes raking over the sharp outfit Nell had helped her pick out: denim flares with snap pockets and a hot-pink polyester long-sleeved tunic with deep aqua geometric shapes.

Nell looked rich in her black polyester double knit slacks without pockets. Hurley stared at his date's top like a hick from Paradise, moving his eyes over Nell's cuffed short-sleeved silk pearl-colored blouse with its long pointed collar and square-cut hem.

Nell laughed right away at their white shoes, pointing to them while her other hand tried to conceal her laughter. "Those shoes!" Nell laughed. "Those are hideous! Now, I have to change into something ugly," she insisted.

"No you don't! It's fine, Nell, let's go!" Hubbard commanded, rolling her eyes at Nell's remark.

"Let's get out of here, then," Nell said, as she hurried to the gray fartmobile.

Hubbard sat close to Mark on the back seat, in contrast to Nell who sat far from Hurley, her head leaning against the front passenger window. Hurley mentioned it before he started the engine. "Ain't ya gonna sit next to me?"

"No...I ain't!" she returned in a mocking voice she knew would make him drive to the football stadium like a madman. And he did.

"You smell really good," Mark told Hubbard softly. Both back-seat passengers could see their driver grinning in his rear-view mirror as he mimicked the compliment to Nell.

"You smell really good," Hurley drawled.

"Shut up, Gunderson!" Hubbard laughed above Nell's laughter. "And slow down!"

Hurley kept turning his head to Nell, which made both girls nervous in a car hurtling down the street.

"Don't worry...he always drives fast. He's a good driver," Mark assured them.

Hurley said to Nell, "I called ya last night."

Nell unwrapped a stick of gum.

"Where were ya?" Hurley asked.

"Out."

"Out where?" Hurley's eyes shifted from the road to Nell's teasing profile.

"Just out!" Nell snapped her gum, teasing her hot-headed boyfriend, especially by not looking at him while he drove.

"She was over at my place, Hurley, doing homework," Hubbard informed him.

"'Til ten thirty?" Hurley frowned.

"No, 'til eleven thirty," Hubbard returned.

"I told you not to call my house after ten!" Nell scolded Hurley, snapping her gum louder.

At that instant Hurley shot Mark a glancing stare in his mirror, a look that Hubbard didn't see.

Hurley said, "I wrote ya a letter last night. I wanted to read it to ya on the phone."

169

Immediately, Nell put aside her indifference toward Hurley and slid over next to him as he downshifted over a slew of railroad tracks. Hubbard saw Nell's arm move as she put her hand onto Hurley's lap and whispered, "You wrote me a letter?"

"I told ya I did, didn't I?"

"Where is it?" Nell begged.

Hurley patted his shirt pocket as if he forgot it, saying, "Gee...I must've lost it."

She was disappointed until finally he pointed to his glove box. Nell scooted over and pressed the latch. The glove box reeked of the Wild Country cologne Hurley had sprinkled inside to make his car smell sexy. She opened the envelope addressed "to Nell."

Hubbard gave Mark a searching look as Nell read her letter to herself while leaning against the front passenger door. Mark turned his face to his window and prayed that Nell wouldn't read it out loud and that Hubbard wouldn't notice his sweating palm in her hand. They all remained silent.

Hurley looked at Nell often, trying to see if he could discern her reaction to the letter.

It took Nell all the way to Robbins Stadium before she finally was done, having read her letter at least three times. As Hurley's farting muffler crawled along the crowded stadium parking lot, Nell folded the letter and put it inside her purse. While they all waited for her response, Mark's knees were firing up and down like the old Ford's pistons. He wished now he had never written that damn letter for the green Andrew Jackson folded inside his front pocket.

Then Nell slid gracefully over to her date and turned his big devilish head to her, whereupon she planted a long wet kiss on his lips that made the back seat passengers yell out in unison, "Hey! Watch where you're driving!"

By the time Gunderson's Ford found a parking space, Nell was crying on Hurley's shoulder and kissing his neck, something her cousin had never seen her do. Hubbard motioned with her eyes for Mark to get out on Nell's side of the two-door.

Once outside, Nell still hung all over Hurley, kissing him wildly while running both of her hands through his thin brown hair.

"Oh, brother, I've never seen her like this with a guy. And to cry...forget it. Nell never cries."

"She must've really liked his letter," Mark stated softly, followed by an ironic half-laugh.

"That's an understatement. I didn't think Gunderson could even write a complete sentence, let alone reduce Nell to tears."

"He's getting better," Mark said. "He's shown me a few things he's written that were pretty good. I know he's crazy about your cousin."

"Yeah."

The way Hubbard said "yeah" and her remote stare into the tree-covered hills high behind the stadium doubled Mark's regret that he had deceived her with his letter. Oh, how he wanted to grab her there in the shaded twilight, even with strangers passing by them like phantoms headed for the stadium entrance. He wanted to scream at her that it was a letter he wrote to her the same day they danced together in her house on Blue Hill.

He so badly wanted to cry out to her face, "Yes, Hubbard, Nell has fallen in love with Hurley by reading the words I wrote to you! Words that told how I never felt alone, truly alone, until I walked back home without you that day...long before we danced! And I wrote about the thousands of hours in Paradise that held thoughts that were only about you and where your life would be going when you were free, free to live your life away from Blue Hill and the memories of frightful/joy that I know I saw on your face when you were there with me at the very top of Blue Hill!"

Now, he felt something related to his terrible loss in Kansas that held him back and kept him from telling Hubbard right then that it was her letter and not Nell's. Perhaps it was the slow-healing bruise on his heart; or, maybe it was some kind of blocked artery that wouldn't allow courage to flow to his heart. Fearful and into his head about why he was feeling this way, he knocked on Hurley's front passenger window and motioned for Hurley to come on.

Hubbard was beside herself, puzzled about why her date was acting so anxious and closed-off toward her.

For Mark and Hubbard, there was plenty of awkwardness around Nell and Hurley's blatant affection, as they followed the hand-holding couple who now both stunk of Wild Country. Mark walked along, aloof and unconscious of Hubbard's desire to hold his hand. So he didn't.

They sat on the visitor's side of the field on concrete block ledges where the band and some three thousand fans from Woodbury cheered for their Wildcats. They outnumbered the home team supporters two to one, though the East High Falcons were favored to repeat as city champs.

When the white-shoed boys from Paradise left to get pop and popcorn for their dates, Nell was eager to hand her cousin the letter from Hurley. Hubbard read it fast.

172

Dear Nell, I know I am only this hick from Paradise and out of your league in so many ways that I can't help but feel that I will lose you one day. I feel so lucky every time I'm with you, though I'm afraid you will move on to someone better than me who can give you the kind of life you are used to. Each time I'm with you I can only think of the time I will be alone again and so far away from my dream girl Nell in the city. Because of your beauty you have forced me to take longer looks at you when I'm with you, even when I'm driving. I know I do that because I have fallen in love with every little thing about you and I look for you to feel the same way too, even though I'm such a bigmouth.

It's not easy being Hurley Gunderson now. It used to be. Until I met you I was just a loudmouth catcher dreaming of playing in the big leagues. Now I dream of Nell Evers watching me make the winning play. Now I dream of being with you and your sweet kisses that I remember more than any game I ever played in. When we lost the league championship to South Woodbury I got over it fast because I thought of the next time I would see you.

I am not able to tell you these things except in a letter that I hope can somehow bring us closer together. I want you to love me too. Your boy from Paradise.

Hubbard handed the letter back to Nell. "That's sweet," she told her cousin.

"Isn't it? I've never gotten such a sweet letter from a boy," Nell gushed.

"It sure doesn't sound like Gunderson."

"I know. But it goes to show ya that you really don't know anybody, do ya, Hubbard?"

"No, I guess not."

To Hubbard's amazement Nell began to cry, getting a tissue from her purse.

"What's wrong, Nell?"

"Oh, I've been so mean to him, teasing him, and leading him on. And here's this guy who really cares about me. You know...I like to keep my options open. I can't be with him and get pregnant, Hubbard. My parents expect me to go to college and marry some rich kid with big plans for the future."

"I know."

"It's hard, Hubbard. I want to be with Hurley. This letter explains why he's so jealous all the time."

"He is crazy about you."

"Don't you want to be with Mark?"

"If I got that kind of letter from him...prob'ly. But he's more scared to than I am. And I've known plenty of girls at Warren House who went all the way and then the guy took off."

"I'm not like you, Hub...I've been with guys before and made them wear protection. I've told Hurley I've been with guys and he gets real mad. He says he'd never wear a raincoat with me," Nell laughed.

"A raincoat? That sounds like Gunderson."

They could see the boys easily from far away, loaded with food and drinks.

"Those shoes!" Nell laughed.

Hubbard laughed, too.

Mark was still distracted by thoughts of guilt over the letter and unformed feelings of loss, as he and Hurley returned from the concession stand.

"I gotta hand it to ya, Wichita...I mean, Mark. You

sure wrote up a storm in that letter. Best twenty bucks I ever spent. If you two hadn't been there I think we'd be doin' it now in the parking lot, on my back seat."

"You think she'll let Hubbard read it?"

"Ya know, she's prob'ly readin' it this very second," Hurley laughed.

"I shouldn't have written that damn letter."

"Why the hell not? You did your buddy a favor. No big deal."

"Maybe not to you."

"You should write Hawkins one of those torch letters. She'll be all over ya...believe me."

"I'm not you."

"Oh, sure...sensitive Mark Freeman. I s'pose you don't wanna get naked with a girl like all us other apes," Hurley flared cynically.

"Yeah, I do, but..."

"But what?"

"Never mind."

"No, I wanna know!"

"I'm scared to...okay?"

"Oh, Wichita! For Christ's sake...it won't hurt ya! Look at me! I've done it. It's nothin' to be scared of."

"I don't want to talk about it. If I do, I do. I'm not going to do it just because you tell me to."

"Suit yourself. But you'll sing a dif'rent tune some day. Mark my words, Wichita."

"Don't call me that."

"Sorry."

Hurley slapped his taller friend on his back and told him discreetly, "After the game we're parkin' at this secret place I found when my old man took me to buy fireworks in South Dakota. It's the coolest spot, Mark. Nobody goes there. It's on this old guy's farm that my dad knows...where he let us shoot fireworks. He said we could go there to shoot fireworks anytime we want."

"We're not shooting fireworks."

"Speak for yourself," Hurley cackled.

About the time the boys started to climb the stadium steps, Hurley could see that a very tall blonde kid in a medal-laden maroon and white letter sweater had stopped near his aisle seat to talk to Nell. He was Todd Menard, a very shy star on the basketball team, who lived close to the Evers house on the other side of Bandshell Park. Todd's parents were friends of Nell's folks.

Nell and Hubbard were enjoying their chat with the polite young man; and Nell, for a change, had no intention of flirting to make Hurley jealous. Todd was craned over, his lanky body bent to hear Nell's voice above the school band. Nell saw Hurley a step ahead of Mark, both with their hands full of loaded compartment trays from the concession stand.

The much shorter but brazen Hurley handed acne-faced Todd his tray saying, "Do ya mind holdin' this for a second?"

The well-mannered kid took Hurley's tray, then Hurley stepped aside so Mark could take his seat. After Hurley sat down next to Nell, she sensed trouble because Hurley just let Todd stand there awkwardly holding the tray.

"Hurley, this is Todd...he's my neighbor," Nell smiled.

Hurley took the tray from Todd and smiled up at him. "Well, Todd, I'm here, now. So you can haul your giraffe ass outta here so we can see the frigin' game."

Nell was stunned and so was Todd, who slunk off like a wounded hound with his neck hunched between his shoulders, just when the roar made by the visiting crowd cheering a Woodbury Central touchdown appeared to be urging on the irascible Hurley.

Above the din, Nell screamed at her date, "What's wrong with you?"

"Nothin' now," he grinned, tossing buttered popcorn into his laughing mouth.

"That guy is the sweetest guy in the world! And you treated him like shit! What is your problem?"

Hurley just sat there eating popcorn and sipping his pop through a straw until Nell's temper climbed to the point of no return.

Finally, at halftime, when Mark and Hubbard went for a walk around the stadium, Hurley apologized. "Okay, I'm sorry."

"You ruined a perfect night with your big mouth. How can you say things like that to people you don't even know?"

"I get all tense when you talk to guys. I just lose it, Nell. I'm sorry."

"You write me such a sweet letter, then you do something like that."

"All I can say is I'm sorry. It's just that I think you're so beautiful, and I know every guy out there thinks so, too. And I'm not really sure about us. You don't let me know."

A few minutes later, Nell softened to him and took his kiss before saying, "What do you want me to do?"

For some reason, his devilish grin and those tiny green eyes were telling her things that made her laugh out loud, covering her mouth with her manicured hands.

Liquor stores in South Dakota were but a hundred yards from the Iowa state line. Nell and Hurley were inside the store buying beer and wine with Nell's fake I.D., when Hubbard and Mark had their first real disagreement; and, of course, it was about Hurley and his behavior at the stadium.

"They obviously made up. If I were Nell, I would not be here now," Hubbard fumed from the back seat, sitting apart from her date.

"If you were Nell, I wouldn't be here either," Mark chuckled alone.

"No...really, Mark, the way he treated that sweet guy...like he was some threat. I mean, she does flirt with guys, I know..."

"To Hurley, he was a threat. I just think that it takes two to make that stuff happen."

"You act like Hurley's not mean to begin with."

"Yeah, I know he's crude and has a sharp tongue...but Nell's no angel, ya know."

"I can't believe you're not mad at him."

"I can't control what he does. I'm not going to let him ruin my night," he drawled.

Not far beyond the vast liquor store's front window, Nell was all over Hurley at the register, kissing his thick neck and rubbing his back as if nothing happened.

"Looks like they're doing better than we are," Mark smiled.

Hubbard moved over close to him, leaning her head on his shoulder, telling him that she didn't want any alcohol.

"Me neither," Mark said and put his arm around her.

Hurley's parking spot was a hidden oasis on the edge of an isolated pasture where one massive oak tree

178

concealed his entire car from the view of the owner's house lights in the distant darkness of rural South Dakota, on this first real cool night before fall officially began.

Hurley left the radio on for them. Petula Clark sang "Downtown" as Mark and Hubbard cuddled close together on the back seat.

Mark thought it was funny how Hurley came prepared, confident that Mark's letter would work for him, so every blanket and pillow in his bedroom had been in his trunk and, now, were spread out on the cold ground on the other side of the tree, out of sight from the rest of the world.

"What are they doing back there?" Hubbard asked.

"Everything."

"I hope she's careful."

"Like us?" Mark smiled and hugged her tighter.

She playfully slapped his leg, adding, "What's that supposed to mean?"

"Nothing, dear."

After their long laugh, "A Lover's Concerto" played on the radio, the song they slow-danced to in her house.

"Nell said I could borrow her car Saturday when I go see Johnny. I could pick you up if you want."

"Okay."

"Nell wants me to get rid of Johnny. She says he's holding me back from spending weekends with her."

"I think it's great how you take care of him."

"Yeah?"

"Yeah."

"I should move him back to my place."

"I thought he liked it at Luther's."

"He does. But some of Luther's hogs get pink eye and pneumonia every fall. I think my vision formula keeps

Johnny immune to it. Doc Jensen keeps tellin' me to patent it and market it to vets all over the country."

"Why don't ya?"

"Money...as usual."

"Maybe Nell's dad would back ya."

"I don't know. Maybe. I just wanna graduate and move back into my house. Maybe I can work at Doc Jensen's clinic. What about you?"

"More and more, I'm thinking about playing ball in the big leagues."

"Like Hurley?"

"Yeah."

"You're better than Hurley."

"He's a good catcher."

"But you can hit the ball better."

"Yeah, but lots of guys can hit," he said humbly.

"You should have Hurley's confidence."

"I guess so."

"You'd be on the road a lot if you played pro ball."

"Yeah, I like the sound of that. I don't see myself around Paradise or Woodbury for long when I graduate. I'm here by accident...or because of an accident."

"Yeah, it's not like you chose to live here or anything," she agreed.

Just then, Hurley let out this shrieking howl that shocked his passengers.

"What was that?" Hubbard asked Mark.

Mark craned his neck around to see through the back window, but he couldn't see Hurley.

"He does that when he's drinking," Mark said.

"I hope Nell's okay."

When Mary Wells began to sing "My Guy," Hurley yelled from behind the big tree, "Hey Wichita! Turn up the tunes!"

"I love this song!" Hubbard squealed, gladly turning up the volume.

After the song, Hubbard turned the volume down once more.

"Isn't it strange how we end up living in the places we do? All because of the random chance of where our parents happen to be in this world," Mark declared.

"Yeah, I often thought how rare it is to live in a place as small and remote as Blue Hill...with so few people. Nell always says you might as well enjoy where you are, wherever that is."

"She's enjoying it here," Mark laughed.

On the drive back to Paradise, Hurley bragged to Mark about going all the way with Nell, and kept thanking his friend for writing the letter for him.

"No more letters, Hurley. Write your own from now on!"

Nell decided to sleep over at Hubbard's mother's house, because she was a bit intoxicated from the wine and her first time with Hurley Gunderson. From under the covers on her bed, Hubbard admonished Nell for her reckless behavior.

"I can't believe you went all the way with that moron."

The more she scolded her cousin for sleeping with Hurley, the more Nell giggled and squirmed under the covers, as if Hubbard's derision was tickling her all over.

"You get pregnant by that jerk and your life is ruined, Nell! Are you crazy?"

"He was careful."

"Yeah, I'll bet! Answer me truthfully, Nell...did you sleep with him because of that letter?"

"What if I did?"

"Oh, brother! He could've copied that from some romance novel, for God's sake! Do you love him?"

"I think so."

"I think so," Hubbard repeated in a mocking, wimpy voice that made Nell burst into laughter.

Stopped by an Angel

October came to Paradise like a raging arboreal fire storm of red and gold mixed with yellow and orange, colors exulting from a thousand century-old maples and oaks that rustled incessantly above the little prairie town every autumn.

Nell didn't let Hubbard use her car to go to Blue Hill, withholding the car after Hubbard told her she wouldn't go on any more parking dates with Gunderson. So, when Hubbard called Mark to tell him she couldn't make it that Saturday, and that Johnny could miss a week of exercise, Mark said he'd walk Johnny, and did so. Hubbard was so happy with his selfless way of helping her that she composed her own love letter to him, a letter that she could not give him.

Time in Hurley's basement was a feast of games for Mark on many weekends. In bed in the quiet Freeman house, there would come a morning knock on Mark's bedroom window that cried out for him to jump from bed with a thrilling appetite for competition to beat his cocky host across the street in something: pool, ping-pong, pinball, even golf putting into the drain hole in the Gunderson laundry room, where Hurley sometimes smoked cigarettes below the open window.

But no knock came this Saturday morning. Right after the usual hearty breakfast Grandma prepared, a treat that Hurley would often devour when invited, Mark donned his coat and set out for the Gunderson basement entrance.

At the bottom of the steps, out of the howling prairie wind that had petrified every tree in town to skeletal gray starkness, Mark held his breath in order to hear the brutal cacophony that was coming from Hurley's bedroom. At first, he thought Hurley was torturing a dog.

To outsiders, Mr. Gunderson seemed a mild-mannered alcoholic, just as his spouse was, except about once a month when the old man exploded from the stress of his business and took it out on his only child. The wailing cries coming from his friend sounded like he was being beaten to death by his 250 pound father. Hurley's repeated pleas of "No! No!" were followed by terrible thuds made by bones when hit by a meaty fist; then came awful, pitiful cries that seemed never to let up.

Mark caught his breath in the cold air at the top of the Gunderson basement steps, feeling the shame of cowardice for failing to help his friend by at least knocking loudly on the basement door, which might have made Mr. Gunderson stop his brutal assault on Hurley. But doubt stopped him from interfering; maybe Mr. Gunderson was punishing Hurley for stealing, or a thousand other things he knew his friend was capable of doing.

Tracing his unconscious steps back home, he thought of how his own father had never laid a hand on him, and if so, how terrible that must be. Compassion for his wayward friend overwhelmed him as he slipped back into the front room and stood in the warm air coming up from Grandpa's floor furnace. In this quiet, safe environment a calming stillness came over him that soothed his nerves. He realized that his home now was a good one compared to his life in Wichita; and, he was certain his life was much better than the one lived by the boy across the street who had been lavished with all the toys.

Sunday, after Mark returned from church, Hurley stopped by to see if he wanted to walk to the river with him. Mark said yes, because he thought Hurley wanted to talk about the beating. It was strange to Mark that Hurley didn't show any physical signs he had been beaten, not a scratch. He decided not to mention what he'd overheard.

On their walk to the river all Hurley talked about was Nell's naked body and how perfect it was. One question to Mark really ticked Mark off.

"Have you gotten tit from Hawkins yet?"

"Don't ask me that stuff. I wouldn't tell ya if I did."

The river looked cold under a gray autumn sky. A pair of railroad tracks ran north and south fifty yards from the river on the Nebraska side, at the western edge of Paradise, just a quarter mile from the cemetery where Mark's mother rested.

A gravel road stretched alongside the tracks some thirty yards away. Beside the tracks, hidden in a tall stand of cottonwoods, the boys from Paradise crouched, waiting for the right car, one that would speed by at 75 mph.

Before they entered the cottonwoods, Mark had patiently watched his rebellious partner search for and find two identical rocks between the railroad tracks; they were gray/flat rocks, oval and about the size of an egg.

Before Hurley's search, they had competed to see who could throw rocks closest to the river's Iowa side some 150 yards away. Gunner went first and splashed his rock about half-way across. Mark's toss was much higher, but seemed to splash close to Hurley's. On their final throw, Hurley let one fly about 20 yards further than any toss, so he lit a cigarette and celebrated his victory.

Then Hurley announced they would have one more throw, this time for accuracy; he explained why as he hunted for the two perfect stones between the tracks. At the end of Hurley's search, the two boys waited in the trees for a passing black Ford Falcon.

Daryl Naylor, age 50, and his son Daryl, Jr., about 30, had been deadbeats on Hurley's paper route. He'd dropped them and cut off their paper. Two years ago, the redneck father and son duo were driving their Falcon at night across the Combination Bridge, an iron waffled surface for vehicles and pedestrians, when they saw their former paper boy hiking the same direction from Woodbury on the narrow pedestrian walkway. The men were drinking and Daryl Jr. threw an open can of beer from his passenger window at the startled Hurley. The can hit Hurley's arm and sprayed beer over his upper body. Hot tempered Hurley fingered them and spewed four-letter words. To Hurley's surprise, Daryl Sr. stopped the Falcon on the bridge.

The rednecks got out of their idling car and stalked Hurley from both sides of the walkway, trapping him with no place to go unless he jumped into the river. They told petrified Hurley that if he didn't jump they'd throw his ass off the bridge, which meant flying through forty feet of darkness into the churning Missouri River. Hurley fought like a cornered animal until they each got a hold of an arm and a leg and swung him high enough over the railing that Hurley peed his pants and begged them to spare his life.

Even now, as he handed Mark one of the egg-size

rocks, Hurley could hear the men's laughter as they dropped him hard onto the iron walkway then drove away, cat-calling at his shivering body.

Mark waited and said nothing even though his left hand was sweating as he turned the rock over and over, its smooth surface gliding from palm to fingertips. They waited for what seemed an hour while Hurley's keen green eyes spotted a dozen approaching vehicles, one after another, and declared them "negative." Mark grew tired from repeated anxiety then relief, after each sped by.

"How do you know they'll come by here now?" Mark asked Hurley.

"I know. They come by here every Saturday about this time. I've missed 'em by inches at least a dozen times. I was either a bit too early, or late, or too high with my aim. I'm ready now," he grinned.

"Why didn't you tell the police what they did?"

"My parents would've grounded my ass if they knew I'd walked to Woodbury and back. Besides, I want God's justice. The Lord doesn't send the law," he grinned and brought his rock to Mark's eye level.

Mark stewed on Hurley's words: "The Lord doesn't send the law"; they unleashed a rush of maudlin waves of loss and regret and anger at God for taking his mother from him. He knew those words had a ring of truth to them, for God had not saved his mother, or prevented her from dying after the accident. Unconsciously Mark's left fist tightened around the smooth stone that, if sent now by his anger, would strike hard and fast at any target he chose.

Building emotions fired a muscle spasm under Mark's right eye, a nervous twitch that last had surfaced at its source in Kansas.

"Are ya with me?" Hurley winked.

Mark nodded yes.

As they stood with the trunk of a cottonwood between them, Hurley seemed to sniff the air to gauge how he would throw. Just then, from a quarter mile away, Hurley heard the familiar whine of the Falcon before seeing its black hood heading north.

"Here it comes!" Hurley barked his joyous warning and gave his orders. "I know when to throw. They're movin' fast, so throw when I tell ya!"

"You sure it's them?"

"It's them."

Mark saw the fierce look of retribution on Hurley's face, his square jaw and menacing mouth set to get even, as the black Falcon closed with whining speed on the gravel road. Both boys were poised to throw when Hurley gave the order.

"Now!"

At that instant, Hurley let fly his rock; Mark's arm went numb from the flashing image of his mother driving her car, and so his rock fell far short of the target. But Hurley's rock hit metal with thunderous ferocity magnified by the Falcon's speed. Daryl Sr. nearly lost control from the impact of Hurley's rock; the car swerved and braked.

Mark backed into the trees ready to run, but Hurley wanted them to see him, so he stood defiantly fingering the two men who had gotten out of their car to inspect the huge dent on the passenger-side door. Their heads turned as Hurley called to them.

"'Member me? You Bastards!" he cackled loudly.

The two shouting men pointed at Hurley and started to run toward him. Mark and Hurley ran for their lives, with Hurley laughing like the devil. Mark followed close behind Hurley, for nobody in Paradise knew every inch of this ground as well as Hurley Gunderson.

They ran between the railroad track for some 300 yards, often looking back at the angry men who stood cursing them from the tree line. The boys dashed toward the river, but stopped when they were out of view of the men.

No way was Hurley going to get trapped on his turf when he saw that the men were getting into their Falcon and driving back toward the boys.

"Follow me, Wichita!"

Hurley led the way, back north toward the river in the direction of their pursuers, until they reached a large sewer drain. Panting hard, Mark could only listen.

"This'll take us to the other side of the road where I hit 'em. Don't worry, it's dry inside and there ain't no rats. C'mon."

Mark looked down to his scuffed and dirty Keds and held back from following Hurley into the sewer pipe until his leader called to him from his duck-walking position to hurry up.

Halfway through the dark sewer that smelled of cold dirt and wet concrete, Mark called, "I can't see ya, Hurley!"

"I'm up here, Wichita! Keep comin'."

On the other side of the gravel road Hurley sneaked a look down the road far to the south and could see the Falcon cruising away from them. Hurley chortled over their getaway, then laughed harder as Mark began cleaning his shoes with licked fingers.

"Don't worry about your shoes, for Christ's sake, Wichita!"

Hurley led them through Paradise on side roads that

were new to Mark. All the way back to Hurley's front porch where they ate peanut butter sandwiches and gulped down a pitcher of cherry Kool-Aid, Hurley gloated about getting even.

"You should have seen their ugly faces when they saw it was me! I got 'em good, Wichita! See...the Lord doesn't send the law! Now, that was real justice!" he laughed.

That night in bed, Mark shuddered at the image of his mother and how it had stopped him from throwing with accuracy. Before sleep, he asked himself, "Could she be my guardian angel? Or am I just a coward who follows orders from a leader who truly lives by conquering his fear?"

Yes, I'm Ready

Mark and Hubbard turned eighteen a week apart, on the 17th and 24th of October. Hubbard's mother let her borrow her automatic push-button Dodge, when Hubbard agreed to wash it on the weekend.

On Saturday, Hubbard felt apprehensive because she had to tell Mark that Nell had hoodwinked her into having a party to celebrate their birthdays at the house on Blue Hill. Hubbard agreed only because Nell threatened to just drop in on them this weekend. Nell and Hurley planned to party at the house next Saturday night, so Hubbard and Mark could be alone there tonight.

"Oh, Hub's ready!" Nell teased her cousin.

"No, Mark's ready," Hubbard laughed.

Mark had dressed in Keds, bell bottom jeans and an olive denim jacket covering his red flannel long sleeve shirt. He waited anxiously on the front porch for the beige Dodge. Old Spice from his grandpa's bottle in the bathroom medicine cabinet burned his peach-hair face after his very first shave left cuts in several places on his neck. His ash blonde hair was yet damp from his bath and spiked with Butch Wax in front.

He stood in the shadows, worrying about Hurley, hoping his pushy friend didn't see him and hoping he wouldn't come over before, or when Hubbard arrived.

Hurley was furious at Hubbard for telling Nell she shouldn't be going out with him. Every time Hurley saw Mark he said negative things about "the pig lover who buried her old man in his hogyard" and told Mark he could do better than Hawkins.

Mark had retorted more than once that Hurley didn't know Hubbard at all, and that if he didn't have anything good to say about her, he shouldn't say anything at all.

Suddenly, for selfish reasons, Hurley now wanted a chance to make friends with Hubbard. Mark had said it was up to her, when Hurley pressed him about a birthday party on Blue Hill.

Then, there she was, pulling the car onto the driveway and steering toward the back of the house. Mark ran through the house, and found Grandma rolling dough on the kitchen table for a rhubarb pie.

"She's here!" he announced.

Out the back door he went, in time to see Hubbard step out of her mother's car wearing the cool green wool sleeveless jumper with a fitted bodice that Nell gave her. Hubbard's lush red hair was styled in a back-combed bouffant. On her feet were a pair of black slides with one inch kitten heels. Mark thought she looked beautiful, and like a grown woman with such conscious eyes; eyes like those he wanted more than anything himself. For he often was too preoccupied with his own thoughts to be fully conscious like this tough farm girl from Blue Hill.

He could see that she liked him, by the tender way her pink-polished fingers moved nervously at their tips and rubbed together, as if she wanted him to hold them.

Hubbard saw that he was afraid, afraid of being

eighteen and still so very shy in this way—as she was. And she understood his distracted state, for she only began to live fully and in the present on the day she accepted that her father's early death was imminent.

"Hi," he smiled.

"Hi."

He was not afraid to take her hand and lead her into the garage where Grandpa was stacking 50-pound bags of salt for the coming winter.

The old man smiled at Hubbard and told her she looked nice. After chatting briefly about her new school and home in Woodbury, Grandpa told Mark to go inside and introduce Hubbard to Grandma before they left.

Once again, Mark took Hubbard's hand as he led her into the Freeman back porch where the good smells of home cooking reminded her of the incredible meals this woman had created for her. In the dim light of the warm kitchen, Grandma Freeman stopped trimming her pie crust to chat with the visitor, smiling with her eyes at how nice Hubbard looked.

Hubbard told the old lady, "I want to thank you for all those great meals you made me. It really helped my state of mind to have such good food while I was there. Thank you, Mrs. Freeman." Hubbard smiled then hugged the much shorter woman.

For his grandma's benefit, Mark smiled and teased his girlfriend, "How about a hug for me, too? Who do you think delivered all those great meals to you?"

Grandma Freeman was tickled when Hubbard hugged Mark.

Before they left, Mark showed Hubbard his room and watched her going from one piece of antique furniture to another, telling him that one day she would furnish her house on Blue Hill with this kind of beautiful old wood.

"Isn't your dad's bed an antique?" Mark asked.

"It's Luther's bed now. I gave it to him for boarding Johnny. And yes, it's certainly an antique. It was my Grandpa Hubbard's bed."

From the ground level basement window that looked out to the Freeman house, Hurley watched Hubbard drive away with Mark in her mom's Dodge. He wondered where they were going all gussied up. Not to the hog farm, he snickered as he lit a marijuana joint.

Mark asked Hubbard to drive the same route he always took when he walked, but they had to turn to the north as they neared Hawkins Cemetery in order to pick up the old highway where they could exit onto Broken Kettle Road.

Not until she parked the bulky Dodge could they hear the sweet/clamor of rustling leaves clinging to the trees around the Blue Hill valley. To Mark it was a more distant sound of leaves blowing in the wind compared to the trees of Paradise, especially the arboreal din made by the lofty trees on Freeman earth.

To Hubbard, the acrid smell of pig manure coming from Luther's place seemed more pungent to her now, since being in the city had sensitized her to these farm smells that once were ordinary and easy to ignore.

As they walked toward Luther's farm she said, "I'm gonna keep Johnny here for the week to see how he feels about being alone, away from Luther's herd. A couple weeks ago I saw him get bullied away from the water tank by a cranky old sow five times his size."

Despite the increasing aroma of Luther's hogyard,

194

the air was charged with an expanding vibrancy that only the Midwest and New England have in October. She wanted to take Mark's hand, but didn't; though they had held hands several times, it had to be his move.

The more she thought about it, the sillier that seemed. So she made the move, and when her fingers touched his, she asked him, "Why do girls always have to wait for the guy to hold hands...to be asked to dance...or to be called by them and have doors opened by them?"

"I don't mind if you don't wait," he smiled, then wanted to squeeze her hand, but didn't.

And he wanted to tell her how beautiful she looked to him just now, but the old feeling of cowardice that he always had around girls he liked stopped his words. And the truth about that letter he wrote for Hurley would not be told, because he had promised Hurley to never tell Hubbard.

Afraid to break his promise, afraid to let the truth come out. It all added up to living in his mind, living in lies about who he truly was at this moment on this western side of Blue Hill.

Luther broke their silence when he hobbled out from his aluminum workshop, an open-sided shed cluttered with oily tools and old coffee tins that held a thousand little things that maintained his operation. The old farmer thanked Hubbard for the bed that, he told them, agreed with his old bones. Hubbard had been most grateful to get the biggest single physical reminder of her father out of her house, and said so. Then she told Luther of her plans to isolate Johnny at her place for the week. The old man said he'd feed and water Johnny for her, but she let him know that she would leave her pet with enough feed and water to sustain him.

"Never seen a pig eat so little as that one. You got him trained to stay skinny," Luther grinned behind his gray stubble.

"My formula keeps him lean and healthy, if he gets just a few grams two or three times a month. Doc Jensen tells me it'll be hard to convince farmers 'round here it would be cost effective for them, since the market pays by the pound, but a leaner animal will be in demand in the future."

"Yep, can't say now that no fat on bacon will be popular 'round here, but my doctor says I gotta reduce my fat intake for my ole ticker. He said somthin' called co-les-trol can clog everything up."

At first, Mark felt reluctant to express his opinion to the crusty old farmer, but he had read an article on the subject in the city paper just last Sunday and Hubbard's presence motivated him. He said, "I read that clogged arteries aren't caused by high cholesterol, that it's plaque from certain fats that stick to the artery walls.

Hubbard agreed and added, "Yes! That's what Doc Jensen says, too. Plaque...that's what Johnny doesn't have. I know because plaque doesn't get on his teeth like other animals."

The bright light of health shown from Hubbard when she turned her gaze on him. Mark again risked himself without worry about saying something wrong, or even about saying something true that he had observed.

"That's where I saw it! Your eyes, Hubbard...they're like Johnny's...with the same light."

He let her look into his eyes unabashed for the first time, without soon averting his away.

"Your eyes have light, Mark."

"Really?"

"Yes! Don't you ever see it?"

"I don't..."

Luther had been listening to them, but now he sauntered off to his shed, and Mark realized he wanted to tell Hubbard something.

"I don't really look for light. And I don't know why. Maybe because most times I don't see it."

She gazed into his pale blue eyes and urged him to continue, softly asking him, "Why don't you look, Mark?"

His chin started to tremble; he allowed her to see these spasms, then hardened the mask he'd worn since Kansas. She could see his light diminish and close off, as if a door to his eyes had been shut in order to protect him from something the heart dare not reveal.

"I saw the light go out in your eyes just now. Why?" she whispered.

Without blinking or dodging those healthy blue eyes of Hubbard Kay Hawkins, eyes that were always lit, he strained his mind to find whatever it was and to let it come out. She waited and watched for the light to come back on, ignoring the storm going on around his jaw and mouth, his nervous eyes, the confusion that only brought more abeyance, like a suspended portal that had closed shut to her.

Mark followed her over to the hogyard gate where Johnny's clean pink snout excitedly sniffed the air, while Luther's bedraggled herd remained listless in a sea of mud and shit mixed with huge clods of hardened dirt.

Hubbard saw that Johnny's hide was dirtier after missing a week with him; the sight of excessive dung caked on his hooves made up her mind for her that he was moving back home for good. He had remained healthy despite living with Luther's doddering stock that seemed always to be getting the antibiotic needle from Doc Jensen.

This time she didn't fasten the rope on Johnny's yellow collar. Her pig stayed close to her while she stopped to tell Luther that Johnny was going to be moving back to her place now, and that she would make sure he had enough food and water for the week, and that Luther didn't need to worry about him.

"I'm gonna try a new formula on him that I'm workin' on."

As they walked away from the old codger, he waved and grinned, his stained brown teeth exposed, "Another experiment, huh?"

On the way home, Hubbard said, "Luther doesn't look so good lately."

"Yeah. He seems to be more tired than usual."

"I think he's afraid to have an operation. He's like my dad...never trusts doctors. My dad said if you need a doctor or lawyer, you're in big trouble."

"That sounds like Luther, too," Mark laughed.

By the time they entered her house they had decided to wash both her mom's car and Johnny. After they changed into some overalls, Hubbard set up her record player by the back screen door and Mark filled two aluminum buckets with soapy water with the garden hose, then dropped in some rags.

To Mark's amazement, Johnny sat as still as a well-trained dog while he took a soft-bristled horsehair brush and scrubbed the pig's tough hide. Shelly Fabares began to sing "Johnny Angel." Hubbard came out singing the words to Johnny, with her overalls rolled up to her white knees. She took over the scrubbing of her angel as Mark, too, rolled his cuffs high, then soaped the car with a rag from the bucket.

During the song he came to believe that Johnny was

loved as much as any creature on earth could be, and without Johnny, Hubbard would never live on the farm alone.

About the time Johnny's pink belly had been scrubbed clean, Mark realized that Hubbard was the first girl he'd ever loved. It was so clear to him that he was not falling in love, but rather, he was in love, and had been ever since he saw her at his game, sitting on the Warren bleachers, when he waited in the on-deck circle. He recalled how his quick look at her revealed that she was looking at him, and his heart felt something that evening, something that was palpable and so very truthful. It felt as if she would always wait for him and support him—no matter where his dreams took him.

And thanks to Hurley's boldness, I'm here with her now, he thought. Because I probably would've gone to the DQ with my dad and Grandpa, if not for Hurley taking charge.

Even now, as "Johnny Angel" ran out of needle grooves on her tinny record player, Hubbard was there, fully present in her absolute abandon, while singing and bathing her Johnny. She was there, in those worn overalls, her red hair up, yet with long strands free and hanging down on both sides of her neck from bending and reaching and scrubbing. She would be a good mother to her children, he knew, as he cleaned the roof of her mother's car.

Then she dried Johnny behind his pointed ears with the sides of her baggy overalls before joining the car washing. The clean pig stood in the autumn sunshine watching the happy couple with a contented smile on his face, while Martha and the Vandellas sang "Heat Wave" near the back door.

"There's a big Halloween dance at the Woodbury

Auditorium," she said, as Mark rinsed his rag in one of the buckets.

"Really? Are you going?"

"I'd like to," she hinted with a smile.

"I'd like to go with you," he smiled.

"That would be fun. Everyone will be in costume."

"Will Nell and Hurley be there?" he asked.

"I don't know. Right now she's worried that she's pregnant."

"Really?"

"She's late...a week, or so."

"I can't see Hurley as a father," Mark said.

"That's for sure. They're both mad at me because I don't want to go out with them together anymore. Has he said anything to you about me?"

"Not really. Just his usual snide comments here and there. He knows I don't like to ride with him when he's drinking."

As the song continued, Mark thought about the letter he wrote for Hurley and how he was partly responsible if Nell was pregnant. But then he dismissed that negative thought, because he had promised Hurley that he'd never tell Hubbard about the letter.

"I don't think she'd marry Gunderson, even if she's pregnant," Hubbard said.

"Oh, God, Hurley would go crazy either way."

"Oh, well, she's prob'ly just late and there's nothing to worry about," Hubbard noted.

"Yeah, I hope so."

The next 45 on the record player was meant to tell Mark how she felt about him. She feared that it was too obvious a message, so before it started to play she told him that it was one of her favorite songs. He waited for the song to begin as he cleaned the hood and she cleaned the trunk. Then Barbara Mason began to sing, "Yes, I'm Ready," a torch song about a girl in love who doesn't know exactly how to hold her boyfriend's hand, but that she's ready to learn how to fall in love with him.

Now, Hubbard wished she hadn't played it. The lyrics embarrassed her, so much so, she found herself unable to look at Mark, and purposely washed the lowest part of her mom's car in order to keep her eyes down and away from him.

Finally, after the interminable song that she now hated was over, he surprised her by telling her it would be a great song to slow-dance to. She nodded in agreement without looking up, knowing how right he was, because she had already imagined them dancing to it here in her empty house.

Wiping dry the Dodge was easy in the soft breezes swirling through Blue Hill. For some reason she thought of and wanted to walk to the pool of water on the southern edge of Blue Hill, where an unfarmable gully held a bath-size, ever-filled pool of iron-rich water that Johnny loved to slurp.

Mark and Hubbard both wore pairs of her dad's old overboots. Both were still clad in the same water-splashed overalls, with Johnny now clean and yellow-collared, a makeshift leash made from an extension cord tied to his collar. On they tramped, laughing about the silly way they looked and walked in the over-sized footwear.

Once they left Broken Kettle and stepped high through a sloping stretch of dry prairie grass, Johnny thought he was in pig paradise. Hubbard let Johnny take the lead, knowing he would head straight for the salubrious pool of water.

On the way, Mark told Hubbard about the night with Hurley when they were in Hawkins Cemetery. He told her how he felt so weak for following Hurley and letting him control every move they made.

"It's like I need a big brother, a leader I can follow."

Hubbard nodded pensively, "I've never had a girlfriend except for Nell. And since you got to Paradise, you haven't had a friend except for Hurley."

"I never thought of that. If we don't hang around with them, we won't have any friends."

"We're friends," she smiled.

"Yeah, that's true."

"Since I'm related to Nell, I have to be around her. Ever since she told me she was going to have Johnny shipped to the Stockyards, I can't stand to be around her."

"When did she say that?"

"Hurley told me she said it."

"Well, I wouldn't believe half the things Hurley said."

"Anyway, I confronted her about it and she just laughed and called me a big rube."

Hubbard let go of Johnny's leash. They followed him for thirty yards down into a weed-choked gully cut by grooved ruts that flowed from the main pool, eight inches deep and maybe six feet long. Johnny waded in and began to gulp the rust colored water. Mark looked around for the pool's source and where it flowed. Hubbard told him that nobody knew exactly where it came from, and that her dad used to soak his feet in it because of the minerals in the water.

"My dad thought the water came from an underground pool made from the ice age."

Mark kicked off his boots and stepped into the pool

of water beside the pig.

"Feels good. If this is the same water that comes from the pipe near the cemetery, I know it has healing powers. I poured some on my blisters and they felt better right away."

Hubbard joined him and their combined movements effected freshet waves, splashings over the rim of the pool that remained constant from its underground source.

Mark grinned at Hubbard. "Hurley's dad uses it on his butt."

Mark looked up and saw a scraggly evergreen growing at the top of Blue Hill's eastern ridge, a juniper tree with bluish-gray cones standing alone, invisible most of its life. He wanted to hike up there with Hubbard and lean against its trunk and kiss her.

Johnny followed their bare feet to the juniper on cool hard ground through stiff grasses. They sat against the dry trunk, their shoulders touching, yet they faced different directions.

"You really have a quiet little paradise out here," he said.

"Yeah," she sighed.

"What's wrong?"

"Oh, I don't know. Sometimes I think I've inherited from my parents the ability to feel blue at times for no apparent reason."

"You think that's possible?"

"It usually hits me when I'm alone...when I'm out here...in the house mostly."

"You sure you want to live here when you graduate?"

"Where else could I live with Johnny? That's really why Nell's so upset with me. She wants me to go to Iowa

State with her, and share an apartment with her. It's a party town...and that's Nell. I hope she's not pregnant."

"Me, too. Couldn't you get a farmhouse in the country near Ames?"

"I don't know, maybe. I really don't want to be around Nell that much...and all that partying she likes to do."

"Poor Hurley," Mark sighed.

"Yeah," Hubbard agreed.

Halloween Dance

Halloween fell on a Thursday, but the big dance was tonight, Friday night. Hurley talked Mark into riding to the dance with him and wearing the same costume, which consisted only of a pungent mask that Hurley created. Two hoboes, nicely dressed in matching white shoes, crossed the street, headed for the Freeman back door.

Grandma and Grandpa wanted to see the boys in costume before they left for the city.

"Hoboes!" Mark smiled excitedly when he answered Grandma's question: "What are you s'posed to be?"

In Hurley's basement, they had plastered their necks and faces with Vaseline and then covered the area with fresh coffee grounds.

Grandma Freeman thought their clothes were too nice for hoboes. She said, "No hobo wears clean white shoes!"

Hurley looked over their clean flares and long sleeve zipper shirts and quipped, "Okay, we're rich hoboes!"

They left the house each holding one of Grandma's caramel apples on wooden spears, still hearing the couple's laughter at Hurley's remark.

It was a perfect chilly night for a Halloween dance,

without the usual biting wind this time of year. Paradise homes were still lit with carved pumpkins on porches when the Paradise hoboes hopped into Hurley's '56 Ford, its dull gray paint faded and ugly, yet distinguishable as Hurley Gunderson's car.

The muffler seemed louder than usual tonight as they cruised out of town. From his ashtray Hurley removed what looked like a thin rolled cigarette and lit it. The smoke smelled sweet to Mark.

"Wanna try a marijuana joint, Wichita?" Hurley grinned.

Mark declined.

Iron Butterfly blared "In-A-Gadda-Da-Vida" from the 8-track cassette player. As Hurley smoked he shouted above the song. "I got it from Nell! She gets it from some rich chick at her school! I tell ya, Wichita, we're just hicks out here, way behind everybody! Don't tell Hawkins I told ya Nell buys it at school, okay?"

"I won't."

"Yeah, we're like in the stone age, Wichita! I tell ya, every time I skip gym and drive over to take Nell to lunch, I'm humiliated! But then we puff on this stuff and it's all just a big joke! She even likes my car when we get high! We laugh 'til our guts ache! And, boy oh boy, Wichita, tonight's the night!"

Hurley turned down the volume after his passenger asked him what he meant.

"Nell's not pregnant. Isn't that great?"

"Yeah."

"Yeah? It's frigin' great news! She might start puttin' out again tonight! Sure ya don't want to celebrate with me...Mark?" he offered again.

"No, I better not."

"It won't hurt ya. It slows everything down. Just try one little hit."

Despite the frenetic beat of the seventeen minute song, Mark noticed that Hurley was driving slower and seemed happier than his usual brooding self.

Just then, as they drove past his mother's resting place, Mark had second thoughts about trying the funny weed. Hurley picked up on it and pulled over to the side of the road close to a deep ditch. He turned off Iron Butterfly and let his car idle like a cement mixer.

"I'll tell ya what, Mark...you try one hit of this. I promise it won't hurt ya...and then I'll tell ya somethin' about Hawkins that'll blow your mind. But! Ya can't say anything to her 'cause Nell made me promise not to tell ya. Deal?"

Mark looked at Hurley's extended right hand and the burning little joint pinched in his left. Hurley added, "Look, you tried beer, and now I know you don't like it much. So I never asked ya to try any of my old man's vodka, 'cause I know that ya wouldn't like vodka if ya don't like beer. Right?"

"I guess."

This time Mark took the joint with Hurley's words, "Mark, you're my only friend, besides Nell. And this is somethin' every man should know about his girl. And after ya try it, ya won't be so hard on her. Trust me."

Hurley relit the joint and passed it to Mark. "Inhale and hold it a bit...ya might cough the first time, so take it easy."

Mark sensed Hurley wasn't trying to lead him in his usual abrasive way, or intending to mislead him, so he inhaled and held the smoke, until he began coughing just like Hurley said he might.

Hurley turned off the engine, but left the Ford's lights on, and took another hit himself. Mark was feeling different, but not in a bad way.

Hurley leaned over to Mark. "Wichita, your Hubbard smokes this stuff all the time...with Nell...and she doesn't want you to know it. Isn't that a kick in the head?" Hurley laughed.

Again Mark took the offered pinjoint, inhaled, and held it in while thinking about what Hurley just told him. He knew now that Hurley was right; he couldn't be so hard on her after he just tried it himself.

"Now, when we meet 'em at the dance, ya can't say anything, Wichita."

"I won't," Mark laughed for some inexplicable reason, which made Hurley bust out into raucous laughter.

"They'll prob'ly be extra happy to see us, if ya know what I mean!" Hurley laughed.

Hurley pressed the rewind button on his cassette player, then spotted something in the ditch. Quick and determined, Hurley got out of his car and opened the trunk. Mark sat still in a musing stupor.

Via his side mirror, at first Mark couldn't see what Hurley was doing. Then, Hurley stepped forward, pointing a rifle barrel into the ditch on his side of the car. Mark turned to see a big taffy-colored tomcat frozen in place in the ditch, illuminated by the Ford's headlights. It's yellow eyes were on Hurley's aim. POP! Mark saw the cat die instantly from one shot, its lifeless body prostrate on its side, its teeth exposed and showing quick, violent death.

Hurley soon returned, slid behind the wheel and drove on as if nothing happened. Mark's lips felt even drier than before.

"You killed that cat for no reason!" Mark exclaimed.

"I don't do nothin' for no reason, Wichita. I'm preparin' myself for Nam," he grinned.

As "In-A-Gadda-Da-Vida" began to blare again from Hurley's speakers, the brutal cat-killing merged with the song in Mark's busy mind.

By the end of the long song they had crossed the Combination Bridge into Iowa. Hurley's scare on the bridge and pitching rocks at the two rednecks in the Falcon suddenly struck Mark as very funny and he began to laugh.

"We're lucky those guys in the Falcon didn't catch us!" Mark chortled above the music.

"Yeah! That was a blast!" Hurley guffawed.

By the time they arrived at the massive auditorium, they had both forgotten about the coffee grounds sticking to their faces. Hurley splashed on Wild Country cologne from the bottle in the glovebox, then tried to find Nell's car in the huge parking lot. Finally, after spotting her ragtop he couldn't find a space to park near it. He told Mark they must've been smokin' weed because her convertible's top was down on this near-freezing night.

On foot, after passing a group of uniformed cops who stood smiling and chatting outside the venue, the hoboes laughed and giggled about their white shoes. Since Nell had purchased their tickets two weeks before, they went right in at one of the five turnstiles.

Thousands of costumed kids from all over Woodbury milled around every inch of the immense auditorium. Every single time he saw some girl wearing a costume that resembled a feline, Mark's mind conjured up the cat that Hurley shot.

Finally, he asked, "How are we supposed to find

them, if they're dressed in costumes?"

"I don't know. Nell wouldn't tell me what her costume was, either. But they'll spot our shoes."

The dance floor was jammed with thousands of howling costumed dancers. A large stage held Paul and the Pioneers, the city's best-known rock band that would occasionally mix in a polka and offend many between "Proud Mary" and "Wipe Out."

This was one of the few times the hoboes from Paradise didn't attract attention with their footwear, though Nell and Hubbard saw them right away. The girls were dancing together to the band's version of The Searchers' tune "Love Potion Number Nine," not too far from the spot where their hoboes entered the auditorium floor.

Nell was in a black witch's costume: pointed hat, black dress and heels with a long rubber crooked nose that had wart bumps on it. Hubbard wore faded denim jeans with a curly-q tail, her "pigs are beautiful" t-shirt and a plastic pig's snout attached to her nose.

Nell was in the same silly condition as the hoboes were and both girls were getting along swell for the first time in a long spell. They too were celebrating Nell's good news, even though Hubbard knew well that her cousin really was a witch during her time of the month.

The witch and the pig purposely moved deeper into the throng of dancers; forcing the boys to hunt for them without being seen by them. Only Hurley walked up and down the floor, swaggering on his bowed legs with his muscled biceps extended out from his sides, a country honcho, a leader among boys, saying without words that his woman better not be dancin' with some city slicker...or there'd be big trouble.

That's why Mark stayed back, waiting on one of

the five hundred folding chairs that bordered two sides of the massive dance floor. Mark sat in the dark arena beside a fat Zorro who kept complaining about the music. Yet Mark chose to be there rather than with Hurley, as his buddy prowled for Nell and she played a cruel game meant to torment his friend.

Soon, Mark began to feel scared, paranoid from the smoke he shared with Hurley and from being surrounded by thousands of normally placid kids now hiding behind their costumes, letting go of a myriad pent up emotions by hooting and hollering and pretending to be free. And his neck was itching like crazy from some chemical reaction caused by the Vaseline and coffee grounds mixed with Grandpa's Old Spice that he had splashed on before going over to the Gunderson basement.

Most of all, his busy mind raced with the words Hurley said about Hubbard smoking pot. Words that were running in his head with a thousand Halloween images before him. Into the span of his eighteen years of unconsciousness, there came a ghoulish, insidious sense of betrayal that was speeding his heart to the music, churning his guts and shooting adrenaline into his sedentary legs, now numb from the dream of wanting to run, but can't.

If only he could run away now, to another life, a life that he would choose this time. Begin again. He was eighteen now, and he could run away and try out for all the minor league teams he could find. First, he knew that he needed wheels and a way to make money so he didn't live like a hobo. He knew his mother was the only one who could hold him back now from living such a life—and she was gone.

"Yesterday" by The Beatles sounded flat and way too loud for a slow song. Hubbard looked for Mark after the cocky hobo found and danced with his witch. Hurley told Hubbard that Mark was feeling good after getting high with him on the way over.

Hubbard put her pink snout up to Hurley's stinky face. "Did you tell him, Gunderson?" she yelled.

"Relax, Hawkins!" the hobo laughed. "I told ya I wouldn't. Would I lie to you?"

But she saw something in his red/green eyes: nothing. They were the vacant eyes of a mean liar who, thank God, missed getting her cousin pregnant.

"Where's Mark?"

"I don't know." Hurley smiled, his hands pressing his witch's buttocks as he continued to grind Nell against his groin to "Yesterday."

Only hot water and lots of paper towels removed his coffee ground mask in the men's restroom. Finally he'd had it with the irritating itching on his neck and face. For an instant, in the mirror, he thought about walking back to Paradise and taking his chances on the bridge. That silliness had worn off and was replaced with a broodiness that wanted to punish Hubbard for living another kind of life in the city that even Hurley knew about.

Yet the more he stewed about it, the smaller he felt. After all, he reasoned, it was her life and she didn't owe him anything. What seemed like an hour cleaning his face was really just enough time for two more songs from Paul and the Pioneers. Before exiting the bathroom, two hot-boxing devils in adjoining stalls made him sneeze and when he inhaled again he sucked a coffee ground into a nostril and felt an immediate caffeine rush. Several times he tried to snort it out, but no luck. One last look into the mirror and he was sickened by the redness in his eyes and the way his mood went south with thoughts of Hubbard's other life.

Hubbard pulled off her pink nose and put it in her pocket, sensing Mark would be upset with her after Hurley broke his promise and told him about smoking pot with Nell a few times. But she didn't smoke any with Nell tonight, instead telling her rich cousin that she'd only consider renewed friendship with her if she dumped Gunderson for good. Nell had said she was getting tired of Hurley anyway, and that she'd break up with him when the time was right. Hubbard knew that her cousin was afraid of Hurley's temper, so she told Nell that she understood her situation, but she just did not like Hurley Gunderson.

Hubbard saw Mark walking alone with his head down, his hands deep into his front pockets as if not wanting to be at the dance at all. She watched him, without a costume, his face red as if wind burned. Then he saw her, ten feet away, facing him, her curly pig tail obscured. He stood in front of her, his eyes so red that she didn't notice his smile or the coffee grounds sticking to his ear lobes.

"Ya wanna get outta here?"

He nodded yes. She directed him to wait while she told Nell she was leaving.

"Can you give me a ride home?" he asked above the music.

"Yes, if Nell lets me use her car."

"Tell Hurley I have a ride, if you get the car."

<u>Moon Over Paradise</u>

Hurley and the witch were fast-dancing. After Nell gave her the keys to her car, Hubbard went right up to the hobo's greasy/grounds face with her hands on her waist and told him that Mark had just asked her why she smoked grass. Hurley stopped dancing and confessed that he'd told Mark because he wanted Mark to get high with him. Hubbard smiled big with her clear blue eyes and said, "Gunderson, Mark didn't ask me anything about getting high! I just wanted you to know that I know you're a gawd damn liar who can't be trusted!"

Then she saw the evil in his eyes and lost any satisfaction about tricking him. She left feeling afraid of him, and understood clearly what Nell meant by waiting for the right time to tell him they were through.

Hubbard returned to Mark, slipped into her jeans jacket, then they made their way out of the crowd. While putting up the convertible's top in the auditorium parking lot, Hubbard decided she was glad she had tricked Hurley into revealing his lie. Yet she was concerned about the evil eye that Gunderson gave her.

They rode in silence until they stopped at the Paradise Dairy Queen. They sat across from each other at a table for two against the clean front window. Each ordered a banana split.

Mark seemed lost in the big vanilla moon that was low and appeared to be right over the Freeman house. Hubbard broke the silence.

"I know Hurley told ya I smoked pot."

He looked into her eyes and said, "It's no big deal."

"I don't smoke that often. Just a few times with Nell. I told her not to smoke it around me so much."

"I tried some."

"I know. I just wanted to tell you."

"It's your life. You can do what you want."

"You sound sad," she said.

"I'm pissed at myself for letting Hurley bait me into trying it."

"Why do you even hang around with Gunderson? He's like this big creep and you're like this sweet guy."

"Same reason you hang around with Nell...it just happens."

"I know I can't tell you who your friends should be, but he's big trouble for anyone around him."

"I know. Last week he said that his dad told him since his grades are too low to go to college, he's making him go into the service."

"What about baseball?"

"His dad doesn't care. I never saw his dad once at any of his games. He's mean as hell to Hurley. If he didn't do what his dad wanted, I think he'd kill him. Mr. Gunderson said he'd take Hurley's car away and he'd have to work in the monument company if he doesn't enlist. Hurley hates that place."

"Maybe the service would be good for him."

"He's afraid of going to Viet Nam. I told him to join the Air Force, or the Navy, but his dad was a Marine and tells him that any other branch of the service is for sissies."

"Your dad's not a sissy."

"I know. But that's one thing you don't call Hurley...a sissy."

"Yeah, I can see that," she agreed.

They stared at the moon while finishing their treat. Soon, they were laughing about the rubber pig tail sticking out from the back of her chair that she forgot to remove. She pulled it off and handed it to him, telling him that he could keep it as a memento to remember her.

"I don't need this to remember you. I'll always remember you."

"You say that now, but what about in ten or twenty years?" she laughed.

"If I live to be old, you'll always be a good memory, Hubbard."

He saw her blush, and thought how this very moment certainly seemed to be a beautiful thing to always remember.

"Your eyes are so red," she laughed.

"What's so great about smoking that stuff, anyway?"

"I did it to avoid reality...like Nell does."

"Like Hurley?"

"Yeah," she said.

Parking somewhere secluded and making out were out of the question for Mark, because his neck and face were itching badly again after his banana split. She hoped he would invite her inside as she drove them down quiet Dakota Avenue toward the Freeman's house.

Just then, they saw it together, a hundred yards before turning onto the driveway, a red fire/rescue ambulance from Warren, its red lights flashing, was backed in and parked as if ready to leave. At first Mark thought it was some Halloween thing his grandpa did for the kids, flashing lights and maybe a ride around the block.

"I hope everything's okay," Hubbard called out to Mark as he leaped out of the car even before she parked beside the foreboding ambulance.

Three volunteer paramedics were blocking Grandma and Grandpa's bedroom doorway, along with a stretcher on wheels that was parked by Grandpa's chair.

Mark ran through the front room, across the kitchen then through the bathroom that also opened to their bedroom. He saw Grandpa sitting on the bed, real quiet, holding his wife's hand. When the paramedics noticed Mark, they backed quietly out of the small bedroom into the front room where Hubbard waited anxiously. One of the paramedics told Hubbard that Mrs. Freeman had been dead when they arrived, apparently from a sudden stroke that took her quickly.

Mark stepped closer to his grandpa and asked him softly, "What happened?"

The old man's voice was shaky. "She was at the kitchen table cutting meat for her fricassee stew and she just slumped over."

Mark's eyes traveled up and down his grandma's cinnamon-colored dress patterned with violets; he was looking for a sign that she was still breathing. He saw no movement. Her eyes were closed and her husband had folded her arms peacefully over her chest.

"Is she gone, Grandpa?"

"Yes. She's with God now."

For the first time since arriving in Paradise, Mark felt the same weakness in his legs he felt when he discovered that his mother had died. Yet this time the feeling was coming more from the loss that his grandpa was dealing with.

"Should I call my dad?"

"It can wait 'til morning. I'm goin' to the funeral home. They know we're comin'."

"You want me to go with you, Grandpa?"

"No. You stay here and call your father in the morning."

Grandpa stood up straight and told the paramedics that he was ready. Mark watched his grandpa's powerful arms gently place Grandma on the stretcher they rolled to her bedside. After he covered his wife's face with a sheet, two of the men carried the stretcher over the creaking linoleum rather than wheel it over Grandma's good rugs.

Hubbard stood with Mark on the cool front porch as they watched the men load her body into the quiet/flashing ambulance with Grandpa riding with her.

As they watched the ambulance exit the drive slowly, Hubbard could see that Mark was in the throes of a night that had gone from bad to absolute loss and shock. He didn't hear her when she murmured, "I'm so sorry, Mark."

He could only hear the dull ringing in his ears, the same warning siren he'd heard in Wichita when that phone call came like an unsent autumn letter. He thought about finding the autumn letters that Grandma had told him about and storing them with his own letters.

Hubbard followed him into the dimly lit kitchen that seemed cool now from all the traffic in and out. He stared at the kitchen table where she died, its top still scattered with seasonings and chopped pieces of beef and celery for the stew that was soaking in lightly salted water in a large green plastic bowl. Absently he said, "I'm glad I wasn't here when it happened."

She rubbed his back, agreed silently, then asked him tenderly, "Do you want me to stay a while?"

"Yeah, that would be nice."

She watched him go into his grandparents' bedroom and stare at the impression left on her patterned bedcovering by his grandma's ninety-pound body.

Mark moved his eyes to their nightstand and the faded-black, leather jacket cover of the King James Bible that they read every night together at bedtime. Beside the Bible he stared at the black and white daguerreotypes, framed photos of their parents.

Hubbard followed Mark's slow steps into his room, where they sat on his bed. Again she rubbed his slumped back as he held his red face in his hands and sobbed with grief. Hubbard sensed that his grief about losing his mother was coming out, yet it was the sight of The Lord's Prayer above his bed that broke the dam.

Hubbard stopped herself from mouthing platitudes: "It must have been her time to be with God"; "At least she didn't suffer after a long life"; and, "I know how you must feel." Instead, she remained still, until his groaning words came out onto his hands.

"How's Grandpa going to live without her? Oh, God, he's lost her. Now...he's all alone."

"He still has you, Mark...and your father."

"No, it's not the same. They were life partners. Don't you see that?"

Again she gave him space, letting him go on.

"I wanted her to see me graduate...and see me do something good that she could be proud of. It was always important to her that I keep my grades up. Now she'll never see me do anything. Why does God take when we're not ready?"

"That's something none of us will ever know...and I don't think we're supposed to."

"Well, I don't have to like it."

"It's the way it is, Mark. It was her time to go. I'm not an expert on God's will...nobody on earth is...but I know if you live in anger at God, it makes the world harder to live in. I've never lost someone that was good like your grandma, but I know it was a blessing when my dad died."

"And how was losing my mother a blessing?"

"I don't know, Mark. I've only lost someone who wasn't much good for anybody. But I know that God isn't some old man with a beard who's punishing you, deciding who dies and when."

He sat up and turned to her. "How did you turn out so nice after living with someone like that?"

She smiled and shrugged her shoulders, then said, "I think it's because I manage to shut out most of the bad noise, and live in the moment, more than I used to."

He let his upper body fall back and onto his soft bed. She looked down at his white shoes and smiled at the memory of seeing them for the first time in front of Nell's house and how cute Mark had looked in them, compared to Gunderson. Then, she too fell back onto the bed and gazed at the ceiling with him. Then she told him absently, "I believe when someone dies, someone you love, it changes you forever. It brought you into my life. And that was a good thing."

"Yeah," he agreed.

Hubbard's idea about how a death changes you, made him see things differently. Suddenly it was so clear to him that after his parents separated in Wichita, he started to be afraid of change. But then, he reasoned, if nothing had changed, he never would have come to Paradise to live with

Grandpa and Grandma...or even know them at all.

Now, he knew he was stronger for having had Grandma Freeman in his life. Two more things became lucid to him: to be angry at God for bad things that happen was a big waste of energy; and, if not for Hubbard he would not be taking his good vision for granted. At this moment.

"Now is all we have, isn't it?" he whispered to the dark ceiling.

He turned his face to Hubbard. She was nodding yes, her eyes ablaze with light. She watched his eyes until she could see his light shining, and she told him so.

Around two in the morning, as they lay on pillows at opposite ends of his bed they heard Hurley's fartmobile returning home with "House of the Rising Sun" sung by The Animals blaring from the car's stereo speakers. They both popped up from the bed to peek at Hurley discreetly from behind curtain edges. He was sitting in his parked car in front of his house taking a hit from a roach with the engine off as The Animals continued to blare. They saw Hurley looking at Nell's car on the Freeman driveway, then over to Mark's bedroom window. They laughed at him when he got out of his car still wearing his white shoes and hobo mask.

Again Hurley's face turned to Mark's window before he headed for the basement entrance at the side of the Gunderson house.

"You s'pose he'll wash that stuff off his face before he goes to bed?" Hubbard laughed.

"I'm surprised that Nell didn't make him take it off," Mark said.

"I don't think he's gettin' much action from Nell anyway."

221

"Is she going to break up with him?" Mark asked.

"She said she is...when the time is right."

"I don't think any time is right with Hurley."

Mark continued as they stood at the window looking at the Gunderson house. "I remember one time I was walking home from school with him, and his dad was just getting home. We were going to play pool, but when he saw his dad he got real scared and upset, and told me he had some chores to do first. As I walked home I could hear Hurley yelling at his dad in his driveway about something he didn't want to do right then. Next thing I knew, Hurley was on the ground and his dad was kicking him real hard. Hurley's mom came out and stopped it. But ever since then, I always felt kind of sorry for him."

"I'm sure that's a big part of why he's so mean."

"He's really spoiled with things. You wouldn't believe all the stuff he has in his basement. He eats his meals down there alone. Very seldom do they all have a meal together. He said his mom doesn't want him messing up the upstairs. Some family, huh?"

"I think Nell liked him because he's such a wild brat. I know she gets a kick outta her dad tellin' her to meet boys that come from a better class than that yokel from Paradise."

"Is that what her dad calls him?" Mark asked.

"Yeah."

"Poor Hurley. He's getting dumped by everybody," Mark drawled.

"He brings it on himself...by the way he treats people. Sometimes, I think he's dangerous."

Hubbard left around three in the morning, telling Mark to be sure to let her know when his grandma's funeral was. Mark had hugged her goodbye on the front porch and thanked her for staying with him. She told him to get some sleep.

No sleep for Mark; he was anxious about calling his father in a few hours. Would he hear his father's loss over the phone, in a groan, a sob, a terrible cry? And would he see it on his father's face tomorrow? And poor Grandpa...what would become of him?

He removed his notebook and pen from the nightstand drawer, shutting down worry from his racing mind as each black word on the paper began its life. Another autumn letter. That's what Grandma called them. A letter full of words that would never reach her. They would be words he had never told her, but hoped she knew. And he would leave these words with her when he saw her again, as he had done in the Paradise Methodist Church at his mother's funeral.

Dear Grandma, I'm still in shock from your passing, and wait for Grandpa's return after I call my dad to tell him you have died. I need your strength to tell him this, and even more strength to help Grandpa with his loss. I figured out that you and Grandpa were here for over 170 years combined and most of those years you were together. Grandma, I cannot fathom what you and Grandpa meant to each other; but I know I must find someone with your kind of faith in God in order to live well in the years ahead. Grandma, I think I have found her, yet I have not told her so. I'm afraid to, and I don't know why. Maybe it's because I'm so young and I fear losing my dream to play pro baseball. I am not ready to risk losing something I know I am good at.

I have to tell you that I did a bad thing for Hurley. I

wrote a love letter for him for twenty dollars. The letter made this girl fall for him, and now I fear trouble may come from it. I know you liked Hurley and I just wish that your spirit could help him or prevent him from doing something bad after this girl breaks it off with him. You'd be like some protective angel. I believe in angels and I believe that Hubbard is a living angel on this earth. She even has a pet pig that she thinks is an angel, though she is the one who protects him.

Grandma, so much of my memory of you was seeing you in your kitchen. I can see you working to prepare your delicious meals, especially your oatmeal/raisin cookies. Your aprons were always covered with flour and butter stains because you seemed to be cooking from sunrise to sunset. My mother didn't cook much, but when she did I enjoyed it. But your cooking was the best, Grandma, for what that's worth.

Please tell my mother that I miss her terribly and that I'm doing well. Another confession: I smoked some funny weed with that darn Hurley Gunderson before we went to the Halloween dance. I didn't really like it. I promise not to smoke it again, and hope you don't tell my mother. She will only worry about me.

And Grandma, I will miss seeing and hearing you walk through the house in your black shoes that always seemed so uncomfortable to wear, the way they were laced so tight and squeezing your ankles. Most of all I will miss the way you made our home smell and look and feel on the inside. It was all part of an absolute sense of real security and order, things that I desperately needed when I came here.

To me you will always be a good memory, and proof that a leaf can fall at night...without a sound to warn us that it's forever gone. I don't think I ever told you that I love you, Grandma. I do. Love forever, Mark.

He folded his letter to Grandma Freeman and put it with his collection of autumn letters in the shoebox stored on the top shelf of his closet.

Unable to sleep, Mark went outside into the cold predawn air wearing his winter coat and Keds without socks.

He could see that the front yard would need one more raking as the last of the maple leaves were scattered about and curled with frost on the dying grass. Paradise was buttoned up for winter, not a car or person or animal was about. He could see that the moon had moved west toward Blue Hill and was partly obscured by scudding blue/gray clouds that were thin and breaking up from powerful prairie winds that chilled his flesh as he walked onto the back yard, over to Grandma's garden that was used up and turned over for the winter. He bent down to pick up a black dirt clod from the garden's edge and crumbled it into his soft left hand. Thoughts of putting some of these crumbs of soil that lay on his flat palm with her letter vanished when stronger winds came and blew his hand clean.

He turned and, for the first time, he could really see the tiny Freeman house, its brindle-colored tile exterior he only just noticed, for it was never the outside of the house that appealed to his senses; but rather, it was her loving work in the kitchen that he would always remember. How did she get pleasure from serving us? he wondered. Her ten thousand little moves during tasks with turns and measurings for just the right effect she wanted. And what did I return? Did I only consume her loving work and go my way?

225

Then, just as that very first trace of lightened darkness swept its hue over the Paradise sky, he could feel Grandma's strong sense of family. And he felt like part of this family, like he belonged there. All because of her and her tireless giving without complaining. That's what she had given him: a needed feeling of belonging to people who knew how to provide a safe home.

There was no doubt at all that Grandma would work to sustain her family 'til the end. Now, he could only imagine his grandpa's new pain. It would surely come to him when sleeping alone in darkness after so many years beside her; and it would follow on his lonely walk in the same darkness when he made his way to the courthouse after skipping his own breakfast. Sometimes, he even returned to her at noon, for the lunch that she prepared just for him. How would he go on?

Chicanery

Christmas vacation began. November had been cold, and so far December was colder, yet there had been no snowfall in Paradise or in the entire Woodbury region. Nearly every adult in Paradise attended Leona Freeman's funeral service. Hurley sat in the last row with his parents directly in line with the front row where three generations of Freeman men sat.

All eyes were on Grandpa Freeman's ramrod bearing transfixed on his wife's open casket as the minister eulogized one of the church's oldest members.

The night before Grandma Freeman's funeral, at the wake held in the South Woodbury funeral home, Hurley witnessed Mark placing a letter under his grandma's folded hands lying crossed upon her chest. The letter reminded Hurley of his friend's gift to put words on paper. Oh, how he wished he had Mark's ability to write, for he was being dismissed by Nell, ever since she found out she wasn't pregnant seven weeks ago.

Even his friend from Wichita was spending less and less time with him. That's why he decided to confront Mark about what he knew about Nell. From his basement window Hurley saw that Mark's bedroom window shade was up. Hurley dressed warm for the cold wind blowing; a thick gray layer of clouds soon would bring snow from the west where sixteen inches of white stuff had shut down every road between Hastings and Ainsworth.

Hurley knocked on Mark's bedroom window before opening the front porch door, whereupon he kicked off his overshoes, entered and closed the front door behind him. Inside the Freeman front room, he listened, then called out, "Wichita?"

Nothing. Again he called out for his friend in a house that seemed obviously barren of its matron, and now was occupied tangibly by men who maintained its temperature much cooler than when Grandma Freeman was there.

The Christmas tree standing against the front room curtain was always visible night and day during the holiday season, from the time he was a little boy until today. Now it was decorated as if hurriedly, without the silver tinsel that he knew Grandma Freeman loved. This close to Christmas few wrapped presents sat under the tree. Hurley Gunderson knew that this was no Freeman Christmas.

He searched the little house and saw no sign of Mark, figuring he was at the courthouse helping his grandpa. At Mark's bedroom door he hesitated then entered. He knew all his answers were to be found in this room. Not inside Mark's nightstand drawer or under his bed, but somewhere. Then he found it: Mark's box of letters. Surely, he thought, there must be clues here about his Nell. Sifting and reading fast, he went from page to page, careful to keep them in order while he sat on the edge of Mark's bed reading his handsome writing, all the while listening in case the author returned home.

November 21st, that was the date on the letter that caught Gunner's eye, because it bore his name:

Dear Hurley, I just returned from having dinner at

Hubbard's mother's and step-father's house in Woodbury. Nell and a friend stopped by after dinner, and Hubbard and I went for a drive with them in her friend's car.

Anyway, I hear that you and Nell don't go out much anymore, but I still feel sort of guilty knowing she likes this guy Robert who works for her dad. Nell wants to tell you but she's afraid of your temper. Nell even asked me to tell you, but I don't want to stir you up if you're getting over her with time.

Hubbard keeps inviting me to go do things with them; I say no because I know how you have feelings for Nell.

Anyway, Hurley, I really hope you are getting over her and meet someone new, because I've heard it said that it takes a new love to get over a past love. Your friend, Mark.

Hurley read it again, his jaw clenching at the part where Hubbard invites Mark to do things with Nell and her new boyfriend.

"Robert," he whispered out loud.

Now, he was certain he had been dumped, yet he felt used and betrayed because he had to sneak in here and find out this way by betraying a friend's trust.

After returning Mark's letters to the closet, he smoothed out the crease his rump made on Mark's bed.

Hurley left the Freeman house and crossed the street with a thousand images of his Nell betraying him with Robert who, he thought, was probably some rich guy from the city.

Pressure had been building up inside Hurley since last August around the time he turned eighteen. His father had told him that during the Christmas holidays they would go together to downtown Woodbury and see the Marine

Corps recruiter about signing up. There was a way to get promoted to E-3 early as part of a special enlistment program offered to high school seniors if they enlisted in the inactive reserves six months before graduation. It was a ploy to get more troops for Viet Nam and his father was gung ho about it.

Yes, his dad thought it was a great idea that right after he graduated he'd go right into boot camp, then have a little over sixteen months left to serve on active duty. Then, his father told him, he could go to any college in the country he wanted, on the G.I. Bill, and play baseball.

Gunner knew that it would be easier to play pro ball with college experience because scouting was heavier at the college level; gone were the days when catchers got signed by the big leagues from tryouts. Too risky, he agreed with his father.

But this thing he had for Nell kept gnawing at his brain, even more now after reading about how she'd moved to another lover. On his bed in his messy basement room, he began to write his own letter to Nell, in his words. Once before, the power of a good letter had captured his rich city girl, and he was willing to give it a try.

For two hours he thought, scrawled, erased, tore to pieces, beginning over and over again, until his final draft was ready. He read his last-ditch effort out loud:

Dear Nell, I know you have a new boyfriend. I cannot believe you haven't told me yourself. Nell, how can you go from me to someone else so fast? I had such big plans for us when I sign with the pros. I was going to buy us a great big house to live in and raise our kids first class the way you are used to. Now I'm beside myself and can only hear those two songs the last time we made love in your parents' bed, when they were out of town. Remember? We each picked a song. My song was "You Really Got Me" by The Kinks. I can't get that song out of my head, Nell. I really don't know where I'm goin'. You really got me, Nell.

But it was your song that really hurts me, "Baby, I'm Yours." You started to cry, remember? I know that you loved me then, Nell, and I don't know why that's changed for you. I still feel the same way, Nell. I can't go off to Viet Nam without knowing you are mine. Say you'll wait for me, Nell. Give me one more chance. Baby, I'm your boy from Paradise.

He put the sealed letter inside the Ford's glovebox that still reeked of Wild Country. Then he sat and smoked some weed before starting the car. While driving out of Paradise he discovered the incredible power of a letter. It was making his palms sweat on the steering wheel as nothing else had. He now could see why Wichita kept written words in secret places. And he knew he was not like Mark Freeman, content with leaving his feelings on paper. Just then, it came to him. He would do it now and worry about it later.

Nell looked beautiful that morning. Her new boyfriend, Robert, was meeting her for lunch in the Yonkers Department Store restaurant. She had wandered the third floor looking for the right gift for Robert, finally deciding to get him engraved cuff links with his initials R.G. That was what her father called his young sales manager: R.G.

Robert Greenburg was a handsome twenty-three-year-old, dark haired Jewish man from the north side; his parents had lived four blocks from the Evers house for over thirty years. Robert graduated from the University of Iowa the previous spring and began working for Mr. Evers full-time right after he graduated. He had worked summers for the Evers Fertilizer Company for four years, yet he had never talked to Nell until he was invited to the Evers home for dinner in November to celebrate the silver anniversary of the Evers's booming business.

Nell was in love at first sight from across the dinner table in her parents dining room. Robert found the younger Nell intelligent and sexy, to say the least, staying much later than he planned and making a date with her the following weekend to drive down to Omaha for a friend's art gallery grand opening in Old Town.

Now, Nell sat alone in a booth in the Yonkers restaurant, waiting anxiously for her date. She was sharply attired in a wool double-breasted jacket with wide collar squared in front and adorned with gold tone metal buttons with lime centers. She smoothed out the false pocket flaps on each side of her jacket while she kept her yellow high heels in perfect feminine alignment.

That's the moment when Mary Wells began singing "My Guy" piped softly through the entire store. Nell hadn't thought of Hurley much since meeting Robert and the song made her feel uncomfortable, because she didn't want to be reminded of the boy from Paradise while she waited for her new boyfriend.

She was thinking about a word Robert used to describe his ex-girlfriend in college: chicanery. That word made these moments listening to Mary Wells restive and full of the lies she had told Hurley in order to manipulate his feelings. She longed for this song to be for Robert more than it ever had been for Hurley Gunderson. Even the outfit she wore now had been picked just for Robert, knowing it would go well with the orange blazers her father's salesmen wore.

As the song continued, she fought memories of the sex she'd had with Hurley, the best she'd ever had...until Robert...she hoped. That damn hick, she thought, knowing she'd led him on all the way and even brought him into her home to disturb her father. Yet she knew that Hurley's cocky brashness was a trait she also saw in her father, along with his big dreams.

Over and over, her regrets piled up as "My Guy" seemed like it might never end, this sappy love song about a girl who adored her boyfriend to the pathetic "no handsome face could ever take the place of my guy."

Finally it stopped, and she berated herself for feeling aroused even momentarily by memories of that hick from Paradise.

"Hi! Am I late?" Robert smiled after kissing her on her cheek then sitting across from her.

"No, no, I got here early."

She handed him his wrapped cuff links.

After he opened the tiny box, he smiled in his orange blazer. "What's this for?"

"They're for you. A thank you gift."

"Thank you for what?" he pressed with charm and showing the whitest teeth she'd ever seen.

She tilted her head as if a bit annoyed, then leaned toward him and teased, "For the good times ahead."

Robert knew a come-on when he heard one and answered back after leaning forward with his reply. "I've got a good three hours until my next appointment."

Nell's smile and raised eyebrows spoke volumes, so he suggested they eat light before going over to his place.

All the way over to Robert's luxury apartment

located on the far east side of Woodbury, Nell had a creepy feeling that they were being followed. Oh, God, she worried, while listening for the loud muffler on the car of an enraged baseball catcher in white shoes who she could see ruining her chances with a great catch like Robert Greenburg.

At five o'clock at the courthouse that same afternoon, Mark had just finished polishing all the mahogany benches and woodwork in the main courtroom. He jogged down the stairs to return the bucket of oily rags and wood polish to his grandpa's workshop. Grandpa Freeman was not alone. Hurley was sitting on a five-gallon bucket of wax stripper near the seated custodian.

"Your friend has big news," Mr. Freeman smiled at his stunned grandson.

"I finally did it, Wichita!"

"Did what?"

"I joined the Marines," Hurley beamed with pride, his chest pushed out like a bullfrog. "All I gotta do is pass a physical, get sworn in, then I fly to San Diego a few days after graduation."

Standing beneath creaking overhead furnace pipes, Hurley showed his friend the signed contract and the details about his special delayed entrance program and how he could go to college on the G. I. Bill after his two-year hitch was up.

After Grandpa Freeman got up and left to lock the courthouse for the night, Hurley went on and on to Mark about what a great deal it was and how after he killed a bunch of gooks in Nam he'd be ready for anything behind the plate the pros could throw at him.

"Ain't ya gonna congratulate me, Wichita?"

"Yeah, but I'm surprised. I didn't know you could sign up so fast."

"Yeah, well, I'd get drafted anyway, 'cause I don't have the grades to get out of it. This way, they gotta let me in college after I do my hitch. These are MY terms, Wichita. It's a great opportunity."

"Yeah...I guess..."

"C'mon...I'll give ya a ride home. I got somethin' I wanna show ya."

They sat in Hurley's Ford. Mark could smell funny weed when he opened the passenger door.

"You smoked before joining the Marines?"

"Just a little," Hurley snickered.

Then he reached over and into his glovebox and handed Mark the love letter he wrote in an unsealed envelope marked "To Nell."

"I want ya to read this...tell me what ya think."

Mark read the letter, then chose his words carefully after his friend again asked him anxiously what he thought of it.

"Well, it's written from your heart. It says you don't want to lose her. Is that what you really want?"

"That's just it, Wichita. After I wrote it, my feelings changed about givin' the letter to her. And then after I signed up for the Corps, I read it again and it sounded like I was this desperate boy...not a Marine at all."

"Then don't give it to her."

"That's what I'm thinkin'. It's like all those letters you write but never send."

"It's called an autumn letter."

"Autumn letter?"

"Yeah, Grandma Freeman said they're letters that

are never sent because the way things change with time and circumstances."

When Mark tried to hand Hurley back his letter, Hurley said, "Look, Wichita, I want ya to do me a favor. Keep this letter for me so I don't change my mind and give it to her. I want you to give it to her when I leave for boot camp. Then I don't have to be around when she rejects me. But at least I want her to know how I feel about her. I know I wasn't usin' her."

"Okay. But let me know if and when you want me to give it to her."

"I will."

Hurley extended his right hand to Mark. While they shook hands, Hurley said, "You're the best friend I ever had."

The holidays were cold. Two feet of snow was dumped onto Northeast Nebraska over Christmas Eve and Christmas Day. Even Grandpa Freeman couldn't remember more snowfall on a Christmas morning.

Hubbard planned to visit Mark on Christmas morning around ten, but she would be late leaving her house in Woodbury because her step-dad was having a difficult time shoveling the wet, heavy snow from their long driveway, especially at the entrance where snowplows had left a two-foot snowbank that blocked the driveway.

Mark watched for her, standing beside the lit Christmas tree in the front room, while Grandpa sat in his chair beside the warm floor furnace reading his Bible. From his vantage point, Mark spotted Hurley braving the cold in a t-shirt, headed for the Freeman front door with a wrapped gift.

"Are you nuts? Where's your coat?" Mark

demanded.

"I'm a Marine, Wichita. Mind over matter."

Hurley removed his baseball cap respectfully and handed Grandpa Freeman the gift labeled from "The Gundersons."

"Merry Christmas, Grandpa Freeman."

"Merry Christmas, Hurley. I'm sorry, I don't have a thing for you," the widower smiled from his chair.

"Open it," Hurley urged.

They watched the old man's massive hands carefully remove the wrapping, a habit his wife imparted to him in order to recycle the paper for another Christmas.

"They're extra large," Hurley declared.

They watched Grandpa slip on the leather dress gloves.

"These fit real good. Thank you."

"You're welcome. Well, Wichita, I gotta get back. My parents don't want me gone long."

"Merry Christmas, Hurley."

Not long after Hurley reached his house, Hubbard drove onto the cleared Freeman drive. When she walked into the warm Freeman front room with her arms full of presents, her cheeks were so red from the cold it seemed she had rouge smeared on her face.

"Merry Christmas, Grandpa Freeman," she smiled as she handed him his present and noticed the white light emanating from his narrow blue eyes the same color as Mark's.

"Another gift?" the old man smiled.

She saw the brown leather gloves on his armrest. "New gloves. Those are nice. Who gave you those?"

"The Gundersons," Mr. Freeman answered.

"Hurley was just here," Mark said.

"Oh. Open your presents!" she ordered the men.

Mark sat on the floor beside the tree and began to open his present from Hubbard, then he stopped to hand a gift to her from under the tree, where two gifts remained for Mark's dad. Larry Freeman was due to arrive soon; they would all have an early dinner prepared by the Paradise church ladies who were keeping their oldest member and his great-grandson well fed each week with a variety of dishes and desserts.

The Freemans were happy with their winter scarves from Hubbard. Larry Freeman got to know Mark's girlfriend, carrying on a long conversation with her for the first time. Mark could tell that his dad really liked her. He overheard his dad telling Grandpa that Hubbard was a very nice young lady.

After dinner, Hubbard left earlier than she wanted to because snowfall picked up again. Provided the roads were clear, Mark made a date with her to go sledding on Blue Hill on the 27th when she checked Johnny.

It had been Grandpa's idea to get the old two-seater sled down from the rafters in the garage. He told Mark where to find a file and some saddle soap in the garage that would sharpen the runners and make them as slick as a greased pig.

As Hubbard backed her mother's car out of the Freeman drive, the headlights flashed across the Gunderson's basement window. Hurley had just gotten up from a nap; he felt dazed from the quick dream that woke him and sent him to the laundry room's window in time to see Hawkins leaving.

In Hurley's dream, Hawkins had been the villain

who kept Nell from seeing him. Mark was aiding the two girls, running away with Hawkins and Nell whenever he saw Hurley approaching. When Hurley showed up at Nell's door in his Marine dress uniform and white shoes, they all laughed at him from behind the Evers locked door. Then, in one crystal/split instant during his dream, he saw something that would deliver his retaliation against the cruel trio who, he believed in reality, would all betray him when push came to shove.

Hurley opened his basement window, lit his rolled reefer and blew its smoke out into the freezing air. His thoughts flowed with dark images of things he could do to make himself known as someone never to mess with...friend or no friend. Yes, he smiled, they think I'm a sap who gets the short end of the stick and just lives with it.

"They'll see," he said, grinning while his mind conjured images with puff after puff.

On the 27th of December, Hubbard and Mark headed for the same place on Hawkins land where the brakes went out in Hubbard's truck. Both were bundled up warm, even though the sun was out and certain to melt exposed snow as the day wore on. They hurried from the Freeman house with Mark pulling the greased double passenger sled with ease over the hard snow.

"Nell wants us to come to a New Year's Eve party at her house," Hubbard said.

"That sounds okay. Will Robert be there?"

"Oh, yeah...she's in love, she says."

"Do you think she ever loved Hurley?" Mark asked.

"I can't say. But I think it was just a fling for her."

"I've always thought that's why you and I have stayed good friends."

"Why?" she asked.

"Because we both know that sex can end a friendship."

"Yeah...it's not as important to me as it is to Nell."

They trudged the deep snow past Hawkins Cemetery to the top of the ridge where they faced a truculent wind from the west, and could see Luther's farm. Hubbard thought it strange that no smoke rose from Luther's chimney, since he usually kept his woodburner going day and night all winter.

The snow was too fluffy for sledding on that side of Blue Hill, so Mark left the sled on the ridge rather than drag it down into the valley and back. Hubbard was anxious to see how Johnny was faring alone in the Hawkins barn away from Luther's herd. They hustled down the hill, bounding over the snow until they reached the Hawkins farmyard.

Johnny waited, having heard their approach, his wet/pink nose sniffing the cold winter air through the iron gate. Everything seemed fine until Hubbard went inside the barn and discovered that Johnny's straw bed hadn't been replaced with fresh straw since her last visit. Luther had said he was bringing a bale over a few days before Christmas.

Mark went into the cold Hawkins house with Johnny to get the woodburner going while Hubbard checked on Luther. She feared that Luther was dead, and she dreaded walking into his quiet house to find another resident of Blue Hill who had died lonely and alone, like her dad.

Upon reaching Luther's driveway from the snow-covered road she knew he had to be dead. Luther really enjoyed getting on his little tractor that he'd converted to a snowplow every winter; he would never let snow pile up to the point it impeded his driveway and Broken Kettle Road.

She knocked. No answer. Though she had a key to his house, the front door was unlocked and the front room was as cold as the outdoors.

"Luther?"

On she went, into his bedroom, where she could see that he died in his sleep. His bedroom was like a freezer, her breath fogged with every exhalation, so there was no overwhelming stench of death. His telephone was so cold that its rotary dial nearly stopped moving counterclockwise after every number dialed as she called the Warren Police instead of Sheriff Hickey in closer Paradise. She told the officer that she found Luther and that Broken Kettle Road was blocked with snow, and that she'd try to clear the road with Luther's plow so they could get there.

She found a pair of Luther's work gloves that were damp and stiff on top of his quiet woodburner, its black iron door open and blackened from countless fires.

As she prepared to leave his house, a plastic hummingbird hovering above the rim of a coffee cup placed on the window sill caught her eye; it was attached by a knitting needle pierced into the Styrofoam cup. She went over to it and stared at its tiny dust-caked brown/green wings, knowing that this dainty thing, the only feminine object about the house, must have had some sentimental attachment to the past for crusty old Luther.

Outside, Hubbard went to the little Farmall tractor parked under the open shed. She climbed onto its cold cast iron seat that was covered only by a worn piece of foam rubber and supported by a rusty spring that creaked and squeaked until the roar from the tractor's engine filled the quietude with a familiar sound that gave Luther's hungry hogs salivating hope for an overdue meal. She wasn't concerned about feeding his hogs, for they were overfed for

Nap Town and could wait until she cleared the road for the ambulance.

Mark opened the Hawkins front room curtains to see Hubbard plowing Broken Kettle Road. Since the wood burner was going well now, he exited the house, leaving Johnny alone and happy to be out of the barn and listening to a country song Mark chose when he turned on Hubbard's portable radio.

Mark ran and slid on her fresh-plowed path until he called out her name at the fork just past the row of mailboxes. She turned and saw him running and sliding on the frozen road. She stopped the tractor. He climbed up and stood on the frame, holding onto the back of the bouncing seat as she plowed on and they shouted above the roar of the engine.

"Luther's dead!"

Mark's jaw dropped.

"I called the Warren Police! They couldn't get here unless I cleared the road!"

"He's in the house?"

She nodded yes while keeping the tractor's front wheels straight as the angled blade pushed and moved snow along the right shoulder.

She yelled, "His hogs are prob'ly wonderin' when their next meal's comin'!"

"How long do you think he's been dead?"

"I don't know! Maybe a few days!"

"God, that's creepy!" he shouted.

"No kiddin'! Seems like everybody dies around here! It makes me sad to think he might have died on Christmas!"

Upon reaching the highway, Hubbard turned around and started to clear the other side of the road. About halfway back to Luther's place, the flashing Warren patrol car and an ambulance came up behind the tractor and followed it until Hubbard cleared a circular path in Luther's farmyard.

When Mark hopped down from the tractor his legs were tired from tensing them on the vibrating tractor frame. He let Hubbard do all the talking while he went into Luther's barn and shoveled feed into the empty troughs, where a hundred snorting hogs gobbled up what could be their last meal.

Not long after Luther's body was driven away in the silent ambulance, Hubbard found Luther's sister's phone number and gave it to the Warren policeman, who told her that since his sister was probably Luther's executor she would be the one to have Luther's hogs shipped to Nap Town. Hubbard told the friendly cop, who knew her past, that she had a key to Luther's house. She gave it to him after explaining that she and Luther had been on such good terms, he helped care for her pet pig.

She was allowed to haul two bales of straw to her farm on top of the snowplow blade. Mark carried the fresh straw into Johnny's barn and broke it up after cutting away the bailing wire; then he shoveled the old straw into a wheelbarrow and made a fresh bed for Johnny.

Later, Mark tramped up the cleared road to Luther's driveway entrance and met Hubbard, who had returned the snowplow to its shed, whereupon they walked back to her house.

"So much for sledding," she said.

"Yeah. Maybe some other time."

It wasn't until she got inside her warm house that she really began to feel the pounding headache in her temples and at the back of her neck. She slumped down onto a kitchen chair, her chin touching her chest as Mark gave her an intense shoulder and neck massage.

She told Mark, "God, what if we hadn't come out today? He'd still be there on his bed."

She grimaced, trying to let go of the tension under his strong fingers.

"I know, but sooner or later you would've come out to check on Johnny."

"Yeah, but still, it's real strange to live alone out here and know you're so isolated if something happens like this."

"At least he had his hogs."

"Yeah. I'd never live out here alone without Johnny."

She broke down and started to cry, letting go of more and more tension as he kept squeezing her neck and shoulders, listening to the choppy words that left her throat in gurgling gasps.

"This is...not about Luther. It's some of the...stuff from my dad. It was all about his pain...whatever that was. And I lived with it, too...every day. It gets stuck on ya...like...some virus. I never want this place...to define who I am."

Hurley parked at the bottom of the hill on the left side of the road that led to Hawkins Cemetery. He wasn't sure his Ford could make it any further on the unplowed surface; and he was smart enough to not trust his judgment after just finishing a fat joint on the way over.

A family of ornery crows observed the stranger in their territory from the top branches of the scraggly pines that lined the cemetery. They watched him don a dark blue wool stocking cap and a pair of leather gloves that he took from his trunk. The big black leader squawked at the intruder. Hurley balled a handful of wet snow and heaved it at the grouchy bird perched atop the pine, as he stayed in Mark's tracks up the snow-covered road. When the crow flew off followed by his boisterous family, Hurley cursed the black birds.

"You frigin' crows! You're lucky I don't get my gawd-damn rifle outta my trunk and blow your black ass into the cemetery!"

Gunner's bowed legs climbed higher and higher, following the set of tracks he knew belonged to Wichita and Hawkins. He had seen them leave the Freeman garage with the sled and wasn't quite sure why he was here now, yet he stayed in Mark's tracks all the way up to the ridge where he stopped beside the sled.

His little green eyes took in the drab Hawkins farm and the wood burner's smoke rising above the roof. He could see that their tracks veered toward the Hawkins place.

Hurley stayed in Mark's tracks down the hill, his mind filled with a pot-induced memory.

He had come this way in the summertime when he was about fourteen. He walked down this side of Blue Hill, alone, headed down to the old pig farmer's place where he came upon Hawkins and her dad unloading bags of feed from their truck into Luther's barn.

"What are you doin' here, Gunderson?" Hubbard scowled.

"I was just walkin' around...wantin' to see this side of Blue Hill."

"Just keep walkin'," she had warned.

Even now, he laughed out loud at the memory of

walking to the back fence of the hogyard, not quite out of Hubbard's view. He had seen a monster sow lying on its side against the mud-caked fence. Between the fence boards he pissed on the napping sow, his urine flapping so loudly on the hog's dry hide that Hubbard could hear it from the truck.

Hurley saw Hubbard scurry over to look at the foamy urine covering the sleeping sow and soaked into the black earth at its teated belly. She whirled around, but could do nothing except watch him heading back up the hill and listen to his laughter. He knew, if she had a gun, she'd have shot him right there. And that's exactly what she told him the next time she saw him in Paradise. He only laughed at her, then pushed his nose in with his finger and snorted at her.

Hurley stopped in his tracks. He was angry because he just knew that pig-lover Hawkins had told Nell about him pissing on that old sow; and now his pot-befuddled mind concluded that had to be the main reason that Nell stopped seeing him.

There was no reason for him to go any further; he turned back up the hill and made new tracks that were deeper, made in angry stomping steps that led back to the sled. He unbuttoned his jeans and pissed all over the sled's antique wood and polished metal runners, his yellow frothing urine steaming then freezing fast from the cold gusts of wind coming from the west.

Again he laughed as he walked away, headed for his car. Hawkins would know it was him, and that was fine, because he hated her now more than ever. Besides poisoning Nell against him, she had taken his best friend away from him. Something had to be done about her meddling in his life. And it had to be more than disconnected images in his dreams, he knew.

While driving home and listening to The Kinks blaring from his eight-track, he wished he hadn't peed on Wichita's sled, only because he wanted a swift and powerful retribution without warning; it had to be something so smart and final, they'd never know what hit 'em.

Just then, it began to snow, coming down in big flakes that he let cover his windshield until it was completely whited out. He turned on his windshield wipers just in time, before driving into the ditch. He laughed at his little daredevil act and smiled at this omen, for this kind of snowfall would cover his tracks on Blue Hill and wash away his business on the sled.

The Mean Season

By early April, Mark and Hubbard were together on most weekends, and beginning to have sex. Most times they would spend the night in her room on Blue Hill. Sometimes she'd spend Friday and Saturday nights in his room, since Grandpa Freeman went to bed early and paid little attention to the business of the eighteen-year-olds. They did know that their grades were slipping and they hardly thought of anything else except their time together and the fact that they were but seven weeks away from graduating.

Nell was in love, too, willing to change her plans about going to college in Ames or Iowa City; instead, she was now open to going to a private school in Woodbury that was just a few miles from Robert's apartment.

The first Saturday in April was truly the most beautiful day of the year. The custodian was already at the courthouse when Mark was awakened by a familiar tapping on his bedroom window. Hubbard was asleep and curled up facing away from Mark when he remembered that he had promised Hurley he'd go fishing with him this morning.

Before Mark could get out of bed, Hurley was standing in the bedroom's doorway grinning at Hubbard's full figure asleep under the covers. Mark got up fast in his white briefs and t-shirt and tried to block Hurley's view of his girlfriend. She woke up hearing Gunderson's snide comment about how things had changed around there since Grandma Freeman died.

Hubbard covered her head with her pillow when she heard Hurley laughing in his boorish redneck way. She listened to Mark explaining in a whisper how he forgot about the fishing date. Gunderson's whining words really angered her.

"C'mon, Wichita! You promised! This is prob'ly the last time we can go fishin' before I ship off! I got a lot of things to tell ya. I'm countin' on ya to go with me. I gotta rod and reel for ya in my trunk and the bait's on me. Besides, I can't stand to fish alone, Wichita."

"Alright, then. Wait in the other room for me," Mark whispered.

"I gotcha...gotta clear it with the little woman," Hurley snickered.

Mark closed the bedroom door behind Gunderson before stepping lightly back to Hubbard, sitting on her side of the bed.

"Hubbard?"

"Go fishin'...I don't care," she said from under the covers, apparently not too upset.

He uncovered her head to gauge her mood. She smiled at him, adding, "No, it's okay...I can handle Johnny...and I need to study for that algebra test Monday."

She got up from bed in her pajamas and dressed fast with him.

"You coming over tonight?" he asked.

"I really should study, Mark."

She kissed him goodbye and left the house without even looking at Hurley, who was sitting in Grandpa's chair with his feet crossed casually and grinning like the devil.

Hurley got up and stood in the bedroom doorway

again as Mark put on his worn Keds.

"That girl doesn't like me. But that's okay. Hey! At least we're goin' fishin'!" Hurley smiled.

"Yeah."

"I hope I didn't getcha in trouble with Hawkins."

"No, she's fine. I forgot...that's all. She has other things to do."

"That's the spirit!"

"I have to stop by the courthouse and tell Grandpa something."

"Leave him a note."

"No, I have to talk to him," Mark said.

Outside, the air felt like April when letting go of winter, just chilly enough to know that the weather is warming and things are beginning to grow and turn green again.

As Hurley's fartmobile drove them to the courthouse, Mark thought of what Hubbard told him about spring. She'd said her dad called this time of year "the mean season" because it was when his sinuses would flare and give him terrible headaches, until he would pass out after drinking himself into a stupor.

Hurley parked against the curb near the basement entrance to the courthouse and told Mark, "Hurry up! There's a big catfish in the Missouri with my name on it."

As he walked toward the steps, Mark sensed the positive charge in the air around Paradise, despite the drab colors of winter that were yet stained on the little one-story homes bordering the courthouse on three sides. It was the second such time he'd seen that people here were not quite ready to be outdoors under the gray/humid sky that many had told him stiffened their joints.

Mark opened the basement door quietly, as his grandpa always did. In the boiler room, his heart jumped as he saw something that nobody was meant to see. Grandpa Freeman sat on his chair with his head forward crying into his massive hands. Other than Grandma, Mark was sure he was the only other person who ever saw him weeping. At first, there was a split second when he could have ducked out without being seen. That never happened.

Mark scuffed the clean concrete floor purposely to be heard. The old janitor quickly grabbed his silver, wire-rimmed spectacles from his desk and tried to answer Mark's question.

"Grandpa, are you okay?

Upon wiping his eyes dry with each sleeve and donning his glasses, he told Mark how he was missing Grandma, that this was the first spring he could remember without her. It was the tone of his voice that made Mark cry. Not the words. Not like all those empty words he stored in a shoebox in his closet. Grandpa's tone was not painful from his loss, but rather, it was the tone of joy he felt for the memories of her during springtime.

Mark sat down on a ladderback armchair nearby and wanted to hear stories.

"Tell me," he said, "tell me something about Grandma, something you remember that happened during springtime."

The old janitor sat up straight, his small chin and muscled jaw line came alive, as if memory accomplished this metaphysical shaping of his countenance.

"I was thinking how Grandma would be tilling her garden today, with that sawed-off hoe I made her. And she'd be wearin' those garden gloves with the little daisies on them."

He had just said more than he ever had to anyone on earth about her since she passed on. Work and his faith in the moment had always sustained him and would continue to give him strength as long as God saw fit to keep him there. That's what he and his wife believed.

"Grandpa, I stopped by to tell you that I won't be home for lunch today. Hurley's waiting outside. I promised I'd go fishing with him."

"Catfish are big this time of year," the old man smiled.

"Anyway, I better go."

"Have fun."

"I will. See ya later."

When Mark left the boiler room, Hurley was just opening the basement door.

"What's the hold-up, Wichita?"

The river ran high from winter's melt-off and was glassy from cold morning rains further north. On the riverbank, the boys from Paradise sat on colossal chartreuse-colored rocks left by the Army Corps of Engineers in the early 1950s; their fishing lines were running south fast with the river's powerful current. They were getting no bites from hungry catfish, only deceptive snags from floating debris that constantly moved with the Missouri.

Mark's mind was on his grandpa's blues and some guilty feelings he was having for not being home to have lunch with him.

"Just seven more weeks, Wichita."

"I know."

"Ya know what ya wanna do yet?" Hurley asked as he reeled in his line.

"I might go to Warren State and try out for the baseball team."

"I'm surprised they didn't already offer ya a scholarship after the summer you had in legion. But they will soon enough after they see ya hit."

"My dad says he'll cover my tuition and Grandpa says I can live with him."

"You can live with Hawkins."

"Na. I can stay there when she wants me to..."

"Wants ya to what?" Hurley cackled.

"Living together...that's not for us."

"Why not? You're sleepin' together. How is she, Wichita? Is she good?"

"I don't talk about that stuff."

"Why not? I tell you!"

"But I don't ask. I like Hubbard...and I can't imagine anyone talking about that stuff when you like someone."

Hurley rolled his eyes and cast out again. "You two are made for each other. You'll end up with a house and kids...all those things I'll bet. Not me. I'm stayin' single...and I'll sow my wild oats when I can."

"It sounds like you got over Nell."

"Nell who?" he laughed. "That reminds me...I still want you to give her that letter."

"When?"

"I'll let ya know."

After a long pause and reeling in snags, Hurley asked, "She still seein' that guy?"

"Yeah."

Hurley's nonchalant manner contradicted his usual agitation regarding Nell.

"She ever ask about me?"

253

"I don't know, Hurley. I don't see her much."

"Just think, Wichita, soon I'll be in Nam killin' those slant-eyed monkeys and you'll be at Warren State hittin' over four hundred and pile-drivin' Hawkins. I always thought I'd be the one playin' ball and you'd be the one to join the service, like your old man. Funny how things work out."

"Yeah."

Another long pause.

"Does Hawkins still have that pig?"

Mark nodded yes.

"We oughta barbecue it before I leave," Hurley laughed and lit a roach from his shirt pocket.

After Mark declined Hurley's offer to join him, Hurley asked, "Does Hawkins still smoke?"

"I don't know. Sometimes, maybe."

"Just not around you, huh, Wichita?"

Hurley was hard to be around, Mark thought; perhaps Hubbard's aversion to Gunderson was rubbing off on him; or was it all part of "the mean season."

"What's that supposed to mean?" Mark demanded.

"No offense, Wichita! I was just sayin' how, if she did smoke, it wouldn't be around you, 'cause you don't like to. That's all I was sayin', Wichita."

"And it's none of your business about our sex life! I better not catch you sneakin' around my bedroom window."

"Relax, Wichita! I wouldn't do that."

"Oh, yeah...like Ruby's window? And I asked you not to call me Wichita!"

"Okay, man! Cool it! I'm sorry...Mark," he drawled and laughed.

Mark shoved the cork-handled rod into Hurley's

side. "You've got a big mouth, Gunderson! You show zero respect for me, Hubbard...or anybody! No wonder Nell dumped you! Who wouldn't? You talk about barbecuing Hubbard's pet and killing slant-eyed monkeys in Nam! God, Hurley, maybe your dad beat you too much and made you a mean son-of-a-bitch that'll only do bad things in this world...but I don't want to be around it. I don't feel good around you...and neither does Hubbard or Nell. So leave us all out of your life and don't ask me to do things with you anymore! I'm done with you, Hurley."

Hurley held both rods, one in each hand, and watched the person he thought of as his only friend walk away. He felt nothing. For a long time he had been dead inside; only the fear of death in Nam made him feel alive. From that moment on, he was free, with no attachments to anyone. Nothing would stop him now from doing what he had to do.

Later that night, from a distance, he looked at Nell's car parked in the Evers driveway. He stood fifty yards away from his parked car in Bandshell Park. Actually, it had been Mark's words that brought him there. "Ruby's window." He had to see it for himself, tonight, a spring night that had suddenly turned winter cold and mean.

One last hit from his roach burned the side of his thumb and forefinger. He wished he'd been thinking as clearly earlier, with Wichita at the river. Now he understood himself so much better: I know why I can't let go of her, Wichita. It's like Einstein said, "There's nothing quite as beautiful as the mysterious"...and Wichita...my mystery girl is Nell Evers. I could never figure her out. She's smarter than me, Wichita. And...Mark...after she made love to me the first time, I knew I could die right then, because I had lived a full life. I could never put it into words like you can, Mark. If I could write like you, maybe she'd be with me right now. And she'd wait for me when I was overseas, because of the love letters I would send to her every day. I would use my talent, Mark. I wouldn't leave my words in some box in a dark closet. I'd use my words to live and to keep love. I wish I could've told you these things at the river today.

When Hurley saw Nell come out of the house and hop into her convertible, he started for his car. He followed her across town, not at all tense or anxious, until he saw her hurry into her lover's apartment like an excited schoolgirl. Yes, his mystery girl, so thrilled to be so close to her new boyfriend's apartment! Hurley's stomach had begun to churn when he saw her combing her hair while driving, gazing into her rearview mirror, then straightening her lush eyebrows that he once loved to touch and kiss when he held her face.

Six times. They had made love six times. And he recalled every single time with Nell vividly, until the whirling images made him cough then vomit out the window down the side of his car.

He bailed out of the car, cursing the mess he made and the ensuing silhouette of Nell embracing her boyfriend behind the white drapes of the first-floor apartment. He felt like stuffing the five-pound slippery catfish that was inside his trunk into her glovebox, but that would alert her to his bigger plan, a plan that was changing and getting better by the day.

Hubbard was stretched out on her side on Mark's bed with one of Grandma's tasseled linen pillows between her knees, her hand propped up her head as she listened to Mark talking about his fishing date with Hurley. Mark paced back and forth on Grandma's vintage floral area rug.

"I can't believe you finally told that idiot off."

"I don't know if it did any good, but at least he won't be bugging me to do things with him."

"That's good."

"But it was so strange, Hubbard, when I was walking away from him at the river, I felt guilty, not good at all about telling him off."

"Well, he is your friend."

"Was my friend. I wish I didn't have to look at his sorry face every day at school."

"School will be over soon. You'll get through it."

"That's just it. I don't want to just get through. I want these last days of school to be good memories with no bullshit to get through."

Mark sat down on his bed and rubbed her bare ankle below her pant cuff.

"Don't you see, Hubbard, in the last two years I've lost two women that I miss terribly and can never see again. Just as you lost your dad and Luther. Hurley's been a big part of my life since I moved here. I know he's a bad person in many ways, and that's what I told him today. He's bound to be hurt and confused. Because if I didn't have you, I'd still be hanging out with him."

"Yes, but Mark, you have to know when to let go of bad people who don't serve you well. I saw Gunderson pee on an old sow who had recently nearly died while giving birth to a litter of fifteen! Only a truly evil person would do such a thing!"

"I just don't like leaving it this way. I don't feel right about it."

"Then write him a letter and tell him everything good and bad, before he leaves for boot camp."

Mark knew that writing a letter was the best way to communicate with Hurley, or anybody, because he'd never been able to act on making things right when something bothered him. Never able to say what he wanted to say unless he wrote it down, after wringing it from his heart; but then, he always put his words away forever, a one-sided attempt to convey his feelings to the people he loved. Even Hurley Gunderson wanted his letters read; he was not afraid to risk rejection by a love who had given him the go-by.

Within seconds after leaving a sealed letter on Hurley's windshield, Mark felt the shameful weight of cowardice. He couldn't remember a step taken to get away, into the garage, to stand in the middle of its dirt floor and breathe in scents he would always associate with his hard-working grandpa: gas and oil and firewood stacked on sawdust.

Fluttering in the spring breeze, trapped beneath a wiper blade, the letter said:

Dear Hurley, I had this dream where I saw your face pressed against my window pane. It was right after I thought I'd never see you again. But there you were...ready to play and playing to win. Don't you know that it hurts me, and it scares the hell outta me to think about you leaving soon to be a soldier. That's what I was trying to tell you at the river. Your friend, Wichita.

Prom Nights and Wild Country

It was May Day and just a couple hours from the Paradise prom dance in the little gym at 8 P.M. Mark was nervous when Hubbard drove onto the Freeman driveway in Nell's convertible and parked alongside his dad's Plymouth. Mark had told Hurley he'd let him dance with "Hawkins" if she didn't mind.

From the Freeman front porch he could see her getting out of Nell's car, her red heels visible in the twilight over Paradise. Her prom dress was red, a shocking red, and appeared to be made of silk; it looked so good against her white skin, and so striking with her beautiful lush red hair that was styled into a beehive with curls hanging down each side of her brow. Her blue eyes were down, watching for and avoiding patches of mud until she reached the front sidewalk.

Mark thought she looked beautiful, though she wore absolutely no makeup, her eyes shining bright from her formula. He opened the porch door for her clad in a rented powder blue tux with a white boutonniere on his lapel. She smiled when he pinned on her white corsage; then she laughed when she saw him wearing his white shoes.

"You want me to wear my black shoes?"

She said no as they stepped, laughing, into the Freeman front room. Mark's dad exited the kitchen ahead of

Grandpa Freeman. Both men grinned as they inspected the happy couple dressed for their prom. Larry was quick to tell Hubbard how nice she looked; Grandpa's smile said the same thing as Hubbard handed Larry her camera. The prom couple posed holding hands and smiling big for four pictures, then Hubbard took three snapshots of the three Freeman generations with Mark in the center.

Later, Hubbard thought it was so cute when Grandpa Freeman slipped Mark a twenty dollar bill and said, "Don't run out of gas."

Larry Freeman watched them walking hand-in-hand to Nell's car, careful to avoid muddy places. He could still feel the joy exuding from the couple as they stood on the front porch while he told them to have fun and be careful.

Someone else was watching them now, from his basement window, as he held in then finally exhaled his smoke. His point of view was different: Hurley saw two of the three people who betrayed him and ruined his life.

He stood watching them, clad in white briefs and t-shirt; he was barefooted and not too happy about going to his prom with Karla Dinkle, the only girl he could get to go with him. Karla was his sixth choice, with Nell, of course, at the top of his list. Nell had obviously moved on, spending nearly every weekend with Robert.

Hurley had stopped spying on Nell; it appeared, to those who knew him, as if his nearing graduation combined with his upcoming move into the Marine Corps now occupied his mind.

Even now, as he watched Mark and his date drive east, on their way to have dinner at a Woodbury restaurant, Hurley was thinking about getting his head shaved in order to prepare himself for boot camp. In the last ten weeks Hurley had put on twenty pounds of muscle by doing push-ups, sit-ups, and lifting dumb-bell weights. Tomorrow night he would begin running the streets of Paradise and into the countryside; maybe he would run to Blue Hill and take that pig for a run. Hurley smiled at his pot-induced thoughts and returned to his room looking forward to the dance...with Hawkins...and the message he had for Nell.

Over dinner, Mark didn't have the guts to tell Hubbard that Hurley wanted to dance with her. He was afraid she'd stay away from the event altogether. Not that he was looking forward to seeing Hurley at their prom; but rather, it was a following through kind of thing, about doing something anyway despite a potential embarrassing situation. That's what he was after—graduation to another level of living, living in the moment and handling every situation as if it were something to be cherished because it was a part of his destiny.

At dinner, there was a tall, thin, white candle standing in their line of vision. Hubbard slid the flickering candle to the side a bit and smiled at her date, a coquettish validation to him that they would spend the night at Blue Hill. She was thinking how healthy his eyes looked now compared to when he first moved to Paradise. She could see that his eyes were like his father's and Grandpa Freeman's in color, and they were eyes that could be trusted to never hurt her intentionally. Yes, she was sure that she loved Mark Freeman more than she'd ever loved anyone. And, she also knew that she was more willing to feel her love for him. Yet something was holding him back from truly loving her. She was certain that his wariness was related to the loss of his mother.

There was some vague lack of courage that she could

feel whenever she was close to him. Courage to love and be loved. She knew well that you can't have one and not the other. And it was something she could never make him do, or even talk about. Life's own journey brings love, or it does not. She was willing to wait for his love for a while, but she did not know how long. These uneasy thoughts filled her mind as they sat at the table separated by tall, fancy restaurant menus that obscured their faces from each other.

Then, from the other side of Mark's menu his words caught her by surprise. "Hurley wants to dance with you tonight."

She changed her impulsive response to, "One dance won't kill me. It has to be a fast dance, though. I won't slow-dance with that creep."

Mark laughed behind his menu until she asked him what was so funny.

"I was just picturing you and Hurley slow-dancing...and you know how he likes to grind his hips."

"Oh, God," she laughed.

In his briefs and wearing his white tux jacket after trying it on, Hurley splashed on too much Wild Country cologne in front of his bathroom mirror. His eyes looked like wrapped peppermint candy; his teeth a stained cream vanilla color from frequent pot usage as he smiled at his devilish reflection thinking of Karla's arrival soon, and how he wished he could get out of buying her dinner after the dance. He smirked at the notion of her large body's big appetite, saying to his reflection, "Gawd, I'll bet she eats like a horse after smokin' pot and dancin' up a storm."

About then, he heard her old Chevy truck parking in front. At the bottom of the basement steps he listened for the doorbell. Soon the door at the top of the stairs opened and his mother's voice called down to him, "Hurley, you're date is here!"

"Send her down!" he ordered.

"What about the pictures?" his mother asked.

"We'll take the friggin' pictures later when we leave! Send her down!"

Even above the Stones music blasting from his speakers he could hear the heavy clomping footsteps of Karla Dinkle's low heels coming down the steps. From the laundry room below the open window he saw Karla turn the corner in her black dress. He noticed how her black beehive hairdo matched her 185-pound figure, a shape that was full and bulging at her chest and waist and tapered down to thin calves and massive feet that were flat and wide.

"I'm here!" he yelled above the music.

He thought her thin/square black imitation leather strapless purse did not go with her full figure, that it only magnified her size.

She first saw him smiling under his open window in his briefs, tux jacket, and black rayon socks; he was pinching and raising a burning joint to his lips and took a deep hit before saying, "You look nice, Karla."

"Oh, so do you, Gunderson!" she laughed and walked over to him, taking his offering in hand.

"I got some Coke and Southern Comfort, if ya want some."

"Sure," she gasped while holding in her smoke.

"Wait here, I'll be right back. Make sure the smoke goes out the window!"

"I will," she nodded.

Hurley entered his messy room and the din of rock

music; soon he returned to Karla toting two glasses with ice, two cans of Coke and a half pint of Southern Comfort that he placed on his mother's washing machine.

"Pot makes me hungry!" Karla declared.

"We'll eat after the dance."

While Hurley mixed their drinks, she said, "But I can't drink that on an empty stomach!"

"How 'bout some ham? You like ham?" Hurley barked.

"I love ham!" she smiled, then inhaled deeply, holding another hit.

"I'll be right back," he told her.

Upstairs, now clad in his white pants and t-shirt, Hurley opened the refrigerator door as his mother entered the kitchen.

"Where's the ham?" he demanded.

"Aren't you going out to dinner?" she asked.

"Karla wants some ham. Do I have to spell it out for ya? For Christ's sake, the girl wants some ham!"

Just then, Mr. Gunderson came into the kitchen to see what the commotion was all about. His wife had uncovered the ham and began slicing off pieces.

"Aren't you going out to dinner?" Mr. Gunderson inquired.

"What is this? Do I have to get permission to have a little ham before we go out to our prom? We want a little ham before we go out...OKAY?!"

Mr. Gunderson walked away shaking his head as his red-faced son headed for the basement door with a plate of sliced ham. Mrs. Gunderson called out to Hurley to be sure to not leave the house before taking pictures. The basement door slammed shut.

Still under the window, Karla was now smoking a cigarette and flicking her ashes into her raised palm.

"I'll getcha an ashtray," Hurley said in the quiet basement after the album ended.

"You have The Kinks?"

Hurley handed her the plate of ham and nodded yes.

After putting on The Kinks he returned from his room with an empty Coke can that he gave his date. He watched her gobble the ham as fast as his mother had sliced it; then, she took a hit from her cigarette, exhaled smoke up to the open basement window and went back to the ham. After Hurley had a piece of ham, he lit another joint.

"Pretty good stuff!" Karla said, referring to the ham and pot, her voice above The Kinks.

Karla, an inch taller than her date without heels, towered a few inches above Hurley's slicked- back hair as she drank her Coke/Comfort.

He showed his date to his bathroom sink, hardly believing she polished off the ham so fast, as she kept apart her sticky fingers before rinsing off the grease. Karla was not the same refined girl as Nell Evers, he knew, and as she washed her hands he fondled her breasts from behind, watching her passive face in the cabinet mirror.

Before long, they were naked on one of Hurley's twin beds going all the way to the music of The Kinks, until the album ended and his stereo clicked off. In the sudden silence, Hurley's mother called down to her son to tell him they were going out to dinner now and to come upstairs so they could take some pictures.

A little later, Mrs. Gunderson opened her refrigerator and gave her son his boutonniere and Karla's white carnation corsage. Mr. Gunderson snapped pictures of the red-eyed couple pinning on their carnations, and smiling side-by-side before exiting out the Gunderson front door.

It was dark and windy when Hurley and Karla climbed into his obnoxious-sounding Ford. Just then, Nell's convertible pulled in and parked on the Freeman driveway. Hubbard was behind the wheel, when she told Mark, "Oh, God, I don't want to go into any public place with Hurley Gunderson, let alone dance with him."

Mark started laughing; via the side-view mirror he could see Hurley and his date crossing the street and headed their way.

Hubbard saw them and exclaimed, "Oh, no, Mark! Tell him we have to go inside...anything. Please!"

Mark was the only one to laugh when Hurley pressed his face to the front passenger window, crossing his eyes and mugging like an insane lunatic.

When Mark rolled down the window, Hurley said, "Mind if we walk over with ya?" He smiled and waved at Hubbard.

She courtesy-smiled back and shrugged her shoulders as if she didn't mind. Yet seconds later she rolled her eyes and shot a disgusted look at Mark, because she could smell the overkill of Wild Country mixed with the distinct scent of pot on Hurley.

Hubbard and Mark walked behind Hurley and Karla. Hubbard couldn't help but pick up the same reeking odors coming from Karla. Hubbard turned her head to avoid the pungent wafts assaulting her nose. Both girls held onto their date's arm on the far right side of the road. Arriving cars increased to a rare traffic jam in Paradise; honking horns and cat-calling seniors directed slurs at Hurley.

"Gunderson in a tux! Ha! Ha! Ha!"

"Squirrely Hurley's gotta date! WHEW!"

"Up yours!" Hurley returned, pointing his middle finger while laughing at passing classmates.

Hubbard must have rolled her eyes at Mark a dozen times from the crude insults Hurley shouted at liquored-up seniors arriving at their prom. All the while, Karla laughed like a tramp on a barstool, which caused her date to get more and more vulgar. Often, Mark would laugh at one of Hurley's lewd remarks and Hubbard had to constantly remind herself that it was his prom, not hers.

She had no friends there, though she knew all the seniors. After her stay in the Paradise jail, they all labeled her the weird redhead from Blue Hill who buried her father in his hogyard. Hubbard heard the circulating rumors that the hogs ate poor old Jake Hawkins, and that his greedy daughter had made a bunch of money from a true crime magazine.

Even now, she could see the gossip flowing from the spiteful young Paradise women on double dates, sitting together on the back seats, their eyes looking up at Hubbard while they covered their mouths, making it even more obvious they were slandering the redheaded pig lover from Blue Hill.

"Look, there's that Hubbard Hawkins. She got away with murder. Her rich relatives in Woodbury got her off."

"Can you imagine! Buryin' your dad in his hogyard and cashin' his disability checks. She's somethin' else. And goin' with that nice Mark Freeman. She's the one who oughta be with Hurley Gunderson."

A rock band from Warren played way too loud for the dinky Paradise gym. When the band played "Yesterday" and Mark and Hubbard were on the dance floor, dancing slowly, he whispered to her, "Don't look now, but you're next."

Hubbard looked up from Mark's shoulder and there was Hurley grinding Karla like a sailor on leave, and Karla appeared to like it.

"Oh, Gawd," Hubbard laughed into Mark's neck. "I'm not slow-dancing with that jerk."

To Hubbard's relief, Hurley never asked her to dance. She was surprised that he was really quite civil for Hurley Gunderson. Even on their walk back home from the dance Hurley told Mark and Hubbard, "Have fun tonight. But be careful."

"And he didn't even try to foist his company off on us," Hubbard remarked to Mark as he changed out of his tux into comfortable clothes. Just then, they could hear Hurley's muffler blaring outside. Hubbard went to the bedroom window and opened the curtain a ways. Hurley was driving away with his date who was sitting close to him and lighting a cigarette.

"He must be poppin' for dinner," Hubbard said.

"I can't believe he didn't bug us about going with him," Mark said, as he pulled on his jeans.

"Yeah, I know. I thought for sure he'd bug me about Nell, but he didn't."

She sat on Mark's bed.

"Well, he's going into the service soon. He's got to be bugged about that," Mark drawled. "Every week it seems that somebody from around here gets killed in Viet Nam."

"I know. That's all you see on the news and in the paper, casualties. When does he leave?"

"I'm not sure. Maybe a week."

Mark thought about Hurley's letter still in his shoebox, the one he said he'd give to Nell. He wanted to show Hubbard the letter, but he remembered seeing Hurley seal it; and he figured that Nell would read it to Hubbard anyway. But a letter like that was too personal to talk about, let alone to betray the sacred trust to deliver such an important memento.

Before they quietly left the Freeman house, Mark put their corsages in the refrigerator in the same sealed container while Hubbard waited at Mark's bedroom door. Then Mark tread soundlessly over to his grandpa's bedroom and listened for his familiar light snoring coming from the other side of the closed door. When he was sure he had heard it, he clicked off the lamp beside Grandpa's chair.

They left the front porch as quietly as possible, holding hands on their walk to Nell's car. He opened the driver's side door for her and held her hand as she raised the hem of her prom dress before gingerly sliding behind the wheel.

When Hurley returned from dinner with Karla in South Woodbury, he saw that Nell's car was gone. He kissed his date and told her to hurry back after she changed clothes. He said, "We got some serious drinkin' and partyin' to do."

When Karla's taillights vanished around the corner, he faced the dark Freeman house and grinned because he knew that Karla would be gone for at least an hour.

Woodbury Central High's prom was the following night after the Paradise prom. Hubbard and Mark wore the same outfits and the same refrigerated corsages as they danced to a live band playing the same "Yesterday." It looked like Nell and Robert were in love, dancing close. Robert looked handsome in his black tux. Nell looked stunning in her ultra-feminine, pink-on-pink, long lace overlay dress with spaghetti straps and grosgrain ribbon belt. Her hair was styled like Hubbard's had been the night before: beehive with a clip of curls dangling on each side.

Tonight, Nell's redheaded cousin wore her hair the way Mark liked it best: down, wild and natural, the way it looked this morning when they walked Johnny around Blue Hill after a perfect night alone in the empty Hawkins house.

As they danced in the crowded Annex to "Yesterday," Hubbard's thoughts were on Luther's desolate farm. His hogs had been shipped to Nap Town, and the only thing she could think about when they had tramped across her old neighbor's land was the funeral he never had or wanted. Luther was buried in the Hawkins Cemetery on the other side of Blue Hill; and Mark agreed to help her find his headstone that Luther's sole surviving relative had ordered from Gunderson Monument Company.

Maybe it was the lyrics to "Yesterday" that made her cry on Mark's shoulder. Then, she told him what she just realized.

"Without you, I'm alone. I don't know what I would do without you in my life. We have to make every day count, Mark Freeman. We can't live lives like my dad or Luther...as if we were never here. We have to support each other's dreams and reach our purpose for being here."

After the prom they enjoyed a catered dinner at Nell's house, spending the late evening sipping champagne and joining the excited conversation about Robert and Nell's engagement announcement that would appear in the paper the next morning.

You Beat Me To The Punch

Right after the Paradise Class of '67 were handed their diplomas and set free, Mark and Hurley trailed Larry and Grandpa on the short walk back from the graduation ceremony. Mr. and Mrs. Gunderson waved as they drove by the Freemans in their new Bonneville, on the way to have lunch with friends in the city. No one commented that Hurley had not been invited to go with them.

Clad in crimson caps and gowns with white tassels, the boys from Paradise, in their white shoes, carried their diplomas with pride and relief, for Hurley hadn't been sure he'd graduate until the last minute.

Yet Hurley was quiet. Mark knew that Hurley was always well-mannered around his dad and Grandpa. Despite that, he seemed more like a Marine with his shaved head and bearing. Now they were all headed for Grandma's kitchen to have pie and coffee, the pie provided by the Methodist Church ladies of Paradise.

"When do you leave for boot camp?" Larry asked Hurley.

"In a few days, sir."

"That doesn't leave much time to celebrate your graduation," Grandpa said.

"No sir, it doesn't. But I want to jump right into boot camp. I'm anxious to serve my country, get it over

271

with and play ball, sir."

Mark discreetly asked Hurley if he still wanted him to give Nell the letter.

"Yeah, but not yet. I may not want ya to give it to her...but I'll let ya know before I leave."

Then Larry asked, "Hurley, where's your boot camp?"

"San Diego, sir."

While the older men went into the Freeman front room, Hurley indicated that Mark should stay outside with him.

"Look, Mark, I know about Nell gettin' engaged. My mom clipped out her engagement photo in the paper and gave it to me. But I'm okay with it. That's just the way it goes. I wanted you to know that there's no hard feelings. I'm over her."

"That's good to hear."

"She beat me to the punch," Hurley said then laughed that sick cackle of his. "Oh...uh...Mark, please tell your dad and grandpa I have some things I gotta do now. And maybe save me a piece of pie."

Mark nodded okay.

From the porch Mark watched Hurley cross the street. Earlier, in line to receive their diplomas, the graduates in alphabetical order, Mark could smell pot on Hurley and knew that just minutes earlier Hurley had gotten loaded in the girls restroom with Karla Dinkle.

Now, Mark could hear Hurley singing the same refrain he sang under his breath while standing in line to get his diploma: "You beat me to the punch, whoa yeah, you beat me to the puuu...unch!"

Hurley sang the lyrics over and over while

descending the basement steps into his room, whereupon he put two 45 records on his stereo and cranked the volume up. The first record spun on the turntable and Mary Wells began singing "You Beat Me To The Punch." He went over to his dart board and removed three darts from the center of the board where Nell's happy face and her fiance Robert's happy face smiled from the newspaper photo that had been riddled with dart holes. He lit a joint.

As the song played, he sang along while he stepped back some twenty feet and crouched like a catcher, firing three darts from his haunches, hitting the engaged couple once each. He walked across the room, took a hit and blew the smoke out his basement window.

The second 45 plopped down onto the turntable as he retrieved his darts. Lesley Gore began to sing "She's A Fool" and Hurley sang along. He walked backwards, crouched, and fired three more darts at the photo, hitting them each time. Then he strolled over to his stereo. Beside it, on a soiled dinner plate were the blackened remains of a burned letter—the letter in his stilted handwriting that Mark had composed to Nell for him...for twenty bucks.

Meanwhile, in Woodbury, Robert and Nell picked up Hubbard and her mother in Robert's new white Fairlane, on their way to the graduation ceremony. Nell and Hubbard wore maroon caps and gowns with white tassels. Nell thought her fiance looked handsome in his black, vested polyester suit with white shirt and black tie. Hubbard thought Robert's British Sterling cologne was way too heavy on him.

Nell turned to the back seat and told her cousin, "I can't believe you're moving back into that house again...with that pig!"

"I'll live there as long as Johnny's alive."

"Thanks for the tip," Nell smirked and added, "God, Hubbard, you're throwing your future away for some friggin' pig. Don't you want to go to school?"

"I can't afford school now. I was always so bored in school. My grades aren't good enough for a scholarship. Not all of us are rich, Nell. Besides that, I don't know what I want to do yet."

"So you're going to live in that shack with a pig?" Nell said cynically.

Hubbard's mother chimed in, "Hubbard, you could sell that place and have money to go to school."

"That's true, Mom. But where would Johnny live?"

"Nobody will rent to someone with a pet pig," Robert agreed.

"What are you saying, Robert?" Nell smiled at her fiance, but there was no affection in her tone.

Robert cleared his throat, not wanting to get into the conversation, but stated, "It's her life, Nell. That's all I can say."

"It's her life. Thank you Mr. Straddling the Fence," Nell retorted. "Well, I hate to say this, Cousin Hubbard, but I hope your pig DIES so you can have a life some day."

Nell was the only one in the car laughing.

Hubbard snapped, "That's not funny, Nell. It's an incredibly mean and cruel thing to say. Besides, what business is it of yours what I do? Have you ever heard of live and let live?"

"Well, you just LIVE with your PIG and your WIMP boyfriend, and you'll never see me come visit you at that place."

"Nell, what's your problem? Didn't get to say goodbye to Hurley?" Hubbard glared at her.

"Hurley? I'm engaged, Hubbard! Where did that come from?"

"Oh, like you didn't know my WIMP boyfriend wrote that letter for Gunderson."

"What are you talking about?"

"You led Gunderson on and let him think he could have you. You used him all the way. I'm not as stupid as Hurley Gunderson."

"What do you care? You can have him if you want him, Hub."

"You're sick."

"Okay, you two...enough! It's your graduation day! Quit bickering!" Hubbard's mother demanded.

"Don't think I don't know you've been stealing my records out of my room," Nell accused, undaunted.

"What are you talking about? I don't want your stupid records."

When Robert finally parked, he announced, "We're here!" As he climbed out of the car, he added a muttered, "Thank God!"

That night, Hubbard and Mark were expected at the Evers house to celebrate their graduation with Nell and Robert along with all of the Evers clan. Hubbard told Mark about her argument with Nell on the way over in her mom's Dodge. Mark tried to be the peacemaker, telling Hubbard that Nell had a lot of stuff going on, her hasty engagement to Robert and the unresolved issues she had with Hurley, which she had to feel guilty about. Hubbard agreed, saying that she hoped once Gunderson was gone and Nell was free to focus on her new life with Robert, things would simmer down and everything would work out for the best.

Still, for the entire evening, Nell and Hubbard

remained aloof and cold to each other. Champagne helped, but the feuding cousins never spoke the entire night, until inebriated Nell insisted that her cousin and Mark spend the night in the guest bedroom, stating firmly with a pointing finger at tipsy Hubbard, "You're not driving tonight. My car's blocking your car in the driveway and I'm not moving it. Robert's driving me to his place. I'm taking my keys with me and I'll be back in the morning to make breakfast for you and Wichita. That's final!"

Meanwhile, Hurley stood at the top of the hill in Bandshell Park in the pouring rain. He was wearing a hooded cotton jacket, old jeans and his white shoes. His fingers were stained with pot resin and smelled of Wild Country as he tipped back the last of his quart of beer into his throat.

After he watched Nell get into her fiance's fancy white Fairlane and drive off, he wiped the beer foam from his mouth and cursed the headache pounding behind his temples. He knew he was running out of time. And he knew he was missing something. It was something related to timing; it had to be perfect, and he hoped to God that it wasn't too early, or late for what he had to do.

"So far, so good," he mumbled and repeated to himself out loud, "I've got time." Then he grinned big at the wise words Grandpa Freeman had imparted to him in the basement of the courthouse that afternoon before closing time.

After one last look at the Evers mansion, Hurley began to hum "Johnny Angel" as he walked toward his gray Ford parked in an isolated spot. Standing beside his car, he let fly his empty beer bottle, shattering it on the cement floor of the bandshell a few feet short of the stage.

Hurley pressed his wet face to the glass on the

driver's-side back passenger window. Grandpa Freeman's burlap bags still covered the back seat, and Johnny lay on his belly against the back door, his yellow collar glowing in the darkness. Hurley opened the door and sniffed the air. From the back seat floor he picked up the leash Hubbard used and ordered the pig, "C'mon you frigin' swine, you're not gonna shit in my car!"

Johnny, already nervous from the downpour, stood gingerly on his hooves, afraid to come closer to his kidnapper, so Hurley grabbed Johnny by his collar and dragged the squealing, struggling pig across the rumpling burlap and tied the rope to his collar. Then he lifted him down to the road.

Hurley led the pig over to the grass and waited for him to do his business in the pouring rain. "C'mon! Shit, you four-legged hot dog!"

The pig stood shivering in the rain and Hurley felt a rush of annoyance at the stupid pink beast. Hawkins had spoiled the animal rotten. But then, the pig looked up at him and something came over Hurley, a kind of stillness in the rain, while the trembling pig's brown eyes were glowing at him.

Hurley stared at the soaking wet pig. "Look, Johnny, you're the key to my happiness in this whole friggin' world. Johnny Angel...that's what you are."

The pig shook with cold and paid Hurley no heed. Angel or no angel, that freakin' pig was not getting back in his car until it took a dump. Hurley shrugged out of his hooded jacket and wrestled it onto the pig, thinking if Johnny was warmer, he'd do his business. Dressing the pig only made him crazy. Johnny pulled at his leash and squealed so loud Hurley thought somebody would call the cops.

To calm the pig, Hurley began to sing. "Johnny Angel...Johnny Angel...you're an angel to me. Johnny Angel, how I love him! Dah...dah...dah. I'm in heaven dah...dah...dah. But I just sit and wait dah...dah...dah...'cause I love him!"

Good boy!" Hurley cackled and led Johnny back to his dry car.

<u>Johnny Angel</u>

By early afternoon the next day, Mark and Hubbard's hangovers still lingered. It had rained hard all night and all morning. Hubbard was upset with Nell because she never showed up for breakfast and wasn't answering the phone at Robert's apartment. Hubbard called Robert at his office and he said that Nell wanted to sleep in, and had told him she'd take a cab back to her house.

Now, after breakfast in a city restaurant, Hubbard parked her aunt's borrowed Buick close to the back door of her house on Blue Hill. She and Mark got out of the car fast in the pouring rain, then they heard it together: Shelley Fabares singing "Johnny Angel" coming from her record player in the house. There were no other cars around. Hubbard looked for tire tracks in the mud. None.

Mark and Hubbard were still dressed in the clothes they had worn at last night's celebration. They were checking on Johnny and bringing some of Hubbard's clothing for her move back home. Mark had grabbed some of her things off the back seat, thinking that Hubbard left the song on for Johnny. Hubbard was certain she hadn't left the song on and the spindle open so that the song would keep playing. The record began to play again.

She hurried in the rain to the locked back door. Quickly, she got her house key from under the doormat and unlocked it for Mark before they were both drenched. Once inside the house, Hubbard called for Johnny above his favorite song. They could both smell old cigarette smoke mixed with the pungent scent of pot.

"Johnny!" Hubbard called again.

Hubbard made a quick search while Mark laid her clothes on her unmade bed.

"He's gone!" Hubbard exclaimed.

One look at her bed, and she said, "Someone was in here. My bed's always made."

Hubbard took her rumpled pillow and put it to her nose. "Gunderson was here with Nell."

She handed the pillow to Mark and he, too, could smell Wild Country mixed with some other scent.

"Ambush. Do you smell it? I gave Nell a bottle of Ambush for Christmas."

"At the party here, Nell and Hurley were in your bed."

"That was a while back, Mark."

"But you haven't slept here since. Did you wash the pillowcase?"

"No. But I made the bed."

The sound of pelting rain on the roof made Hubbard think of Johnny being out in this weather and how susceptible pigs were to pneumonia. Then, on the floor Hubbard saw then picked up a saucer with three of Gunderson's butted cigarettes.

"Winstons?" Mark asked.

"Yeah."

"Why would Nell be here with Hurley?" Mark whispered out loud.

What did they do with Johnny? The unspoken question was all over Hubbard's face as the music tormented her mind. She hurried in her low heels to turn off the record player. Mark followed behind her, his black dress shoes making a loud/slick ominous sound on the wood floor.

"Maybe they took him for a ride, or just let him outside. Nell didn't like Johnny in the house," Mark suggested.

Hubbard's worse fear appeared in her mind before she finished saying, "Where would they take..."

The image of Nap Town made her voice quake as she answered her own question. "The stockyards."

"They wouldn't really do that," Mark scoffed.

"Oh, wouldn't they?!" Hubbard yelled.

"Hubbard, they probably just let him out and Johnny wandered over to Luther's."

"His leash is gone!" Hubbard exclaimed, as she inspected the kitchen and found an empty wine bottle and empty beer cans in the garbage can. She saw a used wine glass in the sink. Hubbard dashed for the door and ran outside.

Mark ran after her in the pouring rain. They searched in the Hawkins barn and muddy hogyard. No sign.

They drove to Luther's farm and searched there, then up and down Broken Kettle. Nothing.

Both were plagued by troubling thoughts as Hubbard sped for the stockyards in her aunt's powerful Buick.

"Why would they..."

"Because Nell's a bitch and Gunderson's a devil!" Hubbard snapped.

"Stop at Hurley's house first! See if he's there!" Mark suggested, his eyes on the Buick's rising speedometer.

There were no vehicles parked at the Gunderson house. Then Mark talked Hubbard into checking at Nell's house, then Robert's apartment, if they didn't find Nell at her house.

When they arrived at Robert's place after several near misses running red lights and stop signs in the city, Robert sounded worried because he hadn't seen Nell since that morning, when he left her for work. And he told them Nell didn't show up for their lunch date at their favorite restaurant.

Concerned, Robert wanted to call the police before Hubbard and Mark left his apartment, but Hubbard told him that she didn't want to get Nell's parents worried about her. Robert agreed, since his boss would be in the picture. Hubbard and Mark said nothing to Robert about the clues left at Blue Hill. Instead, Hubbard relieved his anxiety by saying, "Robert, you know Nell. She does things on the spur of the moment. She might be in Omaha on a shopping spree."

"It's still not like her to not call me," Robert said.

"Well, if she doesn't show by tonight, I'll tell my aunt and uncle."

Robert nodded in agreement and soon watched from his open front door as the Buick sped away.

"Where now?" Mark asked, concerned again about Hubbard's speed on the rain-swept highway.

"Nap Town," she said.

"Nap Town?"

"That's right!"

"How are you going to find Johnny there?"

"I'll find him."

"Nell wouldn't get herself or her car dirty," he said,

when she ran a stop sign.

"How about Gunderson, Mark? Does that answer your question, Mark?" she screamed at him. "I can just see that bitch havin' one last fling with Gunderson before he leaves for boot camp. They get all drunk and stoned and they take Johnny..."

"You don't know that!"

"Well, I gotta find out! I'm not gonna do nothing if HE IS THERE!"

It kept raining all the way to the massive stockyards. Hubbard ran two red lights and raced at 60 mph over several sets of railroad tracks on a pot-holed road. She kept hearing "Johnny Angel" playing in her head along with the image of Hurley pissing all over that poor old sow. All the while Mark was plagued by the image of the big orange tomcat Hurley shot dead on their way to the Halloween dance.

Hubbard stayed focused and emotional, and could not get to Nap Town fast enough; whereas Mark was filled with fear about what would happen once they got there. He kept looking down at his best clothes: a long sleeve white shirt tucked into black slacks and the gold-colored tie Grandpa gave him for Christmas. The frazzled driver was wearing a woven off-white cotton/rayon summer dress, a shaped shirtwaist with two side-front pleats and a fold-over cowl collar with fringed side ties and short sleeves.

Mark wanted to say something to her, mostly about what she was going to do when they arrived at Nap Town. She had told him so many terrible things about the place, he was beside himself with fear and apprehension.

She knew right where the holding pens were, and parked her aunt's Buick beside the careworn wooden fence that ran for as far as any eye could see in both directions.

In the deluge, Mark followed Hubbard up to the fence; she was oblivious to getting her nice clothes dirty, allowing her dress to touch and rub against the fence's slippery surface. Yet, when she looked deep into the uncovered holding pen, now dark and ominous as the clouds that drenched them, she startled him with her barely audible, awe struck words.

"Oh, my God!"

Mark's eyes could now see what she was referring to: thousands and thousands of hogs crammed in together, a sea of swine in what had to be hundreds of holding pens, a jigsaw puzzle of worn timbered sectioned pens with a wide aluminum gate for each pen. Hubbard was scanning each pen before her, knowing that her small/clean Johnny would stand out, and especially if he was wearing his fluorescent yellow collar.

The noise was deafening from ten thousand hogs getting rained on.

Mark yelled, "There's too many, Hubbard!"

She ignored his words and continued focusing on the hogs in the holding pen in front of her while moving slowly down the fenceline. She told Mark to walk in the other direction until he reached the cattle holding pens.

The rain was hurting their chances to find Johnny, because now all of the hogs were cleaner. Every color of swine on earth was there: red, black, white, pink, brown, and every spotted combination thereof. Endless hogs, some as big as 450 pounds, all standing in a sea of shit and piss and mud that smelled like the world's largest cesspool.

Mark and Hubbard, completely soaked, moved farther and farther apart down the fenceline. Then, deep into the holding pens, Hubbard saw a stockman in a red baseball cap running for cover, reaching a platform that led to the foreman's office not far from the black, gaping entrance to Nap Town. The rain was coming down too hard for anyone to notice the two of them, she knew.

It was impossible to tell that Hubbard was crying in the rain as she scanned pen after pen; she could not get Shelly Fabares out of her head. Over and over, the song played in her head as if the spindle was left off, playing above the din around her. With "Johnny Angel" louder and louder in her head, a thousand memories spread over ten years kept producing tears.

Before long, she realized she was running out of pens to check and knew they'd have to go deeper into the adjoining pens that were a city block wide. She was glad it was raining so hard, for it would keep the yardsmen inside the foreman's office where, her father had told her long ago, they played cards, smoked like fiends and drank bad coffee like maniacs until the rain let up.

Hubbard imagined the Nap Town kill floor men in their white hardhats and their blood-splattered aprons; they were standing in tall black rubber boots to their knees as they skillfully sharpened their butcher knives and saw blades, ready to greet the doomed pork yet alive inside the moving conveyor belt. She imagined the animals being gassed quickly with a potent ether mist just before their throats were cut at the other end of the belt. She knew because her father had been one of them.

Just then, it dawned on Hubbard that they should be at the entrance to Nap Town and working their way back here. Yes, they should be at the entrance to the gas chamber to see if Johnny was in imminent danger; out here was safe.

She ran for Mark, waving to get his attention and

then yelling his name. "Mark! Mark! We have to go to the entrance to Nap Town where the hogs are gassed! We have to start there and work back!"

Before he could protest, she was mounting the fence that divided two holding pens. She began stepping side to side on the lowest fence board to keep her feet from being trampled by the sandwiched hogs, all the while crouching below the top fence board in order to keep from being seen by any of the yardsmen.

"Do you even know where it is?" Mark yelled after her.

She didn't answer. Perhaps she couldn't hear him. He hesitated at the top of the fence before letting his soaked slacks touch the stinking boards. His black dress shoes were slick on the slippery wood. Down his eyes went, into the waste-filled holding pen, where bloated, grunting sows were crammed together like sardines.

He could see that Hubbard was nearly across the first section to the next, her white underwear visible under her wet dress. Quickly he unbuttoned his white shirt's top two buttons and stuffed his new tie inside his shirt.

The squealing and grunting sounds increased the further he went into the holding area. On both sides of the fence there wasn't any room to touch the ground without being stepped on; and he knew if he slipped and fell he would be trampled to death without being seen or heard. And he knew for certain that he would never do such a crazy and dangerous thing as this if not for Hubbard leading the way. That's when he realized he was playing again the familiar role of a follower. He had been led by Hurley and now even his girlfriend was leading him...toward the unknown, to something he would never do on his own. That's how she and Hurley were alike, and that's why she and his friend clashed: they're both leaders, he realized.

Then he lost it. Because he was into his head, both of his dress shoes slipped together on the slick bottom slat, causing his chin to slam down hard on the top board, cutting a gash that bled fast onto his white shirt. The shock of tough pig hide rubbing against his legs made him jump high, so high he used his arms to guide his airborne legs up to the very top of the fence where he landed hard, straddled over the board on his crotch.

The pain was unbearable. When it eased a bit, he looked ahead down the fenceline, hoping his girlfriend couldn't see him in such agony. Then he realized he hadn't been looking into the holding pens for Johnny, figuring Hubbard had.

By now, Hubbard's dress was smeared black with mud from hem to shoulder. She stopped riding the fence, turning to see if there was any sign of Johnny in the direction of the ominous bridge that led to the tunneled gas chamber of Nap Town. Up ahead, she had to be careful, because she had to pass the foreman's office in order to continue on. If she and Mark were spotted, the men would certainly try to stop them. There was no way to conceal themselves; she could see that they'd have to continue on top of the fence since hogs were crammed nose to butt.

Just then, a yardman came out of the foreman's shack wearing a hooded yellow rain slicker. Hubbard stayed low and motionless atop the fence, her legs quivering from exhaustion and cold rain. When she looked back at Mark, she tried to signal him to stop moving, but it was too late. She could see that the man had spotted Mark; then he saw her.

The noise from the rain and squealing hogs was too loud for her to make out anything the man was barking at

287

them; however, his body language, flailing arms and mouthed expletives told them to get out.

Hubbard continued even faster down the fenceline knowing they would be forced to leave before long, since the yardsman was hustling for the foreman's office. In one of the last pens, she peered around to see exactly where the entrance to Nap Town was. She saw it a bit to the left and way down into the shadows where a terrible hissing noise from compressed steam was coming. By now, there was but one more holding pen to pass before reaching the largest pen before Nap Town.

Mark was so spent he had no clue that the yards foreman and three of his yardsmen were coming toward him on a narrow walkway just one pen down from him. All of the men were toting electric cattle prods, stainless steel sticks of terror to Nap Town livestock that were zapped with enough voltage to cause a stampede.

"Hey! What the hell are you doin' in here?" the foreman demanded to know from Mark.

Mark's fatigued and stupefied look at them brought three more words from the foreman, "Get outta here!"

When Mark looked down the fenceline for Hubbard, she was gone. He craned his head as high as he could, but still there was no Hubbard in sight. His response was panic; he thought she had fallen into a pen. That fear made him continue on, slipping and jumping back onto the fence several times during which time his adrenaline output was so high he didn't notice the slivers of wood gouged into his palms from the slippery fence.

Meanwhile, Hubbard had discovered a walkway, a narrow path that the yardsmen used to herd livestock into the holding areas. She couldn't see if Johnny was among the biggest herd; she would have to mount the fence again if she was ever going to spot her pint-sized pig in this maelstrom of goliaths. And she'd have to do it fast, for when she looked behind her she could see that the foreman and his crew were all over Mark after yanking him down from the fence onto the walkway.

Then, perhaps 200 feet away, she saw the bridge and the belt of steel moving ever so slowly under a tunnel of gas that led to the butchers of Nap Town. Her father's description of it was not as shocking as the reality of unbearable noise, hissing blasts of steam and a million squealing tons of living bacon and sausage being roughly herded into the tunnel by two yardsmen with the long electric prods they wielded from a covered overhead roving platform.

Mark was pinned on his back by three men as rain poured onto his haggard shivering body.

"What are you doin' here?" the foreman demanded, standing over Mark's ringing head.

Mark could not speak, his breathing was too fast to form words.

The absolute terror all around Hubbard was causing her legs to shake from fear. But just then, she thought she saw a speck of yellow against the fence all the way over on the other side of the giant holding pen.

"Johnny!"

Then, the yellow would disappear as if a mirage. Again she thought she saw the yellow collar, and this time, she left the fence and entered the sea of swine.

One of the yardsmen standing over Mark pointed toward the last pen as if stunned by something he'd never seen before; a tall redheaded girl in a dress was inside the big holding pen with the herd.

All the men turned from Mark to watch her climbing

on her hands and knees from hog to hog, straddling one sow, then two hogs at a time, while moving in the direction of the malevolent bridge. The men stood frozen in gape-jawed wonder at how cool she was in this violent storm of swine, keeping her balance and her bare feet off the ground while talking to and scratching 400-pound sows and normally furious boars.

Mark got up from the mud to see what Hubbard was doing, while the foreman led his men to the other side of the pen to cut off the girl. Mark could see one of the men pointing to him as if asking what to do about him. The foreman's gesture hit Mark hard. It was all in a pathetic wave of the foreman's arm and an inaudible scurrilous comment that said loud and clear, "Don't worry about that worthless wimp! She's the one we have to stop!"

It made him cry. Because it was true. He literally could not get over the last fence, or even climb it for fear the men would come back for him.

He tried to justify his inaction by telling himself that it was her pet, not his.

In the din of terror, as she climbed painstakingly from back to back, from one hog to the other, her bare feet elevated, "Johnny Angel" assaulted her mind, bringing memories. She saw again her dad bringing her here and telling her about the downer calf he saved before he was fired. She started to cry when she realized that Johnny had been her father's gift to her, his gift of love; and it had been Johnny she loved like she wanted to be loved by her father. And through Johnny, she would have made her father healthy with her formulas. And her father would have SEEN this and would know that she could rescue his dying body. But, NO! He hadn't wanted to be rescued! He chose to be miserable and die; and she had dumped his lifeless body into a hole she dug, a grave she made in anger, wanting to cover him with Hawkins earth and pig shit.

"Just like you buried me, when Mom left you!" she screamed. "You made me watch you kill yourself! Day after day! I was angry at you! I buried you there because I hated you! Not because that's what you wanted! I hated you! You angry bastard!" she cried while convulsing on the backs of two hogs.

Mark could see the men trying to call out to her. Then he saw her trying to explain to the men that she was looking for her pet pig that had been brought here by mistake. And he could tell that they were not interested in her story. They only wanted her out of the pen, and fast.

Just then, Hubbard lost her balance and fell out of view. Without hesitation, Mark used his legs to vault high over the fence and onto the sea of hogs. He ran lightly and fast in his dress shoes from one hog's back to another, at times skipping two and three hogs at a time until he slipped and fell hard between two frenzied hogs that beat his hands with their hooves. He got to his feet fast.

Hubbard struggled to her feet and rode the back of one big hog as she searched for Johnny. The foreman ordered one of the men on the platform above to use his long electric prod to zap hogs close to the girl, parting enough space for two of the yardsmen to run into the cleared space and drag the girl back to the fence kicking and screaming. When they got Hubbard on her back and pinned to the ground, as they had with Mark, Hubbard yelled, "Check the entrance, Mark! Make sure he's not going into the tunnel!"

Mark continued on toward the Nap Town bridge where a bottleneck of hogs were being prodded from overhead onto the moving belt. The foreman gestured to the platform prodders to stop Mark from going onto the bridge.

Adrenaline made Mark go; no thoughts or fears, just go to the bridge since he thought Hubbard had spotted Johnny. He rode the backs of two black and white hogs, where now, so close to the bridge, unbearably loud noises made by blasts of steam and compressed air drowned out the squeals from the hogs up ahead who were the last to fall from the gas.

The men on the platform, Hubbard, and the others could only watch in horror as Mark rode two runaway hogs onto the bridge where he fell and disappeared from view on the conveyor belt.

"Mark!" Hubbard screamed.

Mark had entered the black tunnel with a dozen squealing hogs, none of which wore a yellow collar. The odorless gas made every hog drop onto the belt's moving surface.

The butchers of Nap Town couldn't believe their eyes when they saw Mark curled up and unconscious on the belt.

An ambulance and a city squad car arrived at the same time. Hubbard was beside herself waiting for Mark to be brought outside. She told the police about Johnny and that she and her friend were trying to rescue him, and that they had broken no trespassing laws by trying to get her stolen property back.

While the cops were trying to figure out what to do with Hubbard, Mark was brought out on a gurney with an oxygen mask covering his mouth and nose. They quickly shuttled him through the open back doors of the ambulance. Hubbard tried to find out from the paramedics how Mark was, but they drove away so fast, with siren blaring, she only had time to ask the driver what hospital they were taking Mark to.

She hadn't told anyone her fears about the Nap Town gas and how she wasn't sure how its ether would mix with the vision formula that all three of them had taken. All she was sure of was that adrenaline mixed with her formula produced in her incredibly restless sleep filled with vivid dreams so intense they had the power to make dramatic shifts in her waking life.

Abandoning her search for Johnny broke her heart, but anxiety about Mark spurred her to follow the ambulance. She dashed for the car and sped after her unconscious friend. She could hear the wailing siren all the way to the hospital.

Killer Dream and Shattered Glass

Hubbard arrived at the hospital exhausted and barefoot. Her clothes and hair looked like she'd been dragged through the stockyards.

When Hubbard entered Mark's private room, he lay unconscious on the hospital bed, an oxygen mask covering his mouth. She cleaned the grime from her face and hands in the bathroom, then waited alone with Mark, until Grandpa Freeman arrived with Larry.

First she told them that Mark's doctor had said he would most likely wake up later that evening after his gas levels came down. They demanded to know what happened and Hubbard related the whole story.

She told the men that her cousin had taken her pet pig to the stockyards, and how Mark was gassed when he tried to rescue Johnny. Both men could not get past the fact that Mark risked his life for a pig. The Freeman men did not seem to care if the yards foreman could have prevented Mark from getting gassed. In each man's eyes, Hubbard saw the absurdity of the whole ordeal...because it had been over a pig.

When she went to get a glass of water in the bathroom so she could swallow aspirin a nurse gave her to ease her aching muscles, she overheard Grandpa Freeman comment that Hurley Gunderson had stopped by yesterday to say goodbye before he left for the service.

Hubbard listened intently from the open bathroom door as the old man said, "Hurley said to tell Mark goodbye. And for Mark to be sure to give the letter in his shoebox to Nell. He said that Mark would know what he was talking about."

Hubbard stepped out of the bathroom and told Grandpa Freeman that she would stop by Mark's room and get him some clean clothes to bring when she returned later that evening.

"Grandpa Freeman," she inquired, "would you mind if I took a bath and changed clothes at your house? The hot water tank doesn't work so well at my place, and I don't wanna explain all this to my mom right now."

"Help yourself. The front door's unlocked. You might get some rest on Mark's bed. You look real tired," the old man said.

"Yeah, that's a good idea," Larry agreed, then asked her if she was okay to drive.

"Oh, yeah, I can drive, but I better go. A hot bath and a nap sounds so good right now."

As she climbed into the Buick, her mind was busy with what she'd overheard in Mark's hospital room, that it could be the proof she needed to confront Nell. Tired as she was, she sped to the Evers house, but Nell's convertible no longer blocked the driveway. Frustrated, she parked her aunt's Buick and retrieved her mother's Dodge.

It wasn't until she entered the quiet, clean Freeman front room that she realized that her dress was still damp and smelled of pig dung and mud. She went into the bathroom and ran hot water into the deep porcelain tub.

Enervated from her ordeal at Nap Town, she undressed, but stood vacillating about whether or not to invade Mark's privacy looking for the shoebox containing Hurley's mysterious letter. She wrapped a large bath towel around her mud-streaked body.

In Mark's room Hubbard found for herself some jeans and a t-shirt, and a pair of white briefs that would do temporarily. Inside Mark's closet, she saw the shoebox on the shelf and brought it down to the bed so she could look for the letter to her cousin from Gunderson. A sealed envelope marked "Nell" rested on top of a pile of letters written in Mark's hand. She resisted the impulse to look at any of the others and focused on the one she held.

She reminded herself of the terrible deed her cousin had done, then opened the envelope and read the note written in Gunderson's awkward handwriting:

Dear Nell, If you're reading this, I must be on my way to boot camp in San Diego. Can you believe I'll be a Marine in just ten weeks? I read about your engagement in the paper. Congratulations...I guess. I'm sorry for being such a jerk when we were together. I have to confess that Wichita wrote that letter I gave you before the game the four of us went to. You know I can't write like that. You probably figured that out anyway. But I know that what he wrote was true about how I felt about you then, Nell.

I guess I didn't want to leave town without saying goodbye and good luck to you. And I did that little thing you always wanted me to do as sort of a goodbye present for you. Well, I better get this over to Wichita before my bus to Omaha leaves without me. So long, Hurley.

Hubbard read Gunderson's letter three times, certain

that "little thing" was the kidnapping of Johnny to Nap Town. The nauseating feeling of arriving too late to rescue Johnny from the butcher's knives made her nearly heave into Mark's shoebox. She needed to think this out. Should she confront her cousin about Hurley's letter?

She went to Mark's bedroom window and parted the curtain. There were no vehicles parked in front of the Gunderson house, or on the driveway. She was sure that Gunderson had gone by now and there was no use in trying to confront the mean-spirited bastard, recalling the time he peed on Luther's sow.

Startled by the sound of running bath water, Hubbard returned the letter and its container to the shelf where she found them and hurried to the bathroom.

Deep and hot bath water was just what she needed to relax her tense muscles, after taking more aspirin she found in the medicine cabinet. Cuts, bruises and scraped flesh beneath dried blood on her arms and legs and feet swelled in the hot Paradise well water. She gently rubbed her bruised cheek with a washcloth where she had fallen hard onto the flank of a terrified hog in the last holding pen. She thanked God for sparing Mark from the deadly fumes in the Nap Town gas chamber.

While she soaked, her fractious mind still raced from the frenzy at the yards; and now this: Hurley's letter proved he had done that "little thing" to her Johnny...to please that spoiled snob Nell. The longer she soaked, the angrier she became at Nell and Gunderson.

Then she let her mind go back to the party at her house:

Gunderson had parked Nell's open convertible near the Hawkins back door. Nell had bought the beer and wine at a South Woodbury liquor store, then she let Gunderson drive her car after she and Hubbard picked up the boys in Paradise.

"That old truck run?" Hurley asked Hubbard as they got out of the car.

"No, it needs a lot of work," she smiled at Mark. All three of her guests watched her retrieve the house key from under the doormat.

"I gotta see this dancin' pig," Hurley said, after opening a can of beer.

"Oh, God, don't tell me you let that filthy pig live in the house now?" Nell asked her cousin.

"Don't worry, he's house broken. And cleaner an' smarter than some people I know," Hubbard answered Nell.

Johnny was standing in the middle of the bare front room, sniffing the air that told him strangers had entered his home. Before Hubbard could put Johnny in her dad's room, Hurley said, "Make him dance, Hawkins!"

"No! Put him outside!" Nell implored while curling her manicured fingers and wrinkling her nose as if repulsed by the pig's presence.

"Hey! This is a party! I wanna see the pig dance, for Christ's sake!" Hurley demanded.

When Hurley tried to pour some of his beer into Johnny's mouth, Hubbard pulled her pet away by his collar toward her record player where she played "Johnny Angel."

Hubbard and Johnny began swaying together, dancing to the delight of Hurley, who whooped and hollered his approval throughout the song. Nell stood, arms akimbo, rolling her eyes at the whole scene, while Mark riffled through Hubbard's collection of 45 records.

After the song, as Hubbard was leading Johnny into

her dad's room, she overheard Nell telling Hurley, "I'll give ya a hundred bucks if ya take that pig and drop it off at the stockyards."

Hurley belched, then asked his girlfriend, "Will ya marry me if I do?"

"Yes!" Nell laughed, then fell into Hurley's arms, causing him to spill beer on the bare floor.

Hubbard focused on breathing slowly to quiet her mind, something she had learned to do at Warren House. A feeling of energy, the power that gave her eyes their light, flowed over her; at first the sensation lasted only for seconds, then longer periods. These immutable traces, that she felt certain was her true essence, and recognized as God's life force, brought stronger and longer rushes of healing waves. They cleared her mind of all thought. Inside these spaces of nothing—that she recognized were everything—she found inner peace that her Johnny was safe at that very moment.

Then, when she was ready, she allowed her consciousness to surface with an awful memory on Blue Hill. She let it keep coming, taking her back to a time during her girlhood just after her mother had left her father, and he was drinking day and night.

On this particular day, her dad was kicking a sow in his barn that had stepped on his foot. Then she saw the image of Hurley Gunderson peeing on the sow. Without judgment, she could clearly see that Gunderson reminded her of her own father. She could see that she had been transferring her anger to Gunderson, who was real easy to hate.

Then, she lost consciousness and fell into a dreamy sleep.

In her dream, Hubbard stood alone in her house while "Johnny Angel" spun on her record player. She saw a letter on her kitchen table beside the stack of Nell's 45 records Hurley had stolen from her cousin's bedroom. Hubbard picked up the letter and saw that it was the original letter in Mark's handwriting that he wrote for Hurley to give to Nell.

After Hubbard read the letter she heard the distant wailing police siren of Sheriff Hickey's squad car approaching from Paradise. At that instant, her hands dropped the letter. She knew that Gunderson had set her up to take the fall, because of the anger and fear she had transferred to him and had been meant for her father.

As the siren's wail neared, she walked in a trance outside, toward then past her lab. The gate to her hogyard was open and her vision began to blur, impaired as it had been before she began taking her vision formula, as she passed through the open gate.

Her squinting blue eyes could see Johnny lying on his belly beside the piece of earth where she buried her father. Johnny was dirty and overweight, and without his yellow collar; as she drew closer she could see that the shovel she had used to dig her father's grave was standing next to Johnny, planted there as if it had been used to dig a fresh grave.

"Nell," she whispered.

She touched the shovel's handle just as the sheriff's siren stopped at the hogyard gate. Footsteps came up from behind her, and she started to dig feverishly with the shovel without a word from the law. Deeper and deeper she went down into the black Blue Hill earth, until she uncovered the blanket she had wrapped around her father's dead body.

She knelt in the grave and uncovered her father's

face that looked old and careworn, the way she remembered him when he was still living his violent storm of a life unlived. Just then, her vision became clear again, and she began to cry a salty river of tears that fell onto her father's dead face. But these were the same tears that held the magic of her hopes and dreams in her formula; these liquid dreams splashed and changed Jake Hawkins's countenance to the same youthful, tanned and handsome face that she remembered when she was a young child, when she was his little girl and he called "Hubby."

"Daddy, I'm so sorry. I buried you here because I hated what you did to yourself when Mommy left. I couldn't save you, Daddy!" she bawled. "Why did you take your life away from me? Why wasn't I enough to keep you happy? Why did you leave me, Daddy?" she screamed. "I wanted to live like other girls...with a father who helped them decide on their own who they become and who they love. But it was because of a boy who lost his mother in an accident far away from here that I was able to love again...like I loved you. Oh, how I wish you were here to see him. He is such a good person...like you were."

Then her clear vision saw a letter under her dead father's folded hands, pressed against his quiet heart. When she reached for the letter, the sky over Blue Hill brought rain that tasted sweet on her lips as she read her father's words:

My Dear Hubby, I left you long before I should've, like that boy's mother in Wichita. The reasons why are not important now, because NOW is all there is and ever was. To look back for too long as I did is foolish because you lose sight of the moment you have right now. I lost the moment, Hubby, and that includes losing you. If you can learn from me and lose the dead past, you will love that boy NOW with all your being, then whatever he does will not hurt you. I loved your mother and you like so many other unconscious people do. But they do not love NOW. They love their imagined future and dwell in the dead past. When you awake from this dream, you will live in the moment only after you forgive me and anyone else who you let steal your here and now...the present. Because, Hubby, the present is a gift...and that's what I give you... NOW. Love NOW, Dad.

Hubbard's eyes opened in the lukewarm bath water. She looked down to her body, and for the first time she saw a beautiful woman's body, a full figured body that felt safe and awake now with tingling aliveness. NOW, she felt like touching herself, surrendering all resistance to letting go of those unconscious thoughts that produced guilt and shame, any thought whatsoever that might induce anything but love of the true beauty that belonged to Hubbard Kay Hawkins of Blue Hill.

As she ran more hot water into her bath, there was no attachment to her mind; she knew NOW that she was not her mind, or any of the stuff she'd done, or anything anyone had done to her.

"I am," she smiled while washing her skin with Grandma Freeman's homemade lavender soap, its sweet aroma and slippery film covering her body with a healing sweet/burn that made her want nothing but how she felt NOW, at that moment, a conscious kind of healing that came from the loving hands of a spirit that yet gave love...in this deep porcelain tub in Paradise.

Hubbard's eyes glowed in the glass of Mark's bedroom window; they were on the Gunderson house.

After her bath she had put on a pair of Mark's white briefs and grabbed a second pair to take to him. One of his white crew-neck t-shirts reached to the bottom of the briefs and felt soft against her belly. She would crawl under his covers and sleep soon.

But first, her relaxed mind began to work for her, showing her what she could do NOW if Gunderson's car was parked across the street. Standing at the window, she imagined that she would put on a pair of Mark's jeans and either his Keds that she'd placed on a chair with his clean briefs and t-shirt, or his pair of white shoes.

Her imagination placed the gray Ford already parked in front of the Gunderson house. Instantly, she found herself standing in the Freeman garage holding a sledge hammer, its oblong head heavy in her hand, the shaft worn from long use. She exited the garage wearing the white shoes and jeans, the t-shirt sleeves rolled up to her shoulders, the hammer riding balanced over her right shoulder as she stalked toward the gray fartmobile.

NOW: she let her subconscious recall everything she labeled as bad that Hurley Gunderson ever said or did around her, and she told herself that each blow would forgive one thing in her past related to him...until all was forgiven.

She raised Grandpa Freeman's hammer high above her head and brought it down hard, smashing Hurley's windshield to spider veins. Then, she went around to every window, shattering them all to pieces, then the headlights and taillights. She wasn't finished. She swung the sledge hard like a baseball bat onto the driver's-side door, saying, "This one's for Mark!"

Then she had one final blow to deliver, to the hood, while standing at the front fender, the mallet high above her head, with all her might: BOOM!

"That was for Johnny," she said.

Still at Mark's window, the image of her revenge gone, she smiled and felt better, trusting that Johnny was safe somewhere in this world, or the next.

Her eyes fluttered when she slid between the cool sheets and covered herself with Mark's comforter. Sleep would come fast for her. Hubbard had only one quick thought: Mark's safe return to her.

<u>Two Birds...One Stone</u>

Still under the spell of Nap Town's powerful ether, Mark lay in his hospital bed in the throes of an incredibly real dream. He felt intensely his lifelong fear of being truly alive, along with his relentless resistance to surrender that fear. Now, his subconscious mind's explosion of drama had manifested in a dream, drama his mind revealed to punish him for living unconscious.

The dream began sometime after he was released from the hospital, because his plastic I.D. bracelet was dangling loose around his bruised right wrist, though he was now asleep in his bed in the Freeman house.

During the middle of the night he was awakened by The Rolling Stones singing "I Can't Get No (Satisfaction)" coming from across the street. He knew that was Hurley's song. When he got out of bed to look out his window he was already dressed and wearing his black dress shoes. In his groggy state, he wondered if the gas at Nap Town had made him goofy.

As he crossed the street he could see that the Gunderson front door was wide open, and Hubbard's old truck was parked behind Nell's convertible in the Gunderson driveway.

Mark stood at the dark entrance to the Gunderson house where he noticed that the song was playing on the large living room stereo. Inside he went, through the big main room and into the master bedroom. He walked to the king-sized bed, his shoes quiet on the thick beige carpet. Hurley's parents were dead. Mr. Gunderson had been shot in the head; crimson colored the pillow case in a blood-red halo. Mrs. Gunderson lay beside her husband with her eyes wide open, frozen in cartoon-like shock.

Back in the living room, Mark lifted the needle from Hurley's 45 record and then could hear the familiar sound of his friend's pinball machine coming from the open basement door in the Gunderson kitchen.

Into the dark basement he went, except now he could see the glowing whiteness from his white dress shoes on his feet. And there at the foot of the steps and lit up above the noisy machine's flipper buttons, Hurley seemed focused on his silver ball in play, when he said, "Hey, Wichita! Record score, baby!"

Mark looked down to the legs of the pinball machine to see if they were propped by anything. They weren't. And he saw that Hurley was also wearing his white shoes. As Hurley kept his ball alive with fingertips and body language, his eyes were flaming like a devil.

"Hurley...your parents..."

"I know, Wichita! I shot the old man with my rifle. My mom woke up an' saw what I did...and she must've dropped dead from a heart attack right there. I didn't have to shoot her. Hey! That's just like with those two boneheads I nailed in the Falcon! Two birds...one stone!" he cackled, then smacked the side of the pinball machine when he lost his ball, smacking its side until it tilted.

"I saw Hubbard's truck in your driveway..."

"Oh, yeah...she came over lookin' for Nell."

"Where is she?" Mark asked, his heart beating so

306

fast he could hear it.

"In my room with Nell."

Mark's legs wouldn't move until Hurley led the way back to his room.

There, on the first twin bed, was Hubbard. Like Nell, she was alive and terrified, with her hands each tied to a bedpost, a gag in her mouth and a blanket covering her.

"Don't worry, she's dressed. I wouldn't touch your girl," Hurley smiled and picked up his rifle, as Johnny sat up grunting between the beds.

"Hubbard wouldn't let you tie her up without a fight," Mark said.

"That's why I told her I was gonna shoot her four-legged sausage," he laughed.

Mark felt himself tremble as Hurley went over to Nell.

"Hurley, why are you doing this?"

"To be free!" he laughed.

"Free? After what you did to your parents?"

"No, Wichita. Free from this..."

Hurley yanked off the blanket covering Nell. Her naked body shivered. Mark saw that her feet were tied together with Hurley's leather belt.

"You ever see such a perfect body, Wichita? No offense, Hawkins!" he laughed while the butt of his rifle rode his hip, the barrel pointing to the low ceiling. "I can't live without that body, Wichita."

"Wh...what are you going to do, Hurley?" Mark stammered.

"Nothin'...if you've got the balls to stop me."

Hurley tossed the rifle to Mark. When he caught the rifle, blood flooded Mark's face in a scarlet glow. In Mark's head sirens and warning bells sounded above the blood banging into the backs of his eyeballs. Then Hurley removed a pocket knife from his jeans, opened the blade and put it to Hubbard's white throat. Hurley looked at his terrified friend who was again wearing the shiny black dress shoes and grinned.

"You got the balls, Wichita?"

"Hurley, don't do this! Please, Hurley!" Mark begged.

Hurley nicked Hubbard's throat and drew blood. She whimpered.

"I can write you a letter!" Mark cried. "It'll be okay! I heard your dad beating you! I can write the best letter ever, Hurley!" Mark pleaded and cried as the rifle shook in his soft hands.

"Can you make Nell love me?" Hurley cried. "After what I've done here? Can you make her love me instead of that other guy?"

The pounding blood left Mark's head and Hurley could see the blazing light emanating from Mark's blue eyes. Mark had suffered enough. Hurley watched Mark go over to Nell and put the barrel of the rifle to her head, his finger on the trigger.

"Is it love, Hurley? Do you really love Nell?"

Hurley's green eyes darted back and forth, caught off guard by his friend's bold move. Tears streamed down Hurley's face as he sat beside Hubbard on the side of the bed and cut the rope, freeing her hands.

He turned to Mark. "Will you still write that letter for me...Mark?"

"Yes."

Mark put the rifle down and freed Nell's hands. Both girls began working at the bindings on their feet.

"You really will?" Hurley sobbed.

"I said I would, Hurley. I'll write the best letter I ever wrote in my life. You'll be okay."

"I love you, Mark," Hurley cried.

"I love you, too."

Hurley and Mark clung to each other, while both wept.

If She Smokes...

At 8 P.M. that night, Mark woke up lucid in his hospital bed; he was noticeably bright-eyed, as if nothing was nugatory after his ether-induced dream. He looked around the room with childlike curiosity.

Grandpa Freeman and Larry were sitting at Mark's bedside. Grandpa Freeman relieved Mark's anxiety about Hurley, explaining what transpired during Hurley's visit to the courthouse with his Marine Corps enlistment papers, before Mark arrived.

"Hurley showed me his papers...and I said to him, Hurley, that's the original contract. Well, he turned red like one of Grandma's tomatoes and said he'd give 'em back to the recruiter once he showed them to his dad. That's when you came in. And yesterday he came in again to see me."

Mark and his dad listened intently. Grandpa's clear eyes smiled and his dentures creaked as he laughed heartily, thinking about what he was going to tell them.

"What?" Mark asked anxiously.

"Hurley asked me, 'Grandpa, what would you do if you really loved a girl and she was marryin' another guy?'"

Larry chuckled at the image of Hurley asking the old man's advice about his love life.

"Well," Grandpa said, "I saw Hurley's cigarettes stickin' out of his shirt pocket and he real quick-like put 'em in his back pocket. So I said, Does she smoke? And he looked at me funny and said, 'Sometimes.' I said, If she smokes..."

"Well, that's when Hurley's face lit up, like he got this great idea. And he jumped to his feet and said, 'That's right! Every time she had sex with me, she smoked!' Then he shook my hand and said, 'Thanks Grandpa. I'm goin' over to that guy's house and get her!'"

"Then what?" Mark asked above his dad's laughter.

"Then he asked if he could borrow a few of the burlap bags in my garage to put down on his back seat. That boy had a plan. I never saw a guy so determined to win a girl," the old man chortled.

"What did he want the burlap bags for?" Larry asked.

"I don't know. I didn't ask. But that boy's eyes, you should've seen 'em. I've never seen such bright, determined eyes in my whole life."

"Where is he now?" Mark asked from his elevated bed.

"I don't know. That's all he told me. So don't worry your mind about Hurley. He's prob'ly got that girl off somewhere...smokin' up a storm," Grandpa's hooting laughter filled the hospital room.

This was all thrilling news about Hurley. But not as thrilling to Mark as realizing that God was inside his own heart. Mark remembered Grandpa's smiling eyes, when he talked about Hurley; were they revealing this spirit of God that was inside everyone? Inside Hurley. Inside Mark, too. Could that be the eternal light people talked about, knowing it was a divine right to be here and live on earth? And Grandpa radiated light...because he didn't live in his mind.

Yes, it all made sense to Mark, now, especially how he had asked himself for courage when he fell into Nap Town, and earlier when he was brave and rode the hogs.

As Grandpa and his dad prepared to leave at the end of visiting hours at 10 p.m., the patient from Paradise told them he wanted to leave the hospital with them. But Mark's dad insisted that the doctor had to check his blood gas levels before he could be released. Mark must wait until morning.

Left alone in the uncomfortable, sterilized environment, Mark kept repeating to himself, "If she smokes..."

Later, he took another restive nap.

Grandpa's Bridge

After an incredibly restless nap, around two in the morning Mark gingerly got out of bed, put on his damp soiled clothes, ripped off the plastic bracelet and walked out of the hospital with no sign that he'd been admitted other than the small bandage on his cut chin.

Outside, it had stopped raining. The air was charged with fresh oxygen compared to the dreadful/sanitary eleven hours he'd spent in the hospital. Mark started to laugh, dismissing the idea of getting a cab, because he felt energized and felt like walking; and, he didn't want to wake Grandpa for cab fare at three in the morning.

It felt good to move his bruised body. He now realized he was looking at the city for the first time. As he walked with a new lightness, his sore feet seemed alive encased in wet socks that felt mushy inside his soggy black dress shoes. Instead of worrying about what he was wearing, he stayed with his breath and held his attention there. Feeling the rush of energy that flowed with each clean breath from head to toes...a thing he always had; yes, it had always been there under the insanity of his jabbering mind, a mind that ruled with relentless possessiveness and had made all strangers the enemy.

He believed what his grandpa had told him in the hospital, that Hurley had something to do with this new aliveness that he now saw in all things, things that appeared to have a dimension he never noticed before. Every thing now appeared to be vibrating with the rhythm of life and with colors. Buildings, street lights, a piece of paper blowing across the sidewalk, things in store windows, the sparse traffic. Before, he was separated from them; before, he had to move past them. But not now. He was truly here, now, in the soft luminosity that appeared to thicken everything he saw, and even made an approaching drunkard appear more meaningful than just a worthless cipher.

Now, he listened to his mind when it would intrude, and he noticed that he missed seeing when his mind chattered away. Yes, it was all so new and fun now, walking fast with a lightness, an effortless energy he'd never known.

"The enemy," he whispered, while crossing an empty street.

A sudden dawning of consciousness told him he had to find Hurley and tell him the thousand things he wrote about him and stored in his dark closet.

"Hurley!" he cried, his steps moving faster without effort.

Now he knew that Hurley Gunderson was his lost brother, a lost soul who also happened to land in Paradise.

"'Cause nobody wants to live in hell," he mumbled and laughed out loud.

Mark knew that Hurley would never find this same inner peace in Nam. And if he did... "Would I ever see my brother again?" Mark cried inside.

He continued to let the emotions come out in tears of grief that ran from his quivering chin to the city pavement that appeared as a moving gray ribbon leading him to the massive auditorium where he and Hurley went as hoboes to the Halloween dance. Visions of that evening flashed as he chose to reactivate the memory...to remember the past through an act of will.

And right then, as the river's black/sparkle appeared in the distance under the dark iron of the Combination Bridge that his grandpa helped build with his own powerful hands—he recalled the time he and Hurley were sitting on the twin beds in the Gunderson basement, just before putting the coffee grounds on their faces.

Hurley had reached under his bed and pulled out a thick scrapbook and sat down next to Mark. The scrapbook held a collection of old newspaper clippings, stories about every crime in Woodbury since the paper had been founded in the late 1800s. Hurley said, "Got 'em at the paper's archives while I worked as a paper boy. Used the microfiche viewer an' copied every one."

One particular clipping from the 1940s was different from the others; it showed a picture of the new Woodbury Auditorium. The story with the picture told of a boy who climbed up on the fifty-foot-high roof of the auditorium and was chasing pigeons when he fell to his death.

Hurley told his friend how the story shocked him so much that he walked all the way to the auditorium...the same night those two rednecks in the Falcon trapped him on the bridge. He went on excitedly about how he discovered himself how the boy got up to the roof.

"I saw the pigeons, Wichita! I prob'ly even saw the very same flock of birds that boy chased just before he died! I felt how excited the boy must've been, Wichita! I went right to the same spot up there where the boy fell...and I chased the pigeons. They took off and flew all together 'round and 'round, making a lot of noise with their wings. I know, Wichita! I could see how a boy would get lost up there...so high...and so thrilled with the birds in flight. And if the kid was a little daffy in the head...he might've thought he could fly, too! I could feel it, Wichita! But Jesus Christ Almighty! The poor guy must've had such a terrible fall at the end...when he found out he was wrong about bein' able to fly with those birds! And, Wichita, I gotta ask ya...if we're all s'posed to be God's creatures in this world, why couldn't God let that boy fly? At least for long enough so he'd land hard but live and know better the next time. Life...it's all so short and...cruel. Don't ya' think, Wichita?"

Now, as Mark neared the cloverleaf ramp to Grandpa's bridge on the Iowa side, he took a shortcut on the lush grass that would take him up to the right-hand side, onto the pedestrian walkway that led to Nebraska. Halfway up the knoll he recalled seeing the liquid tears in Hurley's green eyes as he talked about the boy and wondered why God couldn't let him fly.

Mark's first step hit Grandpa's bridge during a stillness of mind and absence of traffic from either direction; at that penultimate moment, before the old emotion of his mother's loss usually overcame him, he stopped it, just long enough to see deeply into the old thought pattern that had haunted him. It had always overwhelmed him, this thought that he had been powerless to stop from becoming a real disturbance. He could not put the feeling into words; he only knew that it was the same fear-based pain he suffered after his parents first split up.

He now saw that he had split, too, into a fractious boy who suddenly had an entire world to conquer...alone. His weapons: fear and a recalcitrant mind that labeled and judged and chattered incessantly about every little thing and emotion that came its way. It all seemed so silly, now.

Then, while Mark walked on the gray/black iron of the waffled surface in the pedestrian lane of the great bridge that led to Nebraska, he knew he was headed for his Paradise; but this time, he was coming on his terms, not banished from Kansas as a frightened boy. He was now arriving on strong legs that had been and were right NOW supported by the steel of his father's people, the side of himself that had made him whole for the first time, and had given him the gift of living in the present.

There was so much more clarity in his field of vision now, and there was more depth to every thing, more depth than his beautiful girlfriend's formula ever gave him. Step after light step, and even though it was dark, he could now see and smell the river in the air for the first time; it was a living, ineffable thing that sparkled in the cloud-scudding moonlight, with whirlpools and rivulets made by moving debris on its way to deeper waters to the far south.

Just then, a semi trailer truck roared past, then an oncoming truck whined by from the other direction, headed for Iowa, as Mark stepped lightly, so far removed from Nap Town. Best of all, he was now able to use his mind when he wanted, he could now stop its streaming images when he wanted, all the while staying present, back and forth, back and forth, until he cried aloud.

"I'm FREE!" he screamed to the girders and cables overhead that Grandpa's hands had made so long ago.

Halfway across the quarter-mile length of the bridge he laughed at his scratched and water-soaked black dress shoes that seemed so pitifully unimportant.

Just then, coming from far behind him, he heard the blaring song, "Goin' Out Of My Head," sung by Little

Anthony & The Imperials. Mark swung his head toward the closing headlights as the music grew louder. Though his body hurt in a hundred places, he knew that it wasn't the gas from Nap Town causing the vision his eyes beheld.

Was it Hurley's car? No. As it rolled closer he saw Nell's convertible; the driver honked at him. The music played loud as the Plymouth screeched to a stop on the quiet bridge. Hurley, behind the wheel, snapped off the song and yelled, "Wichita! What in God's hell are you doin' here?"

Mark stepped closer and could see real light blazing from his friend's eyes for the first time. He said to himself, "It's Hurley Gunderson's Paradise."

That's what Mark repeated to himself when he saw Nell, drunk and high, lying on the back seat on Grandpa's burlap bags, petting Johnny and kissing the pig's scruffy pink cheek. And Mark stayed in the moment, neither admonishing nor admiring Hurley's conquest.

"Mark, you're a mess! What happened to ya?"

Mark took over without hesitation. "I'll tell ya later, knucklehead. Let me drive."

Mark got behind the wheel of the convertible and drove slowly toward Paradise.

"Tell me everything," Mark demanded.

"Well, Wichita...I mean Mark..."

"You can call me Wichita."

"Well, Wichita, I went to see Grandpa Freeman..."

"Grandpa told me. What did you do exactly?"

"Let me tell ya, Wichita...ya friggin' pussy!"

Mark laughed, too, as Hurley reached down for a beer that rolled under the front seat. Hurley said, "Grandpa gave me the idea to just go claim Nell. So I got the notion to go out to Hawkins's place and see if she'd be Nell's maid of honor once I convinced Nell to elope."

"Elope!" Mark yelled.

"So, since Hawkins wasn't there, I took Johnny as insurance."

"Insurance?"

"Yeah, ya know, like leverage to convince Hawkins to convince Nell to marry me...somethin' crazy!"

"We're married, Wichita!" Nell screamed, showing Mark the wedding ring she bought with her charge card at a city jewelry store.

"Johnny was our best man!" Nell laughed and petted the happy pig who was wearing Hurley's hooded jacket and was slightly drunk from the beer the groom had been giving him.

"Let me tell 'im, for Christ's sake...Mrs. Gunderson!" Hurley laughed.

Nell laughed, too, then leaned forward and shouted in Mark's right ear, "Oh, God! Wait'll my parents find out!"

"And Robert!" Hurley cackled.

"Go on. You drove over to Robert's apartment with Johnny..." Mark prompted.

"Yeah, and I camped there all night with Johnny Angel here, and after Robert went to work, I went in through the patio door...and did her right in Robert's bed!" Hurley chuckled.

"Oh, God! Don't tell him all the details!" Nell yelled at her husband and slapped his shoulder.

"No, this is our honeymoon and he's my best friend...and I'm gonna tell him...BITCH! Or sweetie!" Hurley cackled, then leaned his head back and kissed his drunken bride on her nose.

"Anyway, Wichita, I proposed...she accepted after

we had a quickie. I didn't just jump her bones. I talked to her and we smoked three cigs in Robert's room...and...IF SHE SMOKES..." Hurley laughed out loud as Nell covered her face on the back seat.

"After we got our birth certificates and bought the rings, we all went back to Hawkins's place to get you and her to stand up for us. An' you still weren't there, so we waited. An', well, we partied...took a pre-honeymoon nap on Hawkins's bed, but then we had to leave for South Dakota before they closed the courthouse."

"Why didn't you leave a note?" Mark queried.

"Hey, I'm no writer, Wichita, you know that."

Mark rolled his eyes, as Hurley opened another can of Grain Belt, saying, "I gotta back up a ways, Wichita, 'cause I left a letter in your shoebox to screw with Hawkins, since she was over there all the time, in case she snooped in your stuff. And I took back the one I gave ya. Anyway, I'm sorry as hell for this, Wichita, but on prom night I took one of them great letters you wrote Hawkins. And I read it to Nell in Robert's bedroom while we smoked..."

"The bastard told me he wrote it!" Nell giggled.

"I told ya Wichita wrote it!"

"Yeah! After we got married!" she laughed.

Hurley continued as he leaned back and gave Johnny a sip of beer that the pig slurped right out of the can, like a pig who'd had plenty of recent practice.

"We spent the whole day until an hour ago in a Vermillion motel, after we got hitched. With Johnny watchin' us," Hurley laughed with Nell. "That pig can really stare at ya!"

On the quiet street in Paradise, Mark was glad to see that Nell's mother's Dodge was parked in the Freeman driveway. Hubbard was at his house. After he parked the convertible in front of the Gunderson place, he convinced the newlyweds to put the top up and to be quiet, because Hubbard was sure to be asleep.

Mark took Johnny by his leash toward the Freeman front porch, while Nell and Hurley giggled down the steps on their way to Hurley's basement bedroom to continue their honeymoon.

At the front door, Mark picked up Johnny and carried him to his bedroom before setting him down on the carpet.

"Hubbard? It's me," Mark whispered in the dark. Hubbard turned on the bedside lamp, leaped out of bed and ran to Johnny, hugging his slim/sturdy body that, inexplicably, was wrapped in Hurley's navy blue hooded cotton jacket.

"You are not going to believe this," Mark smiled. "Hurley and Nell got married. And Johnny was their best man."

Hubbard could see the light shining in Mark's eyes. She thought about all the possible reactions she could choose, and said simply, "I love you."

"I love you, too," he smiled.

The basement light glowed in Hurley's room. He stood under the laundry room window smoking a cigarette. Nell slept on his twin bed. Her steady breathing reminded him that he had to take down that engagement photo with the three darts in it before his new bride awoke and saw it.

His bright green eyes were new as he gazed across the street at Mark's lighted bedroom window, then down to the hundred-dollar gold wedding band Nell had bought him. Since he'd kept his Marine Corps enlistment papers, he was going to tear them up and go to work for his dad in the monument company. Maybe he and Nell could get their own little house. He thought about getting a cat for Nell, one from the pound, and give it a good life, he chuckled.

Now, his glowing green eyes smiled at Mark's window, where it all began for him, and led to this chance to live a real life with a woman he loved and knew had always loved him. Nell made him see and feel what Wichita saw and felt with Hubbard—a needed side to himself that could fill a void during this awful/wondrous time in Paradise.

Right then, the green lights dimmed a bit in eyes that recalled the pain that had been reflected back to him when Grandpa Freeman, with his total presence, had allowed him to see for himself that his runaway mind had been holding him hostage. Grandpa's quiet mind was able to hold Hurley's attention long enough for him to become wholly aware of what he had always been running from: his true Being.

Now, as Hurley moved his gaze to the majestic maple tree in the Freeman front yard, he chose a trace memory of the boy who couldn't fly safely away from the high roof of the auditorium. And he felt new waves of compassion ripple down his face. When he had gone to that same spot on the roof, Hurley Gunderson knew that he was chasing God; and he also thought about flying off that roof, just to end the pain and madness of his dreams, such terrible dreams, scenes and images that showed him destroying his parents and himself. They were nauseating images during restless sleep that he had never wanted to recall, until now.

Always, his mind had recalled those dreams at the worst possible moment: when he was catching during a game, when he sat with his parents at Grandma Freeman's funeral, and many times before, when he stood right here and blew his negative thoughts out of this window. But not now. Now, he looked out at the maple tree. Before, he never saw it as a living thing, it was just another object that was separated from his bustling mind.

It had been Grandpa Freeman who made him see that his busy mind was not in charge.

"Not the mind," he whispered, and smiled when he imagined lifting the needle off the broken record and hearing...nothing...but his breath coming and going...and that maple across the street, its leaves rattling low and so soft and alive in the predawn darkness. And he thought that boy on the roof could've been like him and evidence of the reasoning behind "there are no accidents."

Then came the loving image of Wichita, as Hurley blew the last drag from his cigarette out the open window into the Paradise darkness.

"Lucky bastard," he mumbled and smiled, knowing that his friend had a good woman and a good family, like he was making for himself, now. And that Mark Freeman from Wichita, Kansas, could've done a lot worse than that house across the street with the big maple, a lot worse, he smiled.

<u>Until I'm Gone</u>

In late October, cool/cold in Paradise, autumn was racing fast toward winter. The four graduates of '67 had all turned nineteen.

Nell's parents, at first took the news pretty hard when they found out from their daughter that their new son-in-law was not Robert Greenburg. Mr. Evers wanted the marriage annulled and talked to his attorney. Instead, due to an overriding consideration, the Gundersons moved into the Evers guest house behind the Evers mansion.

Hurley's parents were surprised, as well, especially Mr. Gunderson, when he found out that Hurley never returned his enlistment papers to the Marine Corps recruiter. The big shocker: Hurley started working at Gunderson Monument Company selling headstones to grieving relatives of the dead. The arrangement worked out pretty well, since Mr. Gunderson never drank while at work and the newlyweds avoided contact with him outside of office hours.

Hurley even threw away his extensive collection of murder/true crime magazines that had been heaped under his basement bed...without being told to do so by his new bride, who kept her husband from being drafted because she was four months pregnant when he received the letter that began: *Greetings...*

All feuds were healed, with the exception of Robert who felt humiliated and requested a transfer to Des Moines. Nell and Hubbard, Hubbard and Hurley made their peace. The cousins cried and hugged each other back to forgiveness. Hurley picked up a stray orange and white tom-kitty in the Woodbury Animal Shelter and gave it to Nell. He named the cat Hawkins, and ever since then, Hurley called Hubbard "Aunt Hub."

Aunt Hub moved back to Blue Hill with Johnny. Soon afterward, she began working for Doc Jensen in Blue Hill as a receptionist/assistant. She bought new living room furniture, plus a king-sized bed and moved her belongings into Jake's old room.

Mark still lived with Grandpa Freeman during the week, while he attended Warren State full-time and longed for the start of baseball season. He spent weekend evenings and nights on Blue Hill.

One Saturday in late October, on the courthouse grounds, Mark raked and hauled the last of autumn's leaves into a big pile on the patch of blackened earth where the custodian burned them every year.

Grandpa Freeman stood in his basement office, happy to have gotten Mark part-time work for the county on weekends. From his window he watched as his great-grandson hauled leaves in a burlap bag and dumped them on the growing pile. He watched Mark turn toward the glorious golden mound of leaves, four feet high and as wide as a parlor sofa, and knew the boy's clear and shining eyes were basking in this last chance to see the splendid heap of autumn colors, unlike any other season's hues.

Then, unaware that he was being watched, Mark

turned his back to the mound of fallen leaves, the heels of his Keds crunching the very edge of the pile. He threw back his head, his eyes going up to the barren gray/brown branches, home for these very leaves for more than half the year. He could see one leaf here, and one leaf there, still clinging despite the wind that had blown the rest to the earth. He wondered if the fallen leaves had let go knowing they would return again; and if that was when they died...on the way down to earth?

Summer nights he had heard them, high above his open bedroom window, alive and dancing in the howling wind all through the night. To get his mind quiet he had listened with all his Being to the sound the leaves made distinctly in summer: they sounded heavier and pattered with moisture taken in from spring rain; and when they waved in the powerful gusts of prairie winds, they held strong, as if in the prime of their lives. Was it all a preparation for letting go, to return to the earth in golden splendor after a life lived well? And was I like that one up there...and there...still hanging on...alone and afraid to join the others by letting the endless flowing rivers of invisible wind take me? Why? Because I had not learned how to live. Because I hadn't really begun my life. But there was another reason I could not let go, could not join the others: because I was told and believed there was a white-bearded God who decided it was time to take my young and beautiful mother to His Paradise...and that I could only see her again when He said it was my time to join her.

Still looking up, Mark's chin began quivering with spasms all around his mouth, his eyes a wet/blue from missing his mother so. Then, his eyes became angry as he looked beyond the forked branches to the azure blue sky where the bearded God was supposed to dwell. Inchoate screams were coming up from his belly, then blocked in his throat again, as it had been at his mother's funeral, when he left his autumn letter on her motionless breast. At that time, he had so wanted to turn to them all, to all of those living/old faces in Paradise who never knew her. They were all like these leaves at his feet...old and withered, with leathered faces that had lived three times her lifespan.

Yet it had been blocked in his throat, this raging fire of held-back screams, screams at the bearded, distant God to Whom he had been faithful, while he had been so alone in Kansas.

And now, to the blue above: Who can say that it wasn't, or was the bearded God Who sent me here to wrest this fear of loss out of me, this unwillingness to accept my own death and know that surely one day I, too, will join them here on the pile, whether or not I learn to accept and let go of my fear of joining them.

Mark's eyes rolled back a bit more, into the clear blue way beyond the branches; his long arms spread out wide and back, back, back...until he let all of himself fall backwards, all of his relaxed weight trusting that all of the colors would catch him and take him unharmed...all the while his eyes were open and on the blue above.

After he landed safely in the bed of gold, he smiled at the blue beyond the branches and yet felt the soothing waves of light rushing through him.

Another old man had been watching him, from his basement window in the quiet boiler room, where overhead pipes waited for his powerful hands to use them for the coming winter cold. The glass of his wire-rimmed spectacles had allowed him to see his great-grandson's youth at play in the pile of leaves he would soon burn on this windless day.

For most of his nearly nine decades he had seldom taken time to play; he had lived to work and loved it each day by enjoying moments like this...from a distance...with an unshakable faith in God that his dear mother had taught him in Germany.

The old man ruminated about how all of the Freeman men had lost their mothers when young, and how all of them had lost that natural maternal inner strength that only faith in a merciful God could replace. As he kept watch over his prostrate great-grandson, lying motionless in the golden palmated leaves of autumn, an autumn that might be his last, a smile came to his mouth and brought with it a munificent feeling of hope for the boy in the leaves, trusting that Mark Freeman would live to see only as many seasons as He desired, until called Home to the true everlasting Paradise.

Now, Edwin Freeman knew it was time, time to read his wife's letter, an autumn letter she had asked him not to read until she was gone. Yes, he told himself, I want Mark to read it to me, then it can go with the leaves.

Her letter was not enclosed inside an envelope; it was covered in foil and sealed with a hatpin. It was written in the style of seven decades ago, in black ink on burnished yellow unlined paper that was narrow. Leona May's letter was dated April 9th in the year 1900. She had been eighteen then, and he had been twenty years old. He recognized that the letter was dated the first day he met Leona May; he had been working on the new Combination Bridge, mounting and installing steel he had forged himself in his South Woodbury blacksmith shop.

Young Edwin was about as strong and handsome as he could be then, on the 9th of April, when Leona May first saw him from the Nebraska side of the bridge. Later that same afternoon, Leona brought Edwin some lemonade. That night, she wrote the letter, a letter she never intended to send—an autumn letter to her beloved.

On the blackened earth on the far west corner of the courthouse grounds, Edwin stood tall beside his great-grandson, overseeing the burning of the dry leaves as he watered the area around the golden rim with a garden hose.

Smoke rose then shifted, wafting the crackling scent of burning leaves into Mark's nose while the two men remained quiet together under the warming Paradise sun that settled lower in the early afternoon sky.

Mark was looking forward to seeing Hubbard that night on Blue Hill and thinking about her, when he stopped his mind chatter. Mark was now clear that whether God was within, or was up there somewhere beyond the blue—there was only one God now...in this moment.

At his feet, between his Keds was his shoebox full of autumn letters. There was nothing in them but words about the dead past, about things and people and emotions that meant nothing to him now. He had told Hurley what he was going to do, and so Hurley had given him the original letter Mark wrote to Nell. Mark also had the letter that Hubbard found, the one Hurley had substituted for the real letter. And Hurley had given Mark the newspaper clipping about the boy who couldn't fly.

They were all inside the covered shoebox, a collection of unread letters, and two that had been read. Mark had told his grandfather over breakfast that he planned to burn the letters with the leaves.

Now, Mark went down on one knee and opened the box. From beneath the pile of letters he withdrew a black and white photo, enclosed in it's original wax paper wrapper. He removed the wrapping and studied the picture that had been taken in Wichita a few weeks before his mother's death.

"Your mother is beautiful," Grandpa smiled.

"Yes, she is," Mark agreed and set the photo aside.

"I have a frame," Grandpa said, "I think will be a perfect fit."

Grandpa Freeman handed Mark a small foil-wrapped packet and asked him to read out loud the letter it contained. Mark remained on his knee, peeling away the old foil, gingerly removing the hatpin with careful fingers. He opened the seventy-year-old letter, cleared his throat and began:

Dearest Edwin, How I long to be able to call you that. Though we met just this afternoon, my heart recognized you and led me to see you again. I rushed home to make lemonade, so I would have an excuse to visit you on the bridge once again. I know that masking my infatuation beneath an act of kindness was wrong. But my heart thirsted for just one more moment with you. I pray that God will forgive this small trespass.

I have never thought about writing such a letter as this. I know in my heart I could never send it. For if I did send this letter to you, my love, you would disavow my attentions as a young girl's foolish crush.

Because of the uncertain times we now face in this new century, and because I pray to God you will never read this...my autumn letter...I have nothing to fear from sharing what is in my soul. I see myself married to you. I know it is absolute madness. Yet, that is the way I feel...I see myself tending a garden beside our home. I see myself cooking for you and washing your clothes, attending to all of the small things that make our home a haven from the world...together, until one of us is called to the Lord.

My love, I will cherish these visions in my heart until God allows them to be fulfilled.

God bless you always, Leona May

Mark folded his great-grandmother's letter and put it inside the shoebox. He remained on one knee, looking up at the old man who stood smiling into the burning leaves, his wife's words yet singing in his mind, a distant love song. Mark looked for a sign from Grandpa Freeman, whether or not he was content with putting the box holding his wife's letter into the fire. A slight nod from the old man's head gave permission.

Mark tossed the full container into the burning pile. Together they stood watching the flames with quiet minds; they listened to the crackling leaves that curled and snapped in front of them and heated their faces. The rising gray/blue smoke made by the letters created a different shade of smoke, one that leaves alone could not make.

Each man knew that his life had begun with such a letter, a powerful letter never meant to be read by anyone...except the writer, the one who felt the greatest need to bring the words into being in this world. These were feelings expressed in words so powerful—a lost and troubled friend could win the girl of his dreams with them, and bring new life and hope out of the darkest side of Paradise.

Together, the two Freeman men watched with shared feelings of joy, as the flames blackened to ashes the last of the autumn letters along with the golden autumn leaves. For an eternal instant, each thought he smelled a trace of Grandma's lavender in the leaves, perhaps a hint that she was watching from somewhere...as the trail of gray/blue vanished into the western sky high above Paradise...and perhaps...below it.

They looked into each other's eyes; both could see the light shining. It was God's light, of pure love, sustained love that Mark knew would burn longer than any pile of leaves in Paradise.

"Grandpa, will I see them again?"

"I see them now."

The End

To my readers:

Thanks to you I keep writing up a storm.

I wrote *Autumn Letters* in response to

your requests for a book that would

touch the heart.

Signed and dated limited edition copies of *Autumn Letters*

personalized to you, or as a gift for a friend

are available for $25.00.

To order:

Make checks payable to Michael Frederick

P.O. Box 12487, La Jolla, CA 92039

email: mfrederick310@aol.com

toll free: 888-810-1952

Please include your personalized message,

your name, or your friend's name for inscription.

Price includes shipping and handling.

Please include state sales tax, if applicable.